Ember

By Sara Gibson

This book is a work of fiction. Names, characters, places and incidents either are the product of the author's imagination or are used fictitiously, and any resemblance to actual persons, living or dead, events, or locales is entirely coincidental.

Printed in the United States of America

Print ISBN: 978-1-951490-70-6
eBook ISBN: 978-1-951490-71-3
Library of Congress Control Number: 2022901600

Published by DartFrog Plus, the hybrid publishing imprint of DartFrog Books.

Publisher Information:
DartFrog Books
4697 Main Street
Manchester, VT 05255

www.DartFrogBooks.com

Join the discussion of this book on Bookclubz. Bookclubz is an online management tool for book clubs, available now for Android and iOS and via Bookclubz.com.

*Special thanks to Meredith, who helped me see that a glass
of yang tastes so much sweeter after a bitter gulp of yin.*

Once there was a latchkey kid
in a land without the "net."
She set off in the forest with a book, two dogs, and a cat.
Along the way she met fine folk who spoke of barracudas and
stingrays,
and a country, long and skinny, called Chile.
As the girl grew, she flew away, to travel far and wide.
In distant lands she made new friends like rainbows and fire.

Now a woman and a mom, no longer in my youth,
I am forever grateful for mentors who gifted me hope.

Sunrise

Ra's rapiers emerged from the sea and set the undulating water on fire. In an instant, the sun banished the dark emperor's minions to remote corners where they shifted and scattered throughout the day, eschewing the light and waiting for their master to summon them once again at dusk. The sun's rays reached a perfectly manicured golf course, awakening the sleepy earth and transforming the dark landscape into a canvas of chlorophyll green, sparkling dewdrops, and warmth.

A boy of about nine or ten ran across the grass but stopped in his tracks. A peacock crossed his path and fanned its tail. The child pointed and laughed at the flamboyant bird, but his smile turned to a frown when the feathered freak abruptly morphed into a six-foot-long monitor lizard. Thick saliva dripped from the monster's mouth and onto the verdant blades of the lawn. A red ladybug ran afoul of the oozing substance and disintegrated in a puff of smoke. The reptile pounced on the boy and consumed him in one large gulp.

A moment later, the beast was nowhere to be seen. In the lizard's stead was a well-dressed gentleman of about seventy years old. A tuft of strikingly out of place strawberry-blonde hair peeked out from underneath his red cap, hinting that he wanted to appear more youthful than he actually was. As the bloke brushed off the lapel of his jacket, a raven-haired woman in designer black yoga pants stumbled into him, falling into his arms.

"Oh my! Excuse me!" she sang out, grasping his arms to steady herself.

"Pardon me," he replied coolly.

The mysterious man's voice had a calming effect on the worried woman.

She inquired, "Have you seen a boy? He's . . . about . . ."

He looked deeply into the lady's eyes and smiled, showing his brilliantly white teeth. "No, but I sure do hope you find your son."

The stylish woman seemed dazed. She scratched her head and walked away slowly. "Now, what was I looking for?"

Orb of Destiny

Far away, on a baseball field on Mount Olympus, Eris, the Grecian deity of discord, crouched at home base and gripped a bat. Pandora, the goddess of grain, stood at the pitching mound and wound her arm around like a saw blade. A fly buzzed around Eris's face, so she tried to blow it away. When the insect landed on her nose, she swatted at it furiously.

Seeing that Eris was distracted, Pandora quickly stooped down and reached into a tiny box. She put the baseball down and picked up a gleaming golden orange. The notorious mischief-maker chucked the gaudy citrus at Eris, who was too busy picking bug entrails from her nostrils. The metallic orange smacked the sidetracked batter square between the eyes.

The cheeky orange taunted Eris. "Ha! Your face is so big I couldn't miss it! Hey, do you know why the banana crossed the road? Because it wanted to make a car peel out! Ha ha!"

Eris punched the annoying orb and it fell to the ground with a thud. She then hurled the bat at Pandora, but missed her target. It bounced off the ground and flew into the sky as Eris rubbed her injured forehead and screamed in anger. The other goddesses erupted in raucous laughter. Eris bent down, picked up the auric relic, and threw it at Pandora.

"You miserable wench! I should banish you back to Earth!"

Instead of meeting its mark, the orb veered up into sky like a rocket.

"Uh-oh," snickered Pandora as she fell to the dirt and rolled around. "Now see what you've done, Eris? The golden orange of discord is headed straight for Earth!"

Eris shrieked, "You started it, you fool!"

The auriferous treat blasted through space, hurtling toward Earth. When it entered the atmosphere, it caused a subsonic boom; it was too low for humans to hear, but it caused animals like elephants, whales, alligators, and peacocks alike to thrash and stir.

The gilded globe abruptly halted at a golf course on a sunny peninsula in Palm Beach, Florida, right at the feet of its new owner—the elderly, shape-shifting gentleman on the golf course, who grimaced and held his ears tightly. His sunglasses had fallen to the ground, and he squinted against the bright morning beams blazing in his face. As the strange gentleman bent over to pick up his shades, his eyes grew as wide as saucers. The golden orange gleamed. He wrapped his hand around the orb and struggled to lift it.

"It's my lucky day! This must be solid gold!"

Like the butterfly effect, Eris's wayward pitch precipitated a chain of events that would change everything for a young lady named Ember, whose existence would soon turn into a quantum conundrum.

Ember's Dream

Ember, a twenty-year-old college student at Western Carolina University, allowed her ash-colored hair to cascade over her face and hide the fact that she was having a difficult time not dozing off in class. To help her stay awake, she penned a little ditty.

Sleep and Dream
Quasar at the bazaar
Black hole from afar
Wormhole
Brings you near
Dear, like a lily-of-the-valley

Nestled 'round my ear
Burst into fractal infrared
Mendeleev mode virtual
Scatter Rayleigh

Sleep and dream
Sleep and dream

There's no free energy
So let's pedal you and me
Take the breeze
Make energy
From a waterwheel

I flew last night
In a dream
Threw out my arms
And careened

Wings swept up by wind
Float through a cumulous
Sirius
Fly away . . .
Sleep and dream
Sleep and dream

Crawlin' crawdads red
Reach out and claw my hand
Slip, slide down mossy dreams
Blazing sun in uncloudy skies
In the shade

There's no free energy
Gibbs me free energy
Gibbs me free energy

Ember closed her eyes, trying to work out the tune in her head, but she ended up lulling herself to sleep after all. Her head fell to the desk, which snapped her attention back to the classroom. Dr. Trimmers, her quantum physics professor, was still discussing Schrödinger's cat.

"Now if you put a domesticated feline, perhaps a tuxedo varietal, in a box with a device that has a fifty percent chance of killing the cat . . ."

The students chuckled. Someone asked, "What the Hello Kitty?"

Ember simply could not stay awake. Dr. Trimmers's monotonous voice swiftly sent her into sand land again. When she opened her eyes, she was surrounded by white on all sides. All was quiet. She stepped back and bumped into something. She spun around. A black box sat on a table. Words in red letters materialized. "Open me."

Ember gingerly placed her hand on the cube. Something inside the container scratched at it right under where her hand was. She jumped back as the box meowed. She was suddenly filled with concern.

"Oh, poor kitty! What did Dr. Trimmers say? The cat can be dead and alive at the same time? But if I open this container, will I find a dead cat? Will that mean that I killed it?" The mouser meowed again. "Since the cat is meowing, it must be alive. A cat that is alive *and* dead surely can't meow. I'll open the box and let this fine kitty out."

The box was silent. Ember nudged it, and the cat purred. As she removed the lid, a swift vacuum sucked her into a black hole.

She shrieked, "Oh no! I forgot that Schrodinger's box has radiation in it!"

Tufts of fur swirled around Ember's face. A cat tongue licked the side of her face. It was wet, rough, and warm.

"Aw, poor kitty." But then she turned to look at it and screamed, for the cat's appendage was not attached to anything.

Ember tried to bat the leathery organ away, but it was glued to her. She felt her cells stretching and mixing with the cat's. Her belly was covered in soft fur.

"I'm going to be pulled apart! I'm dying, lost forever in this awful abyss!"

Ember started to drift out of consciousness when a light ripped through the darkness. A deep male voice said, "Never fear, dear, for I am here to save you."

A mysterious figure with chalky skin—making him look almost as if he were made of marble—appeared above the stranded student. It was a man with a great curly beard and a mane of silver waves. He stretched a chiseled arm toward Ember, who was trembling, and pulled her of the black hole and into a blue sky. He then extracted the cat from her cells and deposited the two on their own cottony clouds. The sable feline hissed at the black hole. The sinister spot turned into a cobra and vanished. The regal grimalkin vaulted onto the gentleman's shoulder.

"Well done, Bast," he praised, stroking its sleek back.

Bast spoke in a sultry voice. "I'm here to serve and protect."

The feline's body stretched and morphed into that of a curvaceous woman. Two stately lions bounded out of the heavens and whisked Bast away into the firmament. Ember was awestruck.

The godlike figure who saved her placed one hand on his hip and puffed out his chest. Ember swooned, and the great gent caught her in his powerful arms. Immediately, Ember drew strength from his oddly electrical embrace and perked back up.

"I feel like I'm going to fall into the pools of your celestial eyes," she murmured before she thought better of it. "Did I say that out loud?"

"Dear, dear," the chap said. "Don't fret. I have that effect on all the ladies."

"Did you really just say that? I was being literal when I said *celestial*. I mean, you look like a nice guy, but we just met . . . and you're old," Ember chortled.

"What? I am Zeus. I'll prove it."

He leaned down to kiss her. Ember turned her head away to avoid his smooch, but his lips managed to land on her cheek.

Ember was instantly shocked. A small bolt of lightning ricocheted off her cheek. Bast and her lions came out of nowhere and pounced on the electrostatic discharge.

Ember was floored. "You really are Zeus!"

But before she could learn anything else about the god, she was precipitously whisked back to reality. Dr. Trimmers stood before her, looking at her with a stern edge to his smirk as Ember wiped some drool off her mouth. The other students broke out in laughter.

"Save your dreams for the lab, Ember. You must learn about quantum theory before you practice it. Otherwise, you could find yourself lost in a black hole with no way out." Ember's jaw dropped while the class snickered again. Someone even snorted. Had she been talking in her sleep or something? Dr. Trimmers winked. "Class dismissed."

After she gathered her things to leave, she looked around for Dr. Trimmers, but he was nowhere to be seen.

The Weekend

Ember packed her books into her Nissan Versa, and then got in the driver's seat. The first thirty minutes of her drive on I-40 West seemed to stretch on forever. She felt invigorated as soon as she entered the first twists and turns of the Nantahala River Gorge, which was called the "land of the noonday sun" because of its Cherokee roots, and the fact that it was so deep that the sun only grazed the river itself for a short period each day. When she was a youth, Ember spent many a day rafting and kayaking the clear, shaded waters of the Nantahala. As she drove past the river, she turned her head to watch kayakers flip and cartwheel through the rapids.

Ember rolled down her window to inhale the sweet fragrance of the giant kudzu blossoms. Although beautiful and green, the vine was an invasive species that robbed the native trees of their sunlight and sustenance. Ember drove past the Nantahala Outdoor Center, stopping to let a group of kayakers carrying their boats pass, and then up the river a bit before she stopped for a barbecue sandwich and a bag of boiled peanuts. A dude dressed as a fairy played the bagpipes on the banks of the river. After dipping her toes in the cool waters, Ember continued to her parents' home.

After about another forty-five minutes, in the little township called Granny Squirrel Gap, Ember turned up the steep hill to a log cabin. As if on cue, her two dogs, Gypsy and Tobias, burst out of the woods, barking blissful greetings. Ember applied the brakes and rolled down her window to greet them.

Gypsy, a terrier mix with a dirty yellow coat, was a wanderer before Ember's family adopted her. The female canine dominated over Tobias, a docile black lab and Cocker Spaniel mix who followed Gypsy dutifully around because she protected him with her ferocious barks. Ember reached forward to scratch her dogs' ears, but before she could, Gypsy darted over to an opening in the woods. Tobias dashed after the terrier.

"What's going on?" Ember stepped out of the car to investigate. She soon spied a massive great horned owl standing in the path at the edge of the wood. Gypsy barked up a storm, but the great bird stood firm and simply hooted at her.

Ember recognized the confused avian. Her name was Judge Judy. Dr. Carl, the town vet, rescued her after she was hit by a car. The owl sustained a concussion and never fully recovered. Although Judge Judy resided in the forest on Dr. Carl's twenty-acre property, sometimes she ventured out into the town during the day.

Ember picked up some flat stones, just the kind that her dogs liked to fetch, and threw them up the hill and away from the owl. Immediately, Gypsy and Toby chased after them.

When Ember reached the top of the hill, she noticed her parents weren't there. "That's strange. They should be home by now. It's after five o'clock."

Ember sent each of her parents a text, but neither responded. She called Dr. Carl and left him a message about Judge Judy. Gypsy and Toby ran to her side, laying rocks coated in saliva at her feet. Ember let the dogs in the house and headed straight to her room, a weird feeling twisting her gut. Were her curtains a different color? Was the bed in a different spot?

"Hmm, I can't put my finger on it, but something feels different in here. I guess it's all relative, just like Einstein said."

Ember took her computer out of her backpack, placed it on her desk, and huffed. Studying was the last thing she wanted to do, so she grabbed her journal and walked outside.

Zum Wald

The forest pulled Ember into a trance. Inspired by nature, she opened her journal and began to write.

From the solitary wine-stained wake-robin, sultry in her stench, to the Dutchman's breeches with its dangling pantaloons, the springtime flowers of the Smoky Mountain forest paint its floor with the bounties of life. The large petal trilliums stand tall in the dappled forest shade and boast abundantly in all arrays of purple, red, pink and white, and become greater and succulent when nestled near the creek beds.

Ember's eyes followed alien-like growths of wild grapevines up a large silver maple. The vines were as large around as the trees themselves, and savagely choked them as they climbed up the trunks and thinner branches to seek the sun's photons. She could almost feel them moving, crawling, clogging the very pores of the trees on which they climbed. When she was young, she and the neighbor kids swung on the giant grapevines. Their parents cut the bottoms of the vines, which eventually killed the plants, but it allowed them to soar through the air like Tarzan and Jane.

Ember plucked a peach daylily and nibbled on its tender and fragrant blossom as she scanned the forest floor for other flowers. Standing tall and erect over a group of ghostly Indian pipes stood the proud Jack-in-the-Pulpit flower, its spadix covered by a canopy. Ember imagined the flower delivering a sermon to the parasitic pipes.

In a deep, resonant voice, she preached, "Pipes, you are looking pale. If only you stepped into the sun, you might grow strong and tall like me!"

Ember spotted a sophisticated yet swollen yellow lady's slipper—*Cypripedium parviflorum var. pubescens*—its corkscrew petals dripping down with sensual symmetry like the Song of Solomon.

She pretended she was the wild orchid and fanned her face with her hand, adopting a southern drawl as she said, "Don't bother the pipes, Jack, for they will fade away if the sun blankets them. Besides, what if they suck up all your chlorophyll at night? At least they won't get picked like me. I'm just sooo beautiful and seductive! See how my glossy, yellow blossoms beckon? Don't you want me, too?"

Gypsy and Toby, tails wagging, smashed the boastful Jack-in-the-Pulpit.

"Puppies!" she scolded. "Get away from the lady's slipper. 'Tis a rare and special flower!" Toby nudged Ember's hand with his slobbery snout. "Tobias Darb Muttenberg, you silly dog."

Ember wiped her digits on some fluffy neon moss and looked up, realizing that she'd wound up at the burial ground of her dead pets: a guinea pig, a cat, a turtle, a few crawdads, and a dog. Feeling spooked, she moved along to where a bigleaf magnolia tree stood. Ember held one of the foot-long leaves in her hand, feeling like she was in the time of dinosaurs. She listened for the call of the Brachiosaurus, but only heard the caw of a crow.

The dogs trotted off and Ember called after them, "Where are you going now? Are you leaving me again?"

The wind blew her hair into her face, and she half hoped that a knight would ride by in shining armor. "No knights in this forest! Plus, you are much too old for fairy tales."

Ember plucked a three-lobed leaf of a sassafras plant and crushed it, inhaling its sweet, spicy scent as she meandered back to her house. Ashton Beauregard Felix, her twenty-five-pound cat, rolled in the cool dirt under the shade of the porch.

"Come here, kitty! I know you'll give me a cuddle."

Beauregard ignored her, so Ember reached under the veranda to pet him. The cat darted further under the porch, where spiders, snakes, and bees hid.

"Phooey," griped Ember. "You left me, too!"

A blue jay cawed. Ember wondered if it was the same bird she raised a few years back. One sunny spring day, when Ember was twelve, she was sitting in her room when she heard a great ruckus. She ran outside to see half a dozen blue jays attacking Beauregard, who scurried to take cover under the car. When the tomcat then darted into the woods, Ember followed him and found a baby blue jay so young that it didn't even have feathers yet. She swatted the cat away and picked up the fledgling, named it Berty, and raised it in a cage in her room, right next to her guinea pigs. Berty was so friendly that he'd perch on her shoulder as she walked through the woods. The blue jay grew into a large, sleek, and healthy specimen that made friends with the wild birds by day and returned to her at night—until he didn't. Year after year, she swore she still recognized his call.

"Berty, is that you?" Ember stared into the distance, moved by the brilliance of the afternoon light that painted the pick-me-nots with fire. She stared into their dragon-like faces, once again imagining that the flowers were animated. "Stand guard! We have an intruder! Three, two, one: fire!" Ember plucked one single *Impatiens capensis* and dramatically ducked as the blossoms spit their seeds at her, sounding silent sirens to the hidden bugs below. "I'm hit, I'm hit! Kitty, Toby, Gypsy—my Prince Valiant—someone save me!"

As Ember rolled around on the ground, she thought of how the splendidly assorted species of Southern Appalachia were ghosts of the glaciers that stretched hither and thither, scratching the spines of trees and sowing spores and seeds. Ember sighed as the wind whispered secrets of bygone times, dragging her fingers and toes slowly through the silky dust, digging down to the cool red clay below, and squishing it between her toes.

Musing

Ember swung back and forth on the porch swing, thinking about how much her life had changed since she started attending college in the fall of 2016. Her first semester was quite the adjustment because she had grown up in a small, economically challenged mountain town. She had been surprised at how privileged some of the other students were, with expensive cars or even houses that their parents had bought for them.

Five months into her studies, Donald Trump became president of the United States, and then Ember's high school boyfriend broke up with her to date another girl who had stayed in her hometown. Determined not to let the breakup get her down, Ember joined the university's outdoor club, which consisted of a group of students who liked to kayak, hike, spelunk, and ski. By the second semester, Ember met a kayaker named Titus.

First, Titus invited Ember to meet him at the Devil's Dip, a Class III rapid on the Tuckasegee River, where he showed her his kayak "rodeo" moves. Next, he invited her to kayak the Ocoee, an even more difficult, yet exciting, river in Tennessee that once hosted the Olympics. When the winter rains invaded the local waterways, they kayaked the overfilled creeks together. The extra water made the runs more accessible and exciting. Titus and Ember developed a special relationship, or so she had thought. One unfortunate day, on the West Fork of the French Broad River, Ember turned over in her kayak and hit her head on the rock on the bottom of the river. She was so dazed that she was unable to flip back up and had to exit her boat. She ended up swimming down a series of rough rapids until she was finally able to reach an eddy and climb onto the bank. Ember crawled out of the river, bleeding from the head. She had to walk back through the woods to the road, hitchhike back to Titus's car, and pick him up at the bottom of the river run. Titus was so disappointed in her skills that he told all of his friends she was a *swimmer* and not to kayak with her. The awkward event was just a hint at what was to come for her relationship with Titus.

One crisp fall evening, Ember saw Titus at an outdoor club social. She was unpleasantly surprised to see that Titus was tenderly holding the hand of a competitive canoeist named Gabriella, who also happened to be the daughter of a wealthy CEO. It turned out that she and Titus hadn't been paddling on the same river after all. He turned out to be just . . . just some dumb dude.

Exasperated with the memory, Ember penned a quick poem in her journal, humming along a tune.

Thinking about unrequited love pissed Ember off. She was not a weak, needy little girl in love.

"I know, I'll use him as an excuse to protect my feelings from here on out," she said to herself. Thinking of Alfred Noyes's "The Highwayman," she made a version of it that placed the blame on Titus, casting him as a thief of hearts.

The Flyawayman

Your wind is a torrent of blackness that hides beneath the breeze.
The moon is a sad strong beacon that buckles my tired knees.
Our road is a ribbon of mercury flowing through poisoned veins,
And my highwayman has picked my plumes and cast them to hell's torrid seas.

He'd a Stratocaster atop his lap and an ale beneath his chin,
A blouse of polyester and breaches of rough denim jean.
They fitted with never a wrinkle; she should have stopped right there!
But he played a melodious jingle,
His fingers strummed and twinkled,

He and his guitar glistened into the deep of night.

Over the dance floor he stumbled and clambered out to see the stars.
And he played softly with his lute, but her heart was already charred.
He guffawed when the shutters shuddered, for inside of the panes
The pastor's blue-eyed daughter, Caress, the pastor's daughter,
She jittered and shivered twining her fine silken hair.

Never to love her again, he left her alone and her heart cold and bare.

Ember sighed and rocked herself, thinking of a dog licking its wounds. "If it were only that simple!" she shouted, pumping her fists in the air.

The delicious, deciduous forest quickly comforted Ember. The dense, late spring foliage sheltered all the neighboring houses, and the gentle mountains enveloped her mind as it again began to wander, much like a tomcat venturing into the forest for the night.

The porch swing creaked in chorus with the chirping crickets and croaking field frogs. Ember's journal slid from her lap and landed with a loud thud, silencing nature's music for a moment.

A neighboring dog barked. Ember imagined a Cocker Spaniel bolting up out of a dusty napping hole, holding its head high like a tattling child. Another dog, maybe a lab, defended the first with a few baritone barks. Gypsy and Toby joined the chorus and bolted off the porch as dogs from the holler in the valley below sang in off-key tenor and bass notes. Finally, the neighborhood hounds ended the concert with long, sorrowful bawls.

Fireflies, like vampires rising on cue, ascended from beds that were still warm from the sun. An avocado-winged katydid crash-landed on Ember's lap, dazed and confused. She picked it up by its papery wings, stared square into its vacant bug eyes, and gave it a nudge to fly off elsewhere. The insect fluttered and landed on Ember's shirt.

A leafy green Luna moth descended from the darkening heavens and drunkenly collided with and clamped its furry feet to the wooden frame of the screen door. Like leaf lettuce with eyes, ferny feelers, and a fat body, it seemed as though it flew straight out of Lewis Carroll's *Alice in Wonderland* and onto the pages of her reality.

A whippoorwill sang. Holding her breath, Ember jumped off the porch. What had once seemed like six feet now seemed like two.

"Ah, the theory of relativity manifests again."

Although it was still twilight, the moon had already risen. Ember recited a poem she wrote as a kid. When her high school boyfriend found it, he had accused her of cheating.

She scolded him, "Read the title!"

"Who Am I?" Said the Moon to the Earth That Day in '09
Twirling and
Turning
The path is
Burning a
Bright blue gaze
And I
See your face
Ever so bright
You light up
The night
Your tug
Churns the seas
You make
The breeze
Spinning around me
As we
Twist through space

Captivated

Ember slid her fingers through the silty dirt underneath the edge of her bedroom window when a gleaming globe caught her attention. She peered closer and shuddered. It was the fat abdomen of a black widow, ominously warning her not to get too close.

When Ember was a girl, she was fascinated by the beautiful beings. She spent hours flipping over rocks to find the biggest specimens and discovered that there were odd varieties in the neighborhood. Some of the black widows had red hourglasses on the underside of their abdomens, while others had orange or yellow fiddles on their stomachs. Once in a while she found black widows that boasted bright markings on their backs, too. Why didn't the field guides mention these? Were they mutants born of the mystic Appalachians? Or were they evolved?

Ember felt the urge to view the mountains from the rooftop, another fun pastime of her childhood. Hand over foot, she climbed up the overlapping logs at the corners of the house that fashioned a three-dimensional ladder. Once she felt the scratchy shingles, Ember swung her legs onto the warm roof. Like Quasimodo, she expertly scampered up to the apex of the expanse, after which she sat down and carefully positioned one leg over each side.

"Oh, how brightly the stars twinkle when viewed far from the city light!"

Ember closed her eyes, wishing that she were on a star, like a little princess with her pet snake, caring for a pilot stranded on her planet. As if the universe were responding to her wayward fantasy, green heat lightning flashed, and loud thunder boomed right after. Ember shrieked and jumped up, falling on the steep side of the roof. For a moment she steadied herself, but then the shingle underneath her left foot came loose and Ember slid. She quickly flattened herself out and dug her toes and fingertips into the sandy shingles, tearing off a little skin from the tips of her fingers in the process. She shut her eyes when her momentum stopped just short of the edge. Her feet hit the gutter. It clinked loudly on the rocks below, warning her what her fate would be if she missed another step.

Ember composed herself and carefully crept back up to the top of the house. But her stomach suddenly soured, and she felt she needed to be on the ground. Thunder clapped loudly, vibrating the roof. Ember often felt comfort during the mountain summer thunderstorms that rocked the heavens, but something seemed different about this one. Seconds later, lightning painted the sky, spreading like roots from a tree.

A ferocious sheet of dark rain barreled down on Ember. She was filled with panic, for she did not want to be struck by lightning. She slid down the steep pitch of the roof as fast as she could. A strange storm cloud suddenly descended and engulfed her until she couldn't see a thing. Out of the darkness a dragon-shaped cloud charged her, mouth open wide to reveal lightning crackling within. She took a blind leap, hoping she would land on the embankment below. The beast missed her, and instead clawed at the roof with its forepaws before dispersing.

A sheet of rain knocked Ember flat to the ground, forcing the wind out of her chest. As she gasped for air, a torrent of water swept her down the bank and dumped her at her door. At last, she caught her breath. Ember picked herself up and stood under the awning, shivering. The normally serene creek that meandered in front of her house had swelled over its banks and flowed furiously. A gigantic orange salamander with long red hair rode on the crest of the creek's surge, screaming for help. Ember blinked, but the salamander was gone.

"Hi, Ember!" hooted Judge Judy as she floated down the river on a paddleboard, waving at her.

Ember hailed the great horned owl, but stopped when she realized she had just waved to a talking bird. Maybe she *was* going crazy. Had she accidentally ingested drugs? Why did she start seeing things that day in Dr. Trimmers's class?

Ember wanted to go inside, but she was covered in thick red clay mud she knew would permanently stain her clothes. Although it was still sprinkling outside, the worrisome weather was waning. A ray of sun hit Ember's face and she peeled off her clothes, letting the cool droplets wash her adrenaline away. A double rainbow painted the sky.

Ember opened the front door and went to her room. She dried herself with a towel and put on some leggings and a T-shirt, then wrapped a blanket around her body and sat on her bed. Her thoughts turned away from the storm as she reminisced about kayaking in the rain with Titus. She missed him. Why couldn't she get him off her mind? She picked up her guitar and strummed a tune.

Can't Get You off of My Mind
Can't get you off of my mind
Can't get you off of my mind
But you say you don't have the time
To fool with a woman like me.

Oh tell me where's your watering hole?
I'll see you there if you please.
Then we'll dance circles 'round the moon
Till the stars go to sleep.

You stung me like a bee
Let loose and flew away free.
Now I'm left here blowing with the wind
Just runnin' 'round, chasin' the breeze.

I don't need your sympathy
I've been to the end and come back 'round again.
So come on baby take a ride with me
'Cause I can't get you out of my head.

Can't get you off of my mind
Can't get you off of my mind
I'll jump so high just to touch the sky
To be a woman for a fool like you.

Couldn't get you off of my mind
Couldn't get you off of my mind
Looks like this time I tried too hard
Cause now I can't get you out of my bed!

Enter Character, Center Left

Thousands of miles away, in sunny Redondo Beach, California, two youths sat in the sand, polishing surfboards. Perched on a piece of driftwood beside them was a golden gecko, soaking up the sun and flicking its tongue. When the taller teen with the golden-brown hair picked up his board, the reptile scurried up his leg and onto his shoulder.

The shorter boy brushed a wisp of sable hair out of his eyes. "Jagger, that lizard you found is so weird."

The gecko withdrew a tiny sword from her waist and began slashing the air at him. Jagger laughed. "Joseph, you know our little sister loves this animal. And her name is Excelsior."

Excelsior ran up Joseph's leg and pointed at the ocean. He grabbed his board and ran into the surf. Excelsior jumped onto the nose, planting all four legs firmly. The boys and the gecko surfed together for about an hour. After they got out of the water, they washed off their boards and walked up a street lined with palm trees.

After about a two-mile trek up the hills, Jagger and Joseph arrived at a stucco house and entered. The voice of a young girl immediately called out, "Where's Excelsior?"

The little girl, who looked to be about five or six, was sitting next to a bejeweled cage, holding a cup of tea and looking both proud and smug. She wore a plastic crown and a purple cape.

Joseph yelled, "Rayne, what did you do? Did you take apart Mom's jewelry to decorate that cage?"

Jagger said, "I don't recognize those jewels. Rayne must have stolen it."

Rayne shouted defiantly, "I didn't steal nothing! Excelsior found them! And she told me that if I helped glue gold necklaces to the chair with Gorilla Glue that I would become her queen in a magic land."

Rayne jutted out her bottom lip and planted her hands on her hips.

Jagger said, "Rayne, you know lizards can't talk!"

"She's not a lizard, she's a magical dragon from a distant land, and she needs me to reclaim her throne and be her queen!"

Joseph said, "Nonsense, Rayne! Stop making up stories! Are you crazy?"

Jagger hugged his sister and glared at Joseph. "Come on, she's just a little girl playing make-believe."

Joseph folded his arms, but then Excelsior levitated, leaving all three siblings shocked and slack-jawed.

The Story

The evening was dark and damp. In her room, Ember turned her giant stuffed Grumpy Bear and a 1964 Tonka dump truck around while she donned comfy yoga clothes. "No peeking, boys," she warned.

Grumpy Bear responded, "You're the one who can't be trusted. What disturbing thoughts for a young woman! I'm a stuffed animal, I couln't care less what you look like under your clothes."

The Tonka truck beeped and said, "I'm a truck. I have my own headlights, and they work really well."

Grumpy Bear's stomach rumbled like thunder and rain. "Need I remind you that I am a cheery child's toy, and your impure thoughts are abhorrent!"

Ember snorted. "Cheery? Quite the opposite! I *must* be hallucinating! Maybe I'm just hungry or stunned from the fall on the roof."

Grumpy Bear pouted, crossed his arms, and then closed his eyes. Ember poked his belly. She sauntered over to the bookshelf her father had made for her when she was five years old. The bookcase was fashioned out of Brazilian rosewood he had cut himself while on a mission trip during grad school. She remembered staying absolutely silent as she watched him make it, for *children are to be seen but not heard.*

Ember wanted the bookshelf to be purple, so she squished elderberries all over it. When her father saw what she had done, he erupted in anger and whipped her with a belt. He called Ember a *loser,* a *deadbeat,* a *nobody,* and certainly NOT *an artist.* He used solvents to try and remove the juice, but the natural phenolic chromophores of the juice had deeply stained the freshly sanded wood. Ember's father then primed and painted the bookcase white, so that *no one else would be embarrassed by her stupidity.*

"You can't paint over your sins, Ember," he'd scolded as she sniffed and cried, cowering in a corner.

Over the years, the berry juice pushed back through the paint, turning the bookcase magenta and then finally a dark plum. Despite the memory of her father's anger and everything he'd said that day, the books on her shelf never failed to whisk her away to different lands, where she could be an adventurer, nomad, doctor, and space explorer who traveled through time.

Ember perused her collection, and a faded green hardback on the top shelf winked at her. She felt her forehead to see if she had a fever; it was the first possible explanation she could come up with as to why she was suddenly seeing things. Ember grabbed the novel, which she had never seen before, and inspected it. Curiously, no author was listed.

"Let's dive into you," she said as she imagined jumping into a sea of pages. The title of the book was *Cinder*. "How cool, a name similar in meaning to mine—or rather, relative to mine. Cinders from the embers." She opened the book and snow fell out of it onto her lap. Ember was flummoxed. "No, that's not right. It can't snow in a book."

A voice rang out in her head. "Of course it can snow in a book, silly."

Startled, Ember dropped the book, stood up, and paced around for a few minutes. Then, as if she just couldn't help herself, she promptly sat down on her papasan chair and picked the book up again. The snow stopped falling, and all traces melted into thin air. Irritated but intrigued, Ember sighed and began to read.

Cinder

Chapter 1: The Student

It was May 1995. Cinder was a freshman in college. She was at home for the weekend to study for midterms. Cinder slumped in the overstuffed chair in her bedroom, having just broken up with her first boyfriend. She threw her old Cheer Bear Care Bear at her brother's Armitron, causing it to clatter to the floor.

Cinder went outside. The crickets chirped in chorus with the croaking of the field frogs. A locust with wings like a butterfly landed on her lap. She tried to remove it, but it buzzed angrily and spit dark juice on her. A leafy brown Calledapteryx, a monotypic scoopwing moth, fluttered down like a falling oak leaf in the autumn. The calls of the nighthawk, the crepuscular cousin of the whippoorwill, gave her comfort.

Ember stopped reading, slammed the book shut, and threw it down. What was happening? How did a strange book emerge out of the blue with a story that mimicked the day she'd just had? And what was an *Armitron*? Ember ran out of her room, shaking and cursing. A quick internet search on her cell phone answered at least one of her questions. An Armitron was some sort of a crude robot arm from the '80s, which were basically the Dark Ages as far as she was concerned.

As if an unknown force were controlling Ember, her legs carried her back to her room without Ember making the conscious decision to return. She felt as if she were having an out of body experience. She stared at the book, afraid and excited at the same time, then turned to page two.

Cinder propped a ladder on the side of the house and climbed its rungs. The roof was still warm from the early summer sun. Thunder rumbled in the distance. Cinder loved the wild, harsh thunderclaps and bright lightning shows of the humid Ozark summers.

Ember wanted to vomit and scream at the same time. It was as if her universe were shifting, and she was lost in some weird dystopia. "What the heck is going on?"

Ember skipped to the next chapter, where she hoped the story would diverge from hers.

Chapter 2: The Book

Cinder perused her collection of books, and a volume on the second shelf called her name—literally.

"What?" Cinder muttered in disbelief. "Books can't talk. They don't even have mouths."

Cinder pulled the mysterious novel from the shelf and examined the cover. There was no title. She carefully opened the book. Still no title. Cinder turned the yellowed page, which unexpectedly turned white, like a field of dancing snow. A spot of blue appeared and then spread across the page. A cloud flitted onto the scene, and then transformed into the shape of a Herculean man. Shadows made up the contours of his face. He beckoned Cinder and she reached out to him, but her hand stopped at the page.

"Madam, I stretch my hand out to you in the invitation to fly. *Podemos aviar.*"

Cinder was ecstatic. Who didn't dream about flying like the birds, soaring through the air above the world?

"Kind cloud, sir, you'll have to accept my apology, but I fear that I am too large to fit inside a book. You are welcome to visit my world, though, for the air is nice here in the mountains."

"That would be jolly!" replied the hazy figure. But then the blue in his eyes became a pale, almost sad, dreary sky. "But I cannot, for it would be my demise. The winds would carry me away into the unknown of your atmosphere. Please, this world is made for all, for it is a book."

Cinder considered this and nodded. "I suppose, then, I could accept your invitation. However, the question still remains. How do I get into the book?"

His face lit up with pleasure. «Oh, that part is easy. Just start reading."

Chapter 3: Step in with Me

Cinder found herself on page fifteen, Chapter 3.

"Step in with me." As she wondered what he meant by that, the cloud chap offered his hand. "Reach into the book and climb toward me."

Cinder extended her hand and was sucked right into the book. She landed with a thump on a dusty mat of yellowing polysaccharides. She was surrounded by a jumbled mass of tall, white trees and chalky boulders.

"Where is that darned dude? He must have tricked me! Am I in a paper forest?"

Ember put the book down and joked, "Will I get sucked into my book, too?"

Thunder boomed so loudly that her entire house creaked.

"Okay, okay! I'll read on if you cut that out!"

The thunder cut off abruptly.

Even though she was irate with him for tricking her, Cinder could not quit thinking about the enchanting lad who led her into the book. Where was he? Just then she heard him whisper, "Ember."

Ember blinked and read the name again, except that now the print on the page read "Cinder." Maybe she'd just misread, like what happens when you read three pages before you realize you were not really absorbing any of the words at all.

Cinder turned toward a light and pushed on a large fiber. It quickly gave way and sent her tumbling into a tunnel. She noticed groups of large Hs and Os connected with strings. Cinder tentatively pulled on one of the strings.

"Ouch!"

"I'm sorry," she said. "I didn't know you were alive. What are you?"

The string replied, "I'm a hydrogen bond, you dolt!"

Cinder backed away from the bond and stepped into a steaming pile of something stinky and sticky. "What in the world?" she asked and then screamed as a giant worm with a very large mouth full of gleaming teeth chomped down at her. "Oh no! A bookworm!"

Cinder darted away, but soon realized there was no way she could keep up her pace. A hydrogen bond reached out and tripped her, saying in its crackling, sinister voice, "Maybe if the bookworm eats you, it will quit eating me! After all, you look like a great source of carbon."

"Mr. Hydrogen Bond—"

"That's *Mrs.* Hydrogen Bond, thank you!" it shrieked.

"*Mrs.* Hydrogen Bond, matter can neither be created nor destroyed. You have nothing to worry about!"

The hydrogen bond laughed humorlessly. "Do you know what it's like being in a chemical reaction? I hate it. I'm fine where I am."

A group of bird-like varmints fluttered up to Cinder and cheeped melodiously around her head. One of them squeaked loudly, like a sad violin, and wove to and fro before her eyes.

"Are you warning me of something?" Cinder asked.

Right on cue, the bookworm lumbered into view. Cinder was cornered by a crumbly page. She pushed on the paper until it gave way. She landed with a thud on page sixteen and waved away the cheeping critters that were still swirling around her head, knocking one of them away. As it squeaked and spun wildly, she realized that the things were not birds at all, but flying music notes.

"Oh golly, am I in a musical?" she muttered, still batting them away.

She ducked underneath a pile of what she guessed was lignin, when a flock of sixteenth notes angrily rushed her, swinging their bars at her head. Then Cinder had an idea. She began to hum "Greensleeves" softly. The notes calmed down and joined in on her melody almost immediately. They followed her as she explored the new page.

But soon, as if controlled by a single brain, or an invisible conductor, the notes stopped and fluttered away.

"Where are you going? I was just starting to like you," she said.

A line of bass notes marched along, answering her query. Like a line of penguins marching to a funeral, they hung their heads and cried somber, low, foreboding tones. But then they grew stronger, intensifying. The fiber forest rustled, and a giant chunk of calcium carbonate crashed down to the ground next to her.

"*Fortissimo!*" Cinder shouted. "Just like the hydrogen bonds!"

A hydrogen bond flexed its muscles in response. Cinder gingerly stepped around it so as not to trip again. As the bass notes boomed louder and louder, a flock of dissonant diminished seventh chords rushed in.

Cinder said, "Okay, I get it, something really bad is going to happen now, right? Well, what?"

The bookworm burst out of the page, baring its teeth and

drooling. Cinder ran away again, this time into a dimly lit tunnel. The pesky high notes followed, flitting about excitedly. She leapt over large fiber logs, batted bonds out of her way, and plunged further into the darkness.

Cinder saw a light high above in the paper canopy and began to climb up a lattice of lignin molecules toward what looked like an opening. She clawed her way up through the filaments with fearful desperation, and finally reached the blue sky. Cinder inhaled the sweet, fresh air, when the silence was ruined by a chord of minor thirds, flat B-D-F-A. A flock of quarter notes swarmed her. As she swatted at them, she lost her foothold and took a spill.

On her way down, Cinder landed atop a gigantic, gnarly silverfish that busily chomped down on clumps of old polysaccharides. When Cinder hit it, they both fell over. The silverfish landed on the bookworm, which was scribbling in a notebook.

The two insects started fighting and quickly became entangled in an agitated mess of music notes, chemical bonds, paper particles, and general discord. Cinder picked up the notebook and saw that the drawings detailed how he was going to torture Cinder before eating her.

Eager to prevent those images from becoming reality, Cinder dusted herself off and wasted no time climbing back up to the top of the page. A group of light, airy, hopeful sounding notes joined her, but Cinder noticed that their music was becoming dark, quickly, and climbed faster. This time she was able to muscle her torso off of the page and into the fresh air. A bass note marched by.

"Oh no! No! Not again!" she screamed as a scaly claw scratched her ankle.

The flying notes were clustered so thickly around her that she was having trouble moving. That was when she began to whistle the theme song to *Rocky*. The notes became so excited that they exited the book, lifting her up with them. As they carried her up, up, up into the sky, she turned back. The menacing claw of the silverfish protruded off of the page, but the book snapped shut before it could make a break for it and flew away into the sun. A gentle wind carried her away.

Ember paused for a moment to read about silverfish on Wikipedia. She was disgusted as she read the passage.

The reproduction of silverfish is preceded by a "love dance" involving three phases, which may last over half an hour. In the first phase, the male and female stand face to face, their trembling antennae touching, then repeatedly back off and return to this position. In the second phase, the male runs away and the female chases him. In the third phase, the male and female stand head to tail, with the male vibrating his tail against the female. Finally, the male lays a spermatophore, or a sperm capsule covered in gossamer, which the female takes into her body via her ovipositor to fertilize the eggs she will lay later on.

Ember looked up "gossamer" and learned that it was like a cobweb. When she clicked on the link for "bed bug," then read about its courtship practice, she retched. Apparently, the male seized the female and pierced through her shell, dumping his seed. The courtship was so violent that the female sometimes died.

A wind howled outside. "What, I need to keep reading?" Ember shouted to her window.

As if in response, the wind blew her window open.

She hurried to shut it and yelled back, "Okay, okay!"

Chapter 4: In the Air

Groups of O's floated around Cinder's head. Some of the O's were singular, while others were linked together in pairs or even triplets. She giggled as the comical figures bumped into each other before joining or splitting apart. It looked like bugs were swarming in the center of each of the figures, but then she noticed the invaders were tiny e's. With her left hand, Cinder accidently struck a doublet O, making it shoot apart.

"You just made my partner leave me. Thanks a lot!"

Cinder exclaimed, "How random! Oh my. I get it. These are oxygen atoms."

The letters He, which Cinder assumed was a helium atom, floated by Ember and uttered in a very scholarly tone, "He, he, he!"

Cinder said drolly, "Very funny."

The helium scolded her. "I wasn't making a joke."

"Well, excuse me, Mr. Macromolecule."

The helium atom chortled. "Don't you know your chemistry? I am an element, a noble gas. A macromolecule is something different entirely."

Cinder giggled. "Yes, I know that a macromolecule is comprised of many elements linked together. I was making a pun because you are so large!"

The helium looked as serious as ever. "I'm the same size as every other helium atom." It stormed away and into the stratosphere.

A cloud of nitrogen atoms surrounded Cinder. The letters were linked together in pairs. She recalled from chemistry class that, at ordinary temperatures and pressures, two nitrogen atoms bind together to form dinitrogen.

The nitrogen pairs whistled and called to Cinder, "Hey, you're looking pretty groovy, lady! Wanna have some fun? If you lend me an oxygen atom or two, we can make nitrous oxide and party all night."

Cinder frowned. "No thanks. Nitrous oxide kills brain cells. I'm afraid I would be a party pooper because I would pass out."

Cinder felt lightheaded. A group of H-O-H and O-O molecules flurried around her, pushing the nitrogen storm away. Immediately, she could breathe again. Cinder opened her eyes wider to inspect the linked elements, noting that the oxygen atoms were larger than the nitrogen atoms.

The water molecules coalesced and wrapped around her. A smooth male voice tickled her ear.

"Hi there, *ma chérie*."

Chapter 5: Damien's Realm

Cinder shrieked. She was standing on a large, fluffy cloud. The ground was straight above her. Or was it down below her? Wispy trails of mist swirled and churned around her, forming a human shape.

"You! You are the one who lured me into the book!"

"Hello, Cinder. My name is Damien. It is a pleasure to make your acquaintance."

Cinder's face felt warm. She wanted to be angry, but Damien was so darn charming. "Oh! My body is made of clouds, too!"

He smiled broadly, exposing impossibly white teeth. "That's because if you want to fly high in the atmosphere with the wind, you must do so in the proper form. It's aerodynamically correct."

Ember seethed. Why were Cinder's defenses down? Damien was clearly full of trickery. "No! Don't trust him!"

Cinder said, "Who was that woman shouting?"

Damien's eyes darted around. "That's just the howling wind. Pesky, isn't it?"

The cloud suddenly became unstable, and Cinder plummeted through the mist. She craned her neck to watch as Damien hurtled after her. In two shakes of a lamb's tail, he had her wrapped in his embrace and was soaring on gust of wind. She clutched him tightly.

"You saved me!" she cried as they rolled themselves up in an aerosol and bounced across the sky.

"We can be the wind," Damien explained. "We need only to jump out of these constricting suits of gases, liquids, and solids."

Ember queried, "Wait, clouds are made of three states of matter?"

Damien replied, "Good question. Yes, clouds are made of water vapor mixed with tiny drops of water and ice particles."

Cinder inspected her arm with wonder. "That is fascinating. But to answer your question, I would love to be the wind. Oh, that would be fantastic!"

Hand in hand, they leapt into the air. Strong currents twisted fervently and became whirling funnels of raw, natural power.

"Damien, you make me so happy. What else can we explore?"

Cinder and Damien explored all the realms of the world, swooping low through the turbulent storms of the tropical seas and flying high into the frigid air above snowy mountain peaks.

One starry night, while gazing up into space, Damien took Cinder so high that they caught a ride on a meteor and flew to the sun. Unfortunately, her oxygen atoms that had fused with his hydrogen atoms began to unravel. The equation reversed, possibly because there were more reactants than starting materials. In essence, she loved him more than he loved her. Le Chatelier, the principal of the atom school, scolded her for overreacting. Cinder amalgamated her atoms together until she was back to her own singular, unimolecular self.

Damien led Cinder to a place he called the Southerly Seas when he halted. "Cinder, I must tell you now. If you choose to dwell in my realm much longer, you will remain in this form forever."

Damien grasped Cinder by her electrons. "Listen, if you do not return to a more complex form complete with cells, tissues, organs, and limbs, you will stay in the form of singular atoms forever. Basically, there will be no more Cinder."

Cinder argued, "But we would be together forever."

Damien shushed Cinder and kissed her elementary particles. He trailed his fingers across her softly, but then she started transforming into a human. Damien carried Cinder tenderly down to the black sea below, coalescing into cold raindrops on her steamy skin in their last passionate dance.

Cinder felt the air around her warm as she tried to climb over the activation barrier, but she did not have the energy. All too soon, she plopped unceremoniously on a hard surface. Cinder stood up, feeling quite dizzy. Damien flickered in and out of view as he hovered in front of her. She leaned forward to embrace him, but he dissipated into a wispy mist and slipped through her fingers into the warm tropical air.

Crazier Than You
Who would've thought?
People could be
Crazier than you?

Oh please,
Oh please, oh please, oh please
Don't go away!
Don't sway
To where the grass is greener.

Rome
Don't you go!
Away
To the wayside!

Stay at home
Don't go away
Away
To the wayside.

Here on this day
I can't even ask you to stay
I just say don't go!
Please don't go away!

I still cannot believe
That you were crazier than me

I cannot seem to see
The floor anymore
The sky is above my feet

How now?
Wow, holy cow!
My love ran away
To the moon
Now he spoons with another

Just please
Don't hurt her, too,
When she says

Don't go away
Stay here today
From May till December

Who would've thought?
People could be
Crazier than you?

I remember now
How crazy I was to you . . .

Chapter 6: Dumped

Cinder made a soft, whistling howl. A warm, tropical breeze teased her face, but then the air was still, and Damien was gone.

Cinder felt hollow inside. After all, she had been in an intense, powerful relationship with a handsome ball of energy. Loving Damien was so good that it almost felt wrong. Was passion worth it if all she had left was a tortuous longing in her heart? It was painful to think about the intense pleasure she'd had with her enigmatic lover, knowing it was gone.

Her breath quickened. Everything was out of perspective. All she could think of was whether she would ever see Damien again or not. He had said no, she could not have him. Cinder was depressed.

Bad Brew
You loved another
In the blink of an eye
She was your lover
So fast as pie,
She was pie!
I pine away
In lethargic pain
That wedge nonhuman
I can't feign that game
A pity that other
Wasn't a girl
Your maiden satin simply
A spirit of this world
She's so bad yet so good
To hasten away your gain
What's left is a crater
Your soul she has slain

Cinder snapped out of the doldrums when a piece of watermelon smacked into her face. She began to laugh because she realized she was acting like a spoiled child who couldn't get her candy.

Chapter 7: The Ship

Cinder brushed the watermelon meat off her face and tasted a piece.

"Oh my goodness, that's tasty!"

Cinder scanned her surroundings. She was standing on the deck of some sort of a pirate ship. Her attire consisted of a rather fashionable bikini made of glittering emerald seaweed. She clapped when she realized she had an actual body again! Curiously, though, she was a little taller, toned, tanned, and more voluptuous than before.

"Although I feel confident, I was completely comfortable being short and having a flat chest."

Cinder then noticed her feet, which were gigantic.

"Okay, I'm all about body positivity. Maybe these are supposed to help me swim."

The air around her head whooshed, and a large blob of sticky red goo landed with a messy plop on her bosom.

"Ha ha, gotcha!" cried a booming male voice.

A striking female with kinky red hair and glowing green eyes pulled on Cinder's elbow and led her behind an old whiskey barrel. Cinder noticed that the girl was wearing an intricately designed glittering seaweed suit.

"Hi, my name is Jade! Have a nip of this liquid courage!"

Cinder smiled. "Don't worry, it's just kelp juice!"

Jade turned a spout and knelt underneath it, taking a few gulps. Cinder followed suit. The liquid was kind of slimy, but refreshing.

Jade commanded, "Bomb them with sea cucumbers!"

"Who?" Cinder asked just before she noticed a pirate ship, full of men, barreling toward them on a wave.

"The attackers, of course!"

Cinder took Jade's advice and grabbed a squirmy green tube out of a bucket of seawater. She laughed, because it was an animated cucumber, not the animal she knew as a sea cucumber. This was a brined vegetable that had a mind of its own, as it launched itself out of her hand, landing square between the eyes of a handsome golden-skinned lad with tabby-likes stripes. He soared through the air toward Cinder as the comical critter exploded into a gooey glob on his face.

Jade cried, "Oh no, Cinder! You're toast! Even worse—French toast, because your bread is fried! He'll make you walk the plank if he catches you! That is, unless you jump ship first!"

On that note, Jade ran to the plank, which looked a lot like a diving board to Cinder. Jade's green eyes flashed wildly at a tall male pirate with blue hair, who stopped in his tracks when he caught sight of her beauty. Like a professional diver, Jade did a double backflip, and tore off her seaweed suit just before she dove deep into the sea below.

Cinder tiptoed to the edge of the plank and peered into the undulating waters below. She was mesmerized for a moment, until the golden-skinned fellow and his dark-haired buddy blasted her with liquid from what looked to be cannons, causing her to fall unceremoniously toward the sea.

"Yum, blueberry juice!" she said as she flopped into the ocean.

Chapter 8: Under the Sea

Under the water, mermaids and mermen swarmed around Cinder. She, too, had a glistening tail with bright scales of many colors. Cinder giggled. "I don't know whether I'm more like a rainbow trout, or Joseph and his coat of many colors."

Jade swam up beside Cinder. She was mesmerizing with her long, red hair that took on a life of its own.

"Cinder, darling, you will find that a few kicks have quite a lot of power, and it does not take long to get used to swimming with a tail. I think it is quite superior to those dangly human legs. Follow me, and I can give you a few tips."

Cinder twitched her tail and swam after Jade, admiring the bright schools of fish that passed. Suddenly, Jade halted and looked at her watch.

"My, look at the time! We don't want to be late for the ball. Rusty invited me. Let's hurry."

"Okay, I guess I could go to a ball. By the way, where do you live?"

"I live in Atlantis, of course. Come on, let's go!"

Taking Cinder's hand, Jade led her through a twisting tunnel of rock that was alit with vibrantly glowing mushrooms. Cinder peered closer into an anemone to find a clown fish performing slapstick comedy for a group of brine shrimp. A rotund fish swished sticks at the shrimp, which just swished them away.

"Oh, how ridiculous," remarked Cinder.

The two mermaids soon came to a dark wall adorned with genies.

"Open, Poppy Seed," commanded Jade in a resonant voice.

The wall opened to reveal the outskirts of a bustling city. Blazing neon lights advertised bordellos, strip joints, and casinos. Laughter, drinks, and sand dollars floated through the hands of loitering dealers, elders, and elegant female figures. A tuna band played popular country tunes under glittering plants and chandeliers formed by plankton.

Jade said, "Stay close, because we just crossed the border into Atlantis. The seedy outskirts will give way to the fabulous city center soon. Tired of swimming? Let's call a cab."

Jade pulled an old, smelly dead fish out of a pocket in her tail, which quickly attracted a pair of limo-eels. Cinder was glad to have a rest and observe her surroundings. Fast-food restaurants with holograms of rotating fish burgers tickled her appetite, but she was quickly distracted as dwellings cobbled together with shark bones and shells gave way to magnificent mansions made of living coral and eerie whalebones.

The eels sidled up next to a moat filled with a dense, silvery liquid and stopped in front of a golden gate that was connected to a long wall-like fence. Jade reached into a pocket of her tail again, this time producing a golden key that she inserted into the lock.

"Now we need to call the golden gator bridge to cross the moat."

"What?" asked Cinder, scratching her head. "Why don't we just swim over the moat?"

A row of dull, menacing metal fins undulated nearby.

"That's Rusty, our moat monster," Jade explained. "He's friendly, but dangerous. If he cuts you with the rusted iron spikes on his back, you could get gangrene. That's why we need the bridge. The golden gator doesn't rust because he's made of gold."

"This is getting stranger and stranger. I thought getting gangrene from rust was a myth. Why can't we just swim over the moat?"

Jade laughed. "Because, silly, the water above the bridge is boiling and will burn you! See the steam streams?"

Cinder frowned. "I see! They smell of sulfur, too."

Jade said, "Outgassing from Hades." She whistled like a dolphin, and a playful, panting, golden bridge bounded toward her.

Cinder had more questions, but Jade seemed tired of explaining everything already.

"Come here, boy!" called Jade.

The golden gator advanced awkwardly, knocked Jade over, and licked her face. Cinder reached forward to pat its golden paw, which was soft as silk. As soon as her hand connected with the animated bridge, its head stretched over and bit the sidewalk, forming a bridge over the moat and to an enchanted path beyond.

Cinder followed Jade across the bridge and stared in wonder when a golden castle came into view. The girls descended into a garden, where they swam through mazes of seaweed as merchildren darted to and fro. Jade led Cinder up to a balcony of the castle and into a luxurious bedroom. A fat catfish lay on the hearth, sucking contentedly on the algae.

Cinder wondered if Jade was a princess. If this city really was Atlantis, then was her father Triton? Jade rang a bell and an enchanted tray of tea promptly swam into the room. The teapot poured a viscous liquid into cups, which then presented themselves to the mermaids.

Jade said, "It's seaweed tea. Drink up."

Platters of food then materialized. Cinder grunted with delight as she downed delicate sushi rolls stuffed with sea cucumbers and tiny wriggling fish. Cinder didn't realize how hungry she was and gobbled down a bowl of jellyfish that was cut like spaghetti. Jade poured shots of sake and roe.

Jade popped a slice of pickled sea fennel into her mouth and chewed. Cinder realized that they both had razor sharp teeth.

Cinder inquired, "Have you always lived here, Jade? In Atlantis, I mean."

"No, I have not. It is quite a different story. Would you like to hear about how I came to be here?"

"I think we have time before the ball. First, I'll sing you a song."

Oregon
Oh, riding on a southbound train
Is where I want to be.
No one there at my side
But a fading memory.

Hop a plane to Atlanta
Then to Switzerland or Spain,
But this twining it ties me
To Oregon.

Born to roam
Like a gypsy,
Oh, this world is where I live!
If I could catch a rocket ship to Mars,
You would no longer
Snare me in your "loving" arms,
Ambrosia Divinity Carrion Infinity.

Oh, dancing in a rainbow rain,
Is how that you see me?
Unduly I accept this life
And long to be free.

My Carolina lover
This love it is insane.
Just forget this displaced fool
In Oregon.
In my distant memories
I feel love and I feel pain.
Turmoil, torture or ecstasy
And capital was gained.

Born to roam
Like a gypsy,
Running wild is how I'll live!
If you want to ride with me
You'll have to set that bottle free.

Ambrosia sweet to the senses,
Honeydew and loving eyes
Buckle my knees
And make me want to cry
Definitively.

Chapter 9: Jade's Story

Before I came to Atlantis, I lived in a creek under a rock in the mountains of the Blue Ridge Mountains of North Carolina. I was a salamander. Yes, in the fourteenth century, a salamander was a mythical species that could endure fire. However, as a modern salamander of the twentieth century, I superficially resembled a lizard with moist skin. I even had gills when I was young, but as a blossoming adult I became sleek and fat and beautiful. My skin was bright orange with wonderful dark beauty spots.

So, filled with pride, I was vainglorious. I did not even want to talk to my other siblings. I often sat on the edge of a pool of water just gazing at my reflection. My brother Sergio warned me that it would be my demise, but I would not listen to him. After all, I knew where the dangerous clawed crawdads lived, and I could run much faster on land than they could with their clumsy exoskeletons.

One day, however, a mean, dirty human boy crept up on me as I sat glistening before a pool of still water. Before I could move, he had me by my beautiful tail. A feeling of utter terror came over me as he lifted me high up in the air. In that moment, I wanted to repent of my vain ways, but I knew it was too late.

Having become so fat, however, my tail broke off at the base. While this ability can be a life-saving mechanism for salamanders, as it allows us to evade predators and our tails will grow back, my pride was damaged. I careened to the ground. I landed on the hard stones of the creek, but my instincts kicked in. I quickly dove into the brisk current, which swept down into a swift channel.

After what seemed like an eternity, something pulled me into a calm eddy. It was Sergio. He had seen the whole incident and followed me to ensure my safety. When he thought we had lost the boy, he helped me into the safety of a calm eddy. I was cold, shaken, bruised, and in shock. My tail was gone.

Sergio held me as I cried, "My tail, my beautiful tail! It is gone, along with my beauty! There is no reason for me to go on living."

Sergio smoothed his front foot over my skin soothingly.

"Dear sister, you are alive and that is a wonder! Now that you have less cause to be vain, maybe you can learn to appreciate the other beauties of our world. In time, your tail will grow back, perhaps even more beautiful than before."

"Yes, you are right, brother," I said, starting to see his point. "Thank you for saving my life."

With a smile, he hugged me again. Then his eyes grew wide. "A crawdad!"

Huge, snapping claws clicked as the crustacean moved closer. Sergio pulled me into the current, but the insufferable invertebrate jumped in after us. Since my tail was so short, the crawdad was not able to latch onto me. However, I was quickly tiring. Imagine my surprise when he stopped to sing a song!

Trouble
Trouble, trouble
Trouble's got me down.
My trouble has doubled
Since you've come around.

This trouble
Has blinded me

So I can barely breathe.
I'm stuck in this rubble,
It's got me on my knees.

When I went downtown yesterday,
I met up with my man.
Then he saw his honey-love
And wouldn't hold my hand.

Trouble, trouble
Trouble's got me down.
When I've gotten way up high
Trouble comes up from the ground.

Oh darlin' oh darlin'
Kiss me yet again!
Although I need you
This trouble you can't mend.
Trouble, trouble
Trouble's got me down.
My trouble has doubled
Since you've come around.

Next, we washed into a current. The powerful backwash of the water held me as a large, snapping claw sliced through the airy bubble. Just as I felt the crawdad's awful appendage's rake against my soft back, Sergio pulled me out of danger, again.

Little did we know that we were just above the treacherous High Falls. What could we do?

Sergio leapt. With all my remaining strength, I flung myself after him, if only to escape the death for another, hopefully less painful one. Closing my eyes, I imagined our tender bodies on the rocks below, then washing away with the water, and perhaps later becoming salt in a foreign sea.

I opened my eyes. Sprays of water sparkled in the sunlight. The world around me was enchanting. That reality shifted, and Sergio and I were transported to Atlantis. The Forces of Atlantis found our tattered souls and saw that there was goodness within. Here, Sergio and I have our own rooms and nourishment.

Chapter 10: The Doldrums

Cinder pondered Jade's tale as they sipped salty drinks. She queried, "And what does Oregon have to do with your story? Why the songs?"

Jade shrugged, "I don't know. Strange, isn't it? It's as if an external force is putting words in my mouth, like someone else is telling the story for me."

Cinder said, "Fair enough. I get that. So, now what?"

Jade's face began to melt like wax falling from a burning candle. Cinder tried to scream, but no sound escaped her mouth. She could no longer move her limbs or tail. All was dark, and Cinder wondered if she was in a void. Was she dead? Would she meet God?

The twang of a banjo playing snapped Cinder out of her thoughts. Cinder was a child again, sitting on a church pew. A little girl seated next to her laughed and cried simultaneously. The sad figure looked up at Cinder with big eyes and said, "My name is Sorrow."

Cinder started shaking when she noticed that blood was dripping from the clothes covering the girl's heart, down her stomach, and onto the floor. Sorrow began to sing, her voice filling the church though her mouth didn't move.

Sorrow

Two little girls, they were sittin' in a pew.
One leaned o'er and said, "Hi, I'm Agate!
How do you do?"

I say, "My name is Sadie,
and you're the prettiest girl I e'er seen.
You must be an angel from heaven, blessed as can be."

The first one said, "Now hush,
I know things you don't know.
I have a little broken heart
that the Lawd I cannot show.
Come along and dance with me,
we'll sing to our heart's delight.
We'll holler with our souls eternally, infernally."

Oh Agate, Agate,
Who touched you?
To make you do the things that you do!

There in the kitchen with a knife to her breast
She laid her troubled life down to rest.

Agate-Lee,
Won't you trust me?
I will give you my hand whenever it you may need!

Down in the kitchen with a knife to her breast,
She tried to lay her little babes down to rest.

Agate, Agate, can't you see?
She said, "There'll ne'er be another lover
never ever more for me.
I done lent my heart once to Eternity!
Life's taken all I needed,
and I can hardly longer breathe."

Oh Agate, Agate,
Won' ya befriend me?
I'll lend a hand, devotion and security.

There in the kitchen with a red ribbon down her breast
She cut open her broken heart
and laid her troubles to rest.

Cinder could barely breathe. The little girl made patterns with red blood on the floor and said, "Do I get to go to heaven now? Can I go now?"

Cinder reached out to Sorrow, but the light faded and the church pew evanesced. Cinder was alone again. She fell forward like a plank, and her face was plastered to the floor as if with some sort of invisible glue. She tried to move, but her muscles didn't work.

All Cinder wanted to do was sleep, but she could not. She closed her eyes and tried to shut off her mind, but it spun out of control. She thought about her childhood, her relationships, and all that was wrong with her life. It was so maddening that she completely lost herself in her thoughts.

After what seemed like many years, Cinder was finally able to peel herself off the floor. Strangely, she was in a dingy apartment with no furniture. The doors were shut, and boards covered the windows, blocking out any light. She had so little energy that she lay down on a piece of cardboard. She wailed, and then words came out of her mouth.

"No one bothers to call or see me anymore. Even the birds in the sky do not sing around my house. If I could only sleep, or dream."

Cinder spotted a refrigerator and opened it. She tried to pour some milk out of a carton, but it had turned into a messy mass of a cheese-like substance. She shrugged, took a bite, and vomited. The energy she had expended left her breathless. She tumbled over, and a can of beans rolled out of the cabinet and hit her in the nose. After what seemed like days, Cinder picked up the beans, opened the lid, and scooped some into her mouth with her fingers. Feeling somewhat nourished, she crawled up the stairs on all fours, burped, took off her clothes, and climbed into bed.

Cinder remained in her bed for seven days and seven nights, her eyes closed though she was not sleeping. On the eighth morning, she was sweaty and shivering, so she decided to take a bath. She soaked so long in the hot water that when she stood, her heart thumped wildly as the blood rushed from her limbs back to her body. Feeling like she was having a heart attack, Cinder collapsed onto the floor.

Cinder woke up next to her wet towel, shaking violently. She drained the cold water from the bath and drew hot water again. The nausea returned. Cinder leaned her head over the side of the tub to reach the toilet and throw up some more. Maybe some ginger ale would help. And where were her friends? She could not find her phone.

The insomnia lasted a week, then another, then another. Cinder forced herself to eat again. Dinty Moore's beef stew, straight from the can. Ramen noodles. She stood in front of the mirror, naked. Her butt was gone, her ribs poked out, and her stomach was a deep hollow. She looked like crap. She needed a haircut. She looked at her ugly face and began crying, which made her even more hideous. Snot hung from her nose in a long, gooey string as her shoulders trembled from the force of her sobs.

Cinder felt sorry for herself, totally preoccupied by her pity party until she heard what sounded like a little girl humming. Cinder quickly grabbed a blanket and found Sorrow huddling under a fern in the forest.

"Sorrow, is that you? Are you okay?"

The girl trembled. "Don't let him touch me!"

Cinder said, "You can trust me, I won't hurt you. Who are you afraid of?"

Sorrow responded, "I was in my bed one night, when someone hurt me really bad. An angel started leading me to heaven, where I would be safe, when an evil dragon snatched me away and put me here. I'm so lonely and scared. I'm glad you're here now."

Cinder tried to lean down and comfort Sorrow, but the little girl turned to mist and dissipated. Cinder scolded herself for thinking only of herself, when other people had real worries.

> ### The Dips
> *I've driven myself into a rut.*
> *As I look around, I frown.*
> *There are others who are really, really down,*
> *Why do I think of little ol' me?*
> *It's as easy not to care as it is to ignore,*
> *To turn away from the shore*
> *And keep on drifting along,*
> *Whistlin' that same ol' darned song.*
> *I want to scratch out my eyes*
> *And replace them with roses.*
> *Piddle paddle there are rapids ahead.*
> *Oh, what to do?*
> *Maybe I need to take a swim anyhow,*
> *A cold, cold swim might make me give a damn again.*

Chapter 11: A Quick Solution

Cinder faded in and out of awareness. The surroundings were pitch black, but at least she knew that she existed and that someone else was there with her. Jade the mermaid was there! Cinder looked down at her legs and noticed that she was a mermaid with a curvaceous figure again.

"What happened?" Cinder asked.

Jade looked confused, too. "I am not quite sure, but someone named the author told me she had writer's block. She said the tragedies of life intervened and stopped the flow. The little girl named Sorrow told me we must convince the author to finish the story, or we might cease to exist without anyone ever knowing about us."

Cinder was perplexed. If what Jade was saying was true, she was only a character in a book that would not survive unless the author published it. She had an idea.

"What do we have to lose? Anything is better than being stuck in this strange purgatory. Maybe we can save Sorrow, too."

"The little ghost girl is dead. How can you save her? Maybe Sergio can save us! He's strong!"

Cinder chortled. "What's Sergio going to do, tease and taunt the author with his imaginary muscles?"

Jade gagged. "Ew, Sergio is my brother! He saved me from the crawdad, remember? Although you might have a point. Everyone should strive to be self-sufficient. Otherwise you might become codependent."

Cinder said quickly, "The author is obviously a woman. Maybe she needs a boost of confidence, some courage, to finish the story. Maybe this story isn't only about self-discovery, but about learning to work together."

Jade looked at Cinder queerly. "What are you going on about?"

"Never mind," said Cinder. "I'm just rambling again."

Jade's face lit up. "I think you should believe in yourself a little more."

A gondola descended from above. The door opened and the golden-skinned man from the pirate ship exited.

"Sergio!" cried Jade, hugging her brother.

"Allow me to introduce you to my friend, Cinder."

Sergio spoke. "We've met, sort of."

Cinder blushed. Sergio beckoned the girls into the gondola, which transported them through a fog and emerged over snow-covered cliffs.

While Cinder did admire Sergio's chiseled chin and unique glowing skin, she was a little bit miffed she had to be rescued. Was this another trick to get the author off topic?

Before Cinder could protest, she fell into a deep sleep, finally breaking her cycle of insomnia.

Chapter 12: The Snow Realm

When Cinder awoke, Sergio was sweeping a lock of hair away from her face. "Hello, sleepyhead."

"Where are we?" Cinder asked.

"The Snow Realm," explained Sergio. "The magical hut is only a hop, skip, and a jump away. It would be, of course, in our best interest to take the snow-doo, for night will soon fall upon us."

"Is a 'snow-doo' a ski-mobile that poops?" Cinder asked, giggling.

It dawned on Cinder that she and Jade were no longer mermaids, but women with legs, and that they wore sleek snowsuits and warm boots. Sergio clapped his hands and the doors of a disk-shaped snowcraft opened, revealing plush, luxurious seats.

"If you would please fasten your seatbelts, ladies, the craft will launch straight into action."

The saucer whizzed down a powdery slope, gaining speed and hopping across the snow. The grade of the slope intensified, and the ship sped faster and faster down the mountain.

Cinder's stomach dropped, and Jade shrieked when the machine hit a cornice. They sailed off a cliff, out into an electric aqua sky. An ocean of glittering, icy peaks lay below them, like waves suspended in time. Cinder imagined the birth of those magnificent beings, the upheaval of the earth, and how their current formations were just snapshots of their lives.

"Relativity," she muttered.

Sergio pulled a lever. The ship morphed into the shape of a boomerang, causing their path to shift and become parabolic. Oddly, they didn't spin around with the saucer.

"Are our seats, like, gyroscopic, or something?" Cinder asked.

"Something like that," Sergio replied.

The flying disc spun around and then landed abruptly, albeit gently, in a soft field of snow.

"I'm speechless," remarked Cinder, wondering why that phrase even existed.

Sergio's eyes twinkled. "How about some real excitement? Are you game?"

"Of course!" Jade clapped exuberantly.

Cinder asked, "What could be more exciting than that last run?"

Sergio said, "The local yetis build ramps for an annual contest. The winner is crowned King or Queen of the Mountain. The contestants are snow penguins that fly and flip around. It's quite an amazing event. The course is perfect for our snow-doo and is freshly groomed."

Cinder asked, "Will the yetis eat us? Will we run over a penguin?"

Sergio looked amused. "I've been given special permission for us to use the course today. Let's go!"

The three humanoids cheered as the snow-doo zoomed down a long slope. Since they were moving so quickly, a modest-looking roller sent their ship soaring high above the land. After what seemed like minutes, they landed on the downward slope which sent them zipping down the mountain at lightning speed. The ship finally slowed to almost a halt.

Sergio said, "Hold on, we're about to descend into gigantic half-pipe!"

The disc tottered on the lip for a moment, then swooshed down into the pipe. The snow-doo flew up vertically and somersaulted above the rim just to speed back down and up to the other side.

They zoomed out of the pipe and sped directly toward a great white wall. Cinder felt like they were going to crash, but the disc slipped through a virtual wall of snow and emerged in a space-aged cave. Shiny, metallic crafts whizzed through the air, changing shape like liquid as they flew. Beams of laser-like fiber optic cables wrapped around their ship, forcing it to a screeching halt. A short, elderly humanoid strode through the air in front of them and gave Sergio the middle finger.

"Is that an elf?" asked Cinder in awe.

Sergio answered, "Yes. He was wearing hover sandals. The elves forge goods in workshops that extend far back into the caves. You'll have to check out the market. As you know, elves make the most fantastic swords, but they also craft other-worldly magi-tech devices."

Cinder's stomach grumbled, "This is amazing, but I'm really hungry."

Sergio said, "Me, too. Let's stop for a bite." Their snow-doo hovered near a dock, and then glided into an enclosure. "The glass is made of diamonds, and if you make contact with it, it sings."

Unable to resist, Cinder placed her palms on the glass, and it sang a beautiful melody with exotic notes that were not possible on Earth. A spread of Mediterranean foods materialized. She groaned in pleasure as she took a bite of piping hot bread that was stuffed with sheep feta and olives and dipped it in tzatziki sauce.

"Yum."

Sergio paused between slurping escargots. "That's their secret. Want one?"

Cinder inspected the snail. "It's raw. Oh, I forgot that you and your sister used to be salamanders."

Jade dipped into a bowl of worms. Cinder decided to focus on her own food and take in the sights.

After they finished eating, they flew off again, whizzing by glowing crystal sculptures and into a large, open room full of gargantuan stalactites and stalagmites that writhed in response to their presence.

The snow-doo cruised out onto a wide expanse of snow, framed by grandiose mountains. The craft came to a stop in front of an ornate wooden castle.

"Wood?" Cinder inquired.

Sergio corrected her, "Petrified."

Jade said, "If you are petrified of this place, why are we here?"

Sergio laughed. "The *castle* is made of *petrified wood*."

As the ship approached a wall of the castle, it opened to let them in.

"Parking garage."

Jade remarked, "Sergio, you seem much more worldly and knowledgeable since I saw you last. How long were we lost in that writer's block?"

Sergio consoled them, saying, "Centuries, but that was in a distant land. It might have only been weeks for you. Time is relative, after all."

Chapter 13: Corralling Cats

As Cinder followed Sergio and Jade out of the ship, they were greeted by a young man with wavy brown hair.

Sergio called, "Alexander! It's so good to see you again."

The men bumped elbows.

Cinder noticed that Alexander had a strange accent as he said, "I've been waiting for all of you to arrive!"

Jade extended her hand in greeting and blushed. "I'm Jade, Sergio's sister, and this is my friend Cinder."

Alexander responded, "I know. I have really been looking

forward to your arrival. I could not be a part of the story without you!"

"Why not?" Cinder inquired.

"That's just how the story goes! My character has not been formally introduced until now. Would you like some refreshments? You are lucky you arrived before nightfall."

"Why?" Jade asked warily.

"Because the giant yetis come out at night."

Loud roars rumbled from the distance outside the castle, prompting Jade to jump into Alexander's arms.

Sergio laughed at her antics. "Never you mind, sister. The petrified palace will keep us safe."

In the parlor, Cinder sank into a chair that hugged her tired muscles like a weighted blanket. She marveled as two suns set over a range of snowy peaks. Before them lay a great still lake that reflected the mountains and setting suns above it. Sergio sat down in a lounge chair next to Cinder, then reached over and caressed her cheek.

"Your face is glowing," he remarked tenderly.

Cinder was embarrassed that Sergio's soft stroke had her skin tingling. "Must be the salamander skin," she muttered quietly.

Alexander returned carrying a tray of steaming hot chocolate and baklava.

As the sun slipped behind the mountains, darkness mercilessly descended. Soon after, a smattering of stars danced into place, twinkling brightly.

Alexander sipped his cup of cocoa and turned to Cinder. "Should we talk about what we are going to do? How are we going to move forward with the story now?"

Cinder said, "Let's think about what happened first. I was at home studying for finals, when a strange man seduced me into the story, and I was literally sucked into the pages of the book. I thought I needed to find my way out of the book, but every step leads to another adventure. After meeting Jade, the plot went way off track. We became lost in writer's block. I was wallowing in my own sorrow when I met a little girl *named* Sorrow—a dead girl who needs to be saved."

Sergio said, "I think we should all work together on a solution. Two, three, or four heads are better than one."

"Yes!" Jade nodded. "You're so right, brother. Now that Alexander is included in the story, we need a plot to keep it going. Otherwise we cannot get to the climax, let alone the end."

Jade giggled and winked at Alexander. Cinder rolled her eyes.

"Exactly," chimed in Alexander. "I have read about the other adventures you have had, which seem fun and all that, but you keep on meandering through fragments of stories. And now here we sit, in a castle made of petrified wood."

Cinder asked, "Why is it petrified? It is very beautiful."

Alexander was happy to supply a brief history of the place. "In the Snow Realm, the trees are alive, so humans are forbidden from using them as shelter or for fire. The ancient dryads crafted this grand castle from deadfall wood, shaped it, and then petrified it for us. The fire for the wood is even petrified, so it never burns out."

Jade cried out, "The ball!"

"Ball?" repeated the others in unison.

Jade looked ecstatic. "I do love a good party."

Cinder's brain hurt. Here they were, wandering away from the plot again. The gears turned so loudly in her head that she feared the others would hear them.

Sergio looked at Cinder oddly and remarked, "Cinder, what's that grinding noise?"

Cinder retorted grumpily, "Never mind! Let's focus on moving the plot forward without getting sidelined again. Jade, can you tell us more about the ball?"

"Yes, yes," said Jade. "Rusty, the master of the moat, invited us to a soirée. He will be the bouncer there."

Cinder gave Jade a sidelong glance. "Shortly after Jade said we needed to get ready for the ball, the writer's block kicked in. Some opposing force must have blown us away from our original trajectory."

Sergio's frowned. "But a ball? What makes you sure this ball is a party instead of some trap that will suck you into a black hole?"

Alexander was flexing his muscles in front of Jade. "Jade, you don't need that thing to protect you. I'm strong. Feel my arms."

"Oooh, you *are* strong," Jade agreed as she ran her hands along Alexander's biceps.

Cinder threw her hands up. "Are we getting sidetracked again? Let's get to this ball, although I hope it isn't until tomorrow. A night of rest would do us a world of good, especially if we are expected to be social and charming at such a grand event."

The ceiling opened, revealing a great crystal dome and the night sky beyond. The moon was shaped like a croissant. Bits of the celestial wonder broke off and floated down into their hands as they roasted the cheese and bread by the fire and had a tasty meal. Alexander produced carafes of white wine.

Eventually, Cinder was too tired to continue the conversation, so Alexander told her, "The floor will light the way to your room."

Alexander demonstrated by walking down a hallway and following a series of lights. Jade stepped forward, and her path went in the same direction as Alexander's. She squealed and ran down the hall as the whole area lit up like a disco ball.

The floor massaged Cinder's feet as her beacon led to the nearest room available. A thick, fluffy down comforter lay invitingly on her bed, but a bubbling sound led her to the terrace, where rose petals floated in a marble bathtub. A pair of warm hands landed on Cinder's shoulders and startled her.

That moment of panic passed; Sergio's voice was deep and soothing. Cinder spun around and looked into his eyes.

He said, "May I kiss you?" Rather than answer him, Cinder kissed Sergio; his lips were firm, yet tender. He whispered in her ear, "You are so beautiful. From the first moment I saw you, I thought you were a jewel. But no diamond could ever sparkle as brightly as you, Cinder."

Cinder descended into the pool with Sergio, and their clothes melted away. "I want to travel the universe with you, Sergio."

"All is yours to decide, my little love," he replied as he stared deep into her eyes. "Remember that you are in charge of what happens next."

Cinder leaned forward to kiss Sergio again, and steam enveloped the two.

Out There
Cataclysmic catastrophe
Strobe of a thousand and twenty glows
Times a mighty number grand
Pluto at the very end
Cosmic dust aglow afar
Anon a view of a birthing star
When we see your picture
You are dead
Is it really so
I rue the truth
We must and could send
Us from beginning to end
Coexist as friends
From different whence and lands

Chapter 14: Late to the Party

Cinder was dreaming about making pancakes and coffee with Sergio when someone tugged on her arm. "Oh, Sergio," she said softly as she opened her eyes.

Although it was dark, Cinder could make out a triangular nose and whiskers in front of her face.

"Wake up!" a scratchy voice hissed.

Cinder sat up like a spring. Something snarled and spat in her face. "Stand up! It's time for you to join the party."

Sharp claws pressed into Cinder's palms. Another set of furry paws clutched around her neck and exerted a surprising amount of pressure.

The scratchy voice warned, "I know precisely where your ventricular vein is located, dearie. Don't fight back, or I will kill you."

Cinder imagined red blood spurting out of her neck. As her eyes adjusted to the dim light, she saw that a motley crew of human-sized moggies dressed in classic gangster clothes surrounded her.

An extremely skinny cat with an eye patch produced a syringe. The cats held Cinder down as they injected her, after which she slipped into a trance.

Chapter 15: Crazy Cats

Cinder sat at a table with a drink in her hand. Dazed and confused, she brought the glass to her lips and sipped. Within seconds, she felt relaxed and mellow. A tall tabby cat dressed in hot pants approached Cinder and handed her a list of drinks, but Cinder didn't want another drink.

"I'm sorry, I don't have any money." She emptied her pockets, hoping that would be enough to convince the striped puss in heels to leave her alone.

"Don't worry, hon," the cat said. "I'll put it on your tab, and you can work it off when your dance shift starts. Don't you remember the rules of the party? Drinking is nonnegotiable. Drink up, or you will be thrown to the tigers."

The tabby unsheathed her claws and scratched the air like she was slashing her own throat.

Cinder nodded and giggled. "Can you put a Tab on my tab, tabby cat?"

The waiter glowered at Cinder, poured half a pint of rum in a glass, and cracked open a Tab. "There you go. Drink up!"

The drinks were infinite. Lemon drops, gin and tonic, cocktails with toes, cosmopolitans, glowing martinis, pilsners, bocks, 100-year-old single malt whiskey, guaro, orange wine, ouzo, egg liquor, ice cream and vodka, and drinks that were lit on fire.

A tall Maine Coon sidled up to Cinder. In a smooth voice, he ordered for her.

"Two mugs of Crown Royal."

Cinder gulped nervously, but after a few minutes she was quite tipsy. She leaned on the cat, admiring his fur.

"You're one cool cat," she said, drooling.

The cat ordered loads of bar food. Cinder continued drinking and ate peanuts, pickles, fries, and dozens of chicken wings. Cinder felt dizzy and bloated. She put her arms around the smooth cat and said, "This is a great party. What's your name?"

The Maine Coon simpered, showing a razor-sharp row of teeth. "I'm Sylve, the king. This is a happening place where you can drink your worries away. It is always a good time in my domain." Sylve produced a flower and handed it to Cinder. "A lotus flower for you, to put in your hair. Come on, let's sing a song!"

A jet-black cat in a suede suit sitting next to them let out a loud cry, and a mob of cats cheered, "Song! Song! Let Sylve sing! The king! The king!"

Sylve stood on the table and, with an *ahem* and a wiggle of the hips, he sang a silly song.

Zanadabee
In the jolly-some land
Of Zanadabee lived a moth
In the cloth of jah-liv-it-a-dee.
Jah-liv, jah-liv, jah-liv-it-a-dee!

The flutterby mutton chops
Soared through the sky,
Quaking and shaking from
Cedar-nut pie.
Tralala trilladee!
Set the sock on the knee
For the cloth in the moth of tranquility.

The dog-dilly-danadoo
Dog with no hair said,
"If you have extra,
could you some for me spare?"

But the cats they just laughed aloud
And puffed up like clouds
In the land of the Zanadabee.
Moth in the cloth who
Makes his brine twisting
The pretzels in knots!

The heat of the sun said,
"So silly be I
for setting away from this
tra-la-la-lie."

Although the song made absolutely no sense to Cinder, she ordered another drink, giggling. Sylve the crooning cat puffed on a Cuban cigar and laughed until he coughed one of his lungs right out of his mouth. The organ was black, slimy, and spotted. It made a few pumping motions and then collapsed. The incident incited a feline frenzy. The cats began to tear the lung apart and eat it. Sylve fed Cinder a piece of his organ, and she laughed along with the rest of the crowd, drunk and delirious.

END Cinder

END Cinder?

Ember flipped through the pages of *Cinder*.

"What? The last half of the book is blank?" Ember was furious. "Stupid story. I can't believe I fell for it. The narrative started out fun, like a whimsical fantasy. Then the story sucked me in and turned dark. Finally, the plot wandered away and off the edge of the earth. The characters are underdeveloped, the plot is nonsensical, and there's no resolution! I could rewrite this book so much better!"

Dejected, yet resolved to do something, Ember flipped to the first blank page. She placed her hand on it, threw her head back, and started laughing maniacally.

"This isn't working. Hand, you're supposed to get me sucked into the book."

As Ember dropped the book onto her lap, snow blew up at her from the pages. Both spooked and intrigued, she opened the hardback again and began to read. The pages of the book came alive as storm clouds painted the sky within and then shifted to form the face of a man. His cheeks were dimpled and his hair rippled with the wind. Gazing into his rainbow eyes caused Ember to become scatterbrained.

The apparition extended his hand toward Ember. He was so close, and she wanted to reach out to him, but her hand just met the page again. Then he spoke.

"Ember, my beautiful Ember. I have waited eons to meet you. Step into the book with me. *Fugere simul.*"

Ember was nonplussed. Latin? Really? She could not trust a handsome man with such an enchanting smile. "I appreciate the thought, and you are a very attractive, uh, man, but I'm not falling for it, Damien."

His demeanor changed completely, "Excuse me? I'm not Damien. He's my evil twin and a trickster who preys on young hearts. I'm the good brother, Xavier. Trust me, Ember."

Xavier's smile melted her brain, and she imagined it flowing out of her ears and onto the ground like a stream of clear water. His green eyes pierced her soul.

"Scatterbrained," she mumbled. "Why would I believe you?"

"Ember, I need you. This whole world does. You are needed to resolve the plot. Without you, we could rot away, doomed forever to be as a forgotten memory, a dream that was never remembered. You are the keystone, for without you, we are nothing."

Ember considered and nodded. "Well, when you put it that way, it both feeds my innate narcissism and makes me feel like I could be doing a good deed. Hmm. If I help, will I still have time to study before finals?"

Xavier scrunched up his face like his eyes were about to well up, just enough to make Ember feel sorry for him. "Is your silly schoolwork more important than saving an entire world? I mean, not to say that education isn't important, but . . ."

Ember was intrigued by Xavier's proposal. "Okay, all right. I need no more convincing. How do I get into the book?"

The lining of Xavier's misty body began to shine silver in the sun. His dark shadows dissipated until he looked like a soft, fluffy lamb.

"Ethereal," she said.

"Ember, it's time for you to help finish the story. What you think you want may not be what you need. Beware the sirens, the subplots, for they will try to lure you away from what you really need to do. If you are successful, you will save the universe. We are all connected."

Ember was wary as she said, "Okay, can I skip the whole forest bit and bookworms? That seems terrifying."

"Ember, you must enter through the portal. You'll have to find your way out of that on your own, but you'll have the help of a few friends."

"Friends?" Ember nervously bit her lip, then gulped and laid her hand on the empty page.

Nothing happened.

"Open sesame!"

Again, nothing happened.

"Hmm. What am I doing wrong?"

Grumpy Bear handed her a pen. "Try this."

"Thanks, Grumps," she said.

As Ember began to write, she felt a tug on her finger. Her digits dipped through the page, and then were lost from view. She tried to pull out her hand, but a force sucked her arm in further. A breeze tickled the tips of her fingers.

Suddenly Toby and Gypsy were by her side, barking. Beauregard the cat stood, tail fluffed and hissing.

"Guys," said Ember. "Get back! You don't want any part of this."

As her arm vanished into the book, Gypsy bit the sleeve of her shirt. Toby bit Gypsy's tail, and then the cat jumped onto Toby's back. With a great deal of squawking, a blue jay flew in through the window and landed on Toby, too, eyeing Beauregard suspiciously.

Ember wailed as she and her four fluffy friends were consumed by the book.

All was dark for a moment, but soon Ember found herself stuck in a tangle of brittle fibers. Tobias and Gypsy pawed at the filaments, and they formed a heap on the ground. A black cat pounced onto Ember's lap and started purring.

"Midnight? What are you doing here?"

Midnight was a tuxedo kitten Ember had when she was a little girl. One evening, Midnight ran into the woods and vanished from sight.

Gypsy barked, "He indicated to me that he's been here for years alone in this awful forest. He's glad to see you!"

Ember nearly lost it. "You can speak?"

Beauregard shot back, "What did you think we were, dumb?"

"Oh my god," Ember breathed.

Midnight stood up on his hind legs, making as if to adjust his bow tie. Ember gulped in awe as the animals stood on their hind legs, standing taller than her. Even the bird was a giant.

She inspected the fibers of the forest. "We really are in the pages of the book! Look, Gypsy, this paper is new. Cinder's book was yellowed and fraying. Does that mean my book is different?"

Something rustled in a dark part of the forest. The cats' tails fluffed again. The canines growled, curling their lips.

A timid voice rasped, "Hello?"

Gypsy, puffing out her chest like a soldier, demanded, "Reveal yourself! Step into the light."

A pitiful guinea pig stepped into the light, his nails clicking on the floor. Beauregard sailed into Midnight's arms, knocking him down.

"I hate mice! And this one is huge!"

Ember recognized the guinea pig. "Pigdor! You're alive! How is it that are you here?" Ember then put her hands on her face and began crying. "I'm so sorry I accidentally killed you that day in the sun! I just wanted you to get to munch on some grass. I had no idea that the heat would overtake you that quickly."

Pigdor's once lustrous coat was now dusty and riddled with pests. "Ember, I forgive you for accidentally slaying me. You were just a child. I did enjoy the fresh air and the grass for a few minutes. There I was, basking in the sun, and I just got so sleepy. The important thing is, you wrote me back to life."

Gypsy said, "Explain yourself, rodent. Why are you here?"

Pigdor responded cheekily, "I don't know, comic relief? What's funnier than a zombie mutant mummified guinea pig?"

A sad bass note bumbled somberly by, prompting Pigdor to catch it and sit on it. "On a more serious note, Ember—"

Ember giggled again, playing an air guitar as she said, "Don't fret."

Pigdor continued, "Reality is relative, and sometimes our tunes play out in a somber relative minor."

Gypsy snorted. "You just said 'relative' twice in one sentence. Tacky."

The notes responded in a relative minor chord progression: A, B, C, D, E, F, G.

Pigdor stepped forward, and Ember embraced him, shedding a few tears. The guinea pig tenderly brushed off the worms that had sneaked from his fur over to Ember's arms.

"I'm so timeworn, or is it time-worm? Wormhole?"

Ember pondered whether she'd created a parallel universe, "More like unparalleled, or perpendicular, but if that's the case, then at some point we'll intersect with ourselves."

Gypsy asked, "Is there a yellow brick road that leads to a magic castle? Where do we go now? Ember, do you have any clues as to what might happen next?"

"I think that we might get chased by giant bookworms and icky bugs."

Gypsy slapped Toby on the back. "Stand tall, soldier!"

Berty flew up high to scan their surroundings, knocking pieces of polymers down that had become too brittle, scattering the scared cats into the polysaccharides and the lignin trees.

Falling into You

Ember ducked into a corner to shield herself from Berty's disturbance in the canopy and was embedded in a woven matrix of hydrogen bonds, cellulose chains, and fibril bundles forged by intermolecular forces between hemicellulose and lignin.

In a soothing voice, Ember called, "Kitty, kitty."

Ember chuckled as the normally stealthy felines teetered out from their hiding places, standing awkwardly on hind legs. Gypsy sniffed the perimeter with Toby close by her side. Toby bumped into the terrier, and she snapped at him with a bark. Beauregard batted at a bond, causing subatomic particles to swarm around her like gnats. The dogs began to bark, and the cat darted away again.

A wind rustled through the paper forest and the great stalks parted. A gigantic face loomed above them. It was Xavier, the green-eyed cloud-man.

Gypsy snarled, "Demon!"

The dimpled man beckoned Ember. "Ember, come with me."

Ember lunged into the forest. Chirping notes collected above her, forming a heart. She followed a path lit with photons.

"Escaped from your excited states, are you?" she hummed seductively, stopping at a translucent wall.

Xavier was standing on the other side of the pellucid pane. Ember lunged forward and pushed on the wall. She tumbled into a tunnel lined with lustrous obsidian. After following a few twists and turns, she broke into a run to find her mysterious lover.

"Jump into my arms, Ember," the voice said.

Ember leapt into a cavern and landed in a large, warm, steaming pile of sloppy stink. She clawed out of the mysterious manure and up onto a slippery stone pillar.

"I'm in deep doo-doo now."

The B Notes

Gypsy ran in circles around the cats, barking, "Obviously Ember was bewitched by that demon. Get yourselves together! We must find her before she does something stupid!"

Toby flanked Gypsy so closely that he kept stepping on her paws, causing her to yelp. Berty flapped his wings, creating a great cloud of dust.

Pigdor yelled, "Everybody just stop moving!" The air cleared, but Tobias barked. Pigdor asked Gypsy, "Why is that dog still just barking? Is he not able to speak? Could you talk to him on Earth?"

Toby whined and looked down as Gypsy gabbed, "Now that you mention it, I haven't been able to make out what he was barking since the day he was run over by a pickup. He rolled out from underneath the back of the truck. I was sure he was a goner. The driver never even stopped. After that he was never the same. I'm the one with the brains, anyway. I always do all the talking and thinking for the two of us. If I took an IQ test, I think you would find that my intelligence is above average, probably even for a human being."

Toby glared at Gypsy, nudging bird notes through his nose. He barked defensively and Gypsy put a paw over his mouth. "Shush, Toby, be quiet."

Berty rolled his eyes, "After that diatribe, you tell him to shush? Look who's speaking."

Pigdor smirked. He picked up a rock and threw it. Gypsy dropped on all fours and bounded after the stone. The terrier ran back with the rock in her mouth and dropped it at his feet. The others laughed.

Gypsy said, "What? Exercise is good for your heart. Have to keep my senses sharp."

A single note flitted by, which Toby tried to bite. It squeaked, and a whole flock of notes arrived, playing a deeply foreboding tune. The notations instantly swarmed the dogs, occluding their views.

"Oh no! They are stinging me!" barked Gypsy.

Pigdor said, "Drat! Bees! I'm allergic; I'll die!"

Gypsy barked, "Uh, you're already dead, but we should get out of here and find Ember. Follow me!"

Pigdor, Berty, Tobias, Midnight, and Beauregard trailed Gypsy up an open path, swatting fibers out of the way. When they had nearly reached a plateau, Toby stepped on a vertical bar with a left-facing colon, and the whole sequence started over again. They were swarmed, at least until they fled up the path another time. Nearing the top, Toby accidentally stepped on another set of the strange dots.

The panting cats disappeared into a crevice to escape the bee notes. Gypsy started up the trail, but when they neared the dots again, Berty pushed them through a crack in the forest, sending them tumbling onto page twenty-two.

"Crushed cranberries!" howled Gypsy. "Now we've no chance of finding Ember! Berty!"

Berty responded drolly, "So you wanted us to keep on repeating that sequence ad infinitum?"

Sniffing his underarm, Pigdor remarked, "What is that horrid odor?" Toby and Gypsy dropped to the ground and began rolling around in a gigantic pile of excrement. Pigdor said, "Now what are you doing?"

Gypsy was on her back, paws up in the air, wriggling in the dung. "Where there are piles of poo, there are beasts. If we roll in it, they won't smell us and eat us."

Pigdor quipped, "Seeing as I already smell really bad, I will just observe your sullying silliness."

Toby ate some of the manure. Pigdor dry heaved. A group of notes playing a cheery tune had surrounded the group.

Pigdor looked relieved. "I have a better idea. These notes seem friendly. Let's all sing together to see if we can excite them enough that they fly away?"

Pigdor cleared his throat and belted out the first line of "Row, Row, Row Your Boat" in a deep bass voice.

The flying notes started to lift him, so Gypsy began warbling in a high soprano. Toby hummed in on the third round, and Berty emitted an off-key caw. The excited notes joined in on the melody and lifted them up in the air, with the giant blue jay flying behind.

Tardigrade King

Ember realized that Damien, Xavier's evil twin, must have tricked her.

"Damn you, Damien!" she cursed, shaking the stinky, fibrous poop off her shoe.

Ember was sitting on a large obsidian rock and surrounded by water. Was she in an underground lake? Something rustled in the darkness. As her eyes adjusted, Ember saw that the whole cave seemed to be moving. Large beasties that looked like stuffed burlap sacks with legs bumbled around. On each of their eight legs were sharp claws. They looked like Oogie Boogie in *The Nightmare Before Christmas*. She made out a circle of teeth set inside a round snout on an eyeless face and realized that she was in a lair of gigantic tardigrades, or water bears.

Ember shuddered. Thousands of the ghastly beasts lined the shore of the dismal, underground lake. Groups of tardigrades were throwing balls into the lake as others crawled out of the water, yawning and stretching. She noticed a similar spheroid at her feet and kicked it into the lake. When the mass hit the water, it began to sizzle and puff up.

"Oh no! They're rehydrating themselves! There must be thousands of them! I'm doomed!"

In response to Ember's utterance, the mouths of the bears on the shore telescoped outward in unison, baring their teeth. Several of the savages latched onto the bodies of their neighbors like lampreys in a horrifying cannibalistic display. Ember covered her ears as sounds of crunching, screams of pain, and grunts of pleasure filled the cavern.

A loud, booming voice interrupted the chaos. "Behold, my kingdom! I have delivered you from your sleep and summoned a beast for you to eat. It is time to feast, my friends."

"Long live the king!" clamored the other tardigrades as they bowed to the looming figure standing three times taller than the others.

The gruesome king was adorned with an ornate gold crown that was dented and covered in grime. He pointed at Ember with a large staff and flared out the purple, rubbery cape he wore, making himself look even more enormous. Tardigrades began crawling into the water, albeit sluggishly. Ember recalled from her studies that they are known as "slow steppers."

Ember didn't know what to do, but she knew she had to do something. "Don't believe him!" she shouted, "I am the one who saved you! I am the one who made it snow. When the snow melted, you were awakened from your sleep. I am your queen! Eat him!"

Some of the tardigrades paused and turned to look at the king, who thundered, "For millennia, I have protected my clan through times of radiation, drought, and famine. It was I, and only I, who summoned this delectable, meaty treat for you to once again thrive and become a great kingdom. Get her!"

The tardigrades extended their quivering mandibles in Ember's direction. Could they sense her fear in the form of biochemical markers? En masse, the crusty bugs lunged for the water and began to swim to her tiny island. Waves from their advances pushed the poop off her rock.

"This is it," she wailed forlornly. Ember was stranded, alone, on a filth-covered island surrounded by hungry water bears that wanted to devour her. She wished that she could at least say goodbye to her pets.

The air began to buzz, and a swarm of unidentified flying objects engulfed her.

"Now what?" she bayed, swatting futilely.

Ember considered jumping in the water but decided to close her eyes and await her fate. Would she be eaten alive by man-eating bees? She sighed and opened her eyes to see the familiar smile of a terrier beneath a furry mustache.

"Gypsy! I've never been so glad to see you!"

Toby nudged his wet, warm nose to her cheek, and Pigdor placed his claw on her shoulder. "Sing!" barked Gypsy.

Together, Ember, Pigdor, Gypsy, and Berty belted out "Row, Row, Row Your Boat" as the flying notes lifted them up in the air and through a tunnel that led to a bright blue sky. The book snapped shut, and Ember's breath caught in her throat when she saw Berty's wing still fluttering in the book.

"No! Berty is stuck in the book! And so are Beauregard and Midnight! Grab it!"

Gypsy pawed at the book, but it immediately flew off into the sun.

Ember was crying for the loss of her friends.

Pigdor tried to comfort her, "There, there. The story hasn't ended yet. If you continue to fill the pages, you will find a resolution."

Ember was pondering how she'd arrived at taking advice from a zombie guinea pig, when a billowing cloud scooped her up and carried her away from her friends. Alone again, she cried tears that crystallized, broke apart, and flew away in puffs.

"Gypsy! Toby! Pigdor!" she called in vain. "They saved me from impending doom and loneliness, but now I am all alone again, stuck in the sky. Poor me!"

Ember flitted along in the sky and eventually cried herself to sleep.

Perplexed

The cats wandered through the intricate fiber forest, playfully batting at globs of small molecular weight plasticized polymers that sat in the interstitial spaces. Berty landed with a thud in front of them, causing the cats' tails to fluff out.

Beauregard said, "Darn it, bird! You scared us."

Berty taunted, "Scaredy cats."

Midnight meowed, "What the fuck is going on?"

"Watch your language! Is this how you talked to Ember?"

Beauregard huffed, "If it weren't for her, we would be sitting at home in the sun eating Meow Mix."

Midnight said, "And how would you eat Meow Mix without Ember?"

Beauregard looked perplexed, then vomited up a white blob.

Berty nudged the vomit with his beak and said, "Too many chemicals! Have you tried insects? They contain healthy minerals and protein."

Beauregard said, "Yuck. Midnight and I have explored the whole page. No matter which way we go, we keep coming back to the same spot. Are you familiar with the story 'Hansel and Gretel'? If we make a path with this paper vomit, and we step in it, we'll know we already walked that route."

Berty squawked, "Maybe you're smarter than I thought."

The animals wandered about the forest, throwing wads of regurgitated paper pulp about until there were piles every way they turned.

Midnight looked exhausted. He sat down and said, "I give up. I'm ready for a nap. It's been hours."

"Good idea," said Berty, "but I'm going to make a nest and stand guard while you two sleep. After that, you can stand watch so I can take a snooze."

Berty quickly fashioned a nest with broken bits of small molecules, pieces of elements, polymers, lignin, and cellulose. The cats climbed up from the ground into a domed structure within a lignocellulosic polymer and purred themselves to sleep.

When the woodland became dark, Berty nudged the cats awake. "It's time for you to watch while I get some rest. I understand that tomcats like you like to wander about at night looking for the next piece of tail, but I don't think you'll find any female cats in this forest. Stay close while I sleep."

Midnight flexed his claws at Berty. "We'd love to 'chase tail,' Berty, but we are 'fixed,' you idiot. Thanks for generalizing, though. Haven't you ever heard about what happens when you assume?"

Beauregard said drolly, "Yeah, you make an *ass* out of *you* and *me!*"

Both cats laughed at Berty.

"My apologies. Your lives are even more pointless than I thought!"

Beauregard threatened, "One more word and I will eat you!"

"Eat this," said Berty as a giant blob of white poop felt down, just missing Beauregard's head.

Berty laid his head down on his nest, leaving one eye open. The nocturnal naturalists wandered noisy around the forest of fibers. Midnight pounced on Beauregard's tail. The two cats yowled as they fought. Beauregard then bit Midnight, who jumped away and up on a ledge made of bonds. As Midnight licked his paw, Beauregard wiggled his large derriere back and forth and then tried to attack Midnight.

Beauregard barely missed the ledge. He hung by his claws, yowling pitifully until the page gave way into shreds. Midnight stretched and sniffed the opening. He inserted his head into the hole and cautiously stepped through. Beauregard followed. His rotund figure was stuck for a moment, but soon the page ripped open wider, allowing his passage.

Berty awoke, mumbling, "Can you idiot cats shut up?"

As Beauregard's tail slipped through the rip, Berty flew down to inspect, after which he scurried after the curious cats.

The Chase

The bright California sun shone through the window of Rayne's bedroom. The girls sat cross-legged on her bed, eating mint chip ice cream straight out of the container. Excelsior lounged in her cage, licking her eyes.

Rayne said, "Excelsior, that's so weird. What else can you do?"

Her room began to shake. Green rays shot out of the golden gecko's eyes and beamed into Rayne's.

With a sinister voice, the carnivore demanded, "Queen Rayne, take me to the beach. Now!"

Rayne flew off her bed, dropping ice cream unceremoniously on the floor as she went, and opened the door of the cage in a hurry. A pair of wings popped out of the gecko's back, and Excelsior flew to Rayne, clasping her talons around the girl's shoulder. Rayne sprinted out of the room and down the stairs, nearly knocking Jagger over in the process.

He scolded, "Hey, watch it, little sister!"

Rayne only dashed out the front door and slammed it loudly.

Joseph's voice carried to his brother from the kitchen. "What's going on?"

"Rayne just bolted."

Joseph emerged from the kitchen, cereal bowl in hand. "What?"

Both brothers lunged for the door, but Jagger spotted her first.

"Look, there she is! She's riding her bike towards the beach. And she's slashed the tires on our bikes!"

Joseph joined Jagger at the door.

In unison, they proclaimed, "Skateboards."

The brothers jumped on their boards and wove through the streets, darting around cars and pedestrians. Rayne was a pink streak, streamers and pigtails flying wildly behind her bike.

Joseph ran over an empty flask of Mad Dog 2020, flew into the air, tumbled onto the pavement, and screamed in pain. Jagger sped on and bolted across a busy street toward the beach. A horn honked, tires screeched, and a car rear-ended another.

Jagger vaulted his skateboard over a set of stairs but didn't stick the landing, causing him to tumble to the sand. Rayne, who was at the shoreline, approached a man who was putting his surfboard in the water.

"May I use your board?" she asked sweetly, batting her eyelids.

The surfer scowled, then laughed and splashed her. Rayne kicked the man in the groin, causing him to double over. The little girl grabbed the board and headed out into the waves.

When Jagger reached the ocean, the surfer was shouting and gesticulating at Rayne, who was duck diving under a wave. Jagger screamed her name as she sank beneath the water.

Quantum Quirkiness

Ember awoke, befuddled. *Perhaps as I egressed the book, I slipped into another dimension.*

Ember remembered that when Cinder hit the air after she left her book, her body had split up into atoms that matched the air. Had the same happened to her? Ember inspected her hand; was it transparent? Feeling quite divided about the situation, she took a breath and observed her surroundings.

Oddly shaped bubbles bumbled about randomly. Inside the strange shapes were letters, mostly capitalized ones. Tiny e's whizzed rapidly by the letters. Upon closer inspection, Ember noted that small, complicated coils, sticks, and particles inside the bubbles were incessantly pulsating and spinning with dynamic swiftness. Ember accidently struck a bubble containing loosely packed atoms that had once made up her elbow.

"Arrrr!" the bubble squeaked. "Can't you be more careful? Bow to me now!"

Ember asked, "Why?"

The argon replied, "I am a noble gas, as decreed by Zeus. With all your different atoms, you ought to know something about that!"

Ember laughed. "Just because you are a noble gas doesn't mean you are royalty. Zeus is just a myth; everyone knows that."

They sky rumbled, and a gigantic lightning bolt flew past Ember's ear.

An ovoid mass containing two spiral shapes wound in the opposite directions, drifting toward Ember. An O in one helix was smiling, while the O in the second was frowning.

The smiling O added, "We are the elixir of life . . . diatomic oxygen. What are *you*, dearie?"

The frowning O grumbled, "You can't be a radioactive element, like plutonium. You're not dazzling enough. You aren't a mutant virus, are you?"

"A virus!" shrieked a negative partner of the neighboring diatomic nitrogen masses. "Let's blow it away from us!"

The elements grew agitated and began shooting photons at Ember.

"Calm down!" she yelled until the elements relaxed back to their ground states.

Ember knew that a wind would only spread a virus, but she was no virus! And anyway, what danger would a virus pose for an oxygen molecule? Why were the atoms and molecules not the cute little sticks and balls that Ember was used to seeing in her school textbooks?

The huge atoms started to blow around more quickly, warming up the air.

The atomized Ember began to form steam. "I guess I am mostly water," she murmured.

Ember accidentally kicked the electron off a hydrogen atom, which excited it terribly. Obviously ionized, naked and upset, the hydrogen fired a photon at Ember. A cool breeze condensed Ember's gaseous particles into water, causing her to fall like many droplets of rain.

Bewildered, Ember felt as if she were coming apart at the seams. Just when it seemed as if her life were ending, she tripped into a hypnagogic trance and dropped out of the sky as dewy orbs of water. A thick thundercloud crackling with lighting surrounded her and sucked her up into its belly.

Bumble Bees
Take a look through my window
Tell me what you see.
I fear there is a quandary,
Bees keep on humming on me.

Well I undid the door,
Too wide you see,

Now don't wanna catch that buzz
Keep your stinger out of me!

Sail in through my skylight
If you can fly that high.
I need some assistance
To get to sleep tonight.
Waiting on the floor,
Alone my mind roams
Airborne autopilot.
It's kind of quiet
Just the way I like it!

Humming bees,
Bumble birds
They really like the honey.
You can do as you please
If you don't want nectar from me!
Gaze into my windows,
See the steel grey rain.
Feel under my overcoat
Rainbow spills I can't contain!

You awoke last night
And shouted in a fright,
Waving at ghost wasps.
You said that I was lost.

I took you by the hand,
Get those bees out of your head.
Come back with me in bed
And rub over me your pollen.

Yes I've fallen into
Dreamin' land again,
Wondering if this road
Will land me on the rails
I wanna ride that train.

So I can get off
At the next stop,
Where I'll meet you
At the peak
Of the mountain.

Bumble birds,
Humming bees,
They really like the honey.
You can do as I please
If you want nectar from me!

Bumble bees,
Hum and drum,
Buzzle me in the trees.
Tickle me like a
Hummingbird's wings.

Bumble you,
Humble me,
As you take my honey.
I'm down on my knees
Nipping the nectar as I please.

The Miasma Man

Ember tingled as the lightning buzzed her molecules.

A soothing voice whispered in her ear, "Hello, Ember. It is I, Xavier."

Something kissed her cool, nebulous hand, sharing his electro-negative set of unshared electrons with her partial positive self.

Ember warmed at the contact. Her atoms became excited and she began to tumble away from Xavier, leaving bits of spent steam in a trail behind her.

Xavier took Ember's hand gently but firmly, and they leapt into the wind, unsheathing their energies. They separated into individual atoms, then divided into electrons and protons. After that, they split into elementary particles such as quarks and leptons. They then diminished into gauge bosons such as gluons, elementary particles that mediate physical forces. The smallest of the smallest of particles seized her soul, whispering about bygone times in worlds far, far away. They told her the secrets of civilizations, wilderness, and grand cosmic gatherings.

After diminishing further, Ember and Xavier ascended to a higher level and slipped completely out of the known universe. They entered an unreality that she would never be able to describe. Even so, a new song flew into Ember's mind. The fact that the words of her poetry were becoming more and more bizarre did not dawn on her.

Horatia

Horatia, you are my lover
Horatia, there will ne'er be another.
I'll take you to the moon a thousand times tonight
Step into my time machine and let's take flight.

We flew to the east and we traveled to the west,
When a thousand dragons

Came flaming o'er a crest.
With fiery breath they charred our tattered rags
We shouldn't have been at a toga party when we took flight.

Horatia, you are my lover
Horatia, I've never known another.
A million sighs I've sighed waiting for your love.
Please don't go down in flames (from the dragon) without
your safety gloves!

Meet me in Machu Picchu
Let's fly to Bombay
To the ancient Parthenon, in B.C. Pompeii
All throughout the universe, we'll travel hand in hand

Horatia, lying in the clover
Horatia, with my kisses you I'll cover.
We'll fold time so we can play in spaceships made of clay.

Horatia, you are my lover.
Horatia, I'll never need another.
Along the way we'll shout and say,
"How we made this day!"

Ember crawled through a thick, gooey primordial stew. The atmosphere above her exploded into copper green bombs as lightning flashed through the air. The static lit the soup on fire. A frog with gills hopped onto her hand.

Ember was a messy mass of floating double helices. Bits of her DNA had exuded into the pond along with Xavier's, causing the pot to boil.

The liquid trebled and chattered and tickled her, cradling her softly and whispering, "I am your true mother, Ember. Forget everything else. Forget your other worlds. You have no higher purpose;

you should stay here where it's easy with Mother. I will take care of you and give you all you need. I am here to provide refection. I am repast for your mind, body, and soul."

Ember sucked her thumb. "Mother."

"Ember," whispered the primordial stew. "Knit me some caps for the babies with your DNA."

Ember made one hat after the other, stitching bits of her DNA together with Xavier's. Xavier began to choke on an amino acid sequence, and Ember stopped her knitting to perform the Heimlich maneuver on him.

After spitting out the sordid stew, Xavier hugged Ember in thanks and whispered in her ear, "Ember, we are in danger! We have landed on some strange siren world! We must get out or we'll remain here forever! I'll distract Mother while you use your knowledge of quantum physics to help get us out of here!" Xavier pulled back and stirred the primordial stew. "Mother, you are the supreme Madonna. Without you, we are nothing. Without you, we are undone. Mother . . ."

Ember's helix intertwined with Xavier's buckyball, and Ember's helix chelated in the center of the buckyball. The power of that combining maneuver allowed them to bounce high up into the atmosphere, at which point Xavier folded over Ember and sped off into space at warp speed.

Ember sighed, but soon a black hole began to pull at them. Since her dream about the black hole, she had learned that spaghettification is what happens when an object is supposedly stretched and ripped apart by gravitational forces upon falling into a black hole.

"Oh no! A black hole!" Ember screamed. "You don't happen to have a black hole invisibility cloak, do you?"

Xavier's eyes lit up. "Why, yes, I do! My father gave me one after I celebrated my six hundred sixty-seventh birthday."

Xavier coughed and spat up a black ball, which quickly unfolded into a large cloak. He wrapped the cloak around Ember and pushed her in the black hole.

"Ember, we need to talk. I'm not ready to settle down. That stew scared the bejesus out of me!"

"What?" screamed Ember as they sped through another black hole faster than the speed of light.

Weightless

The atmosphere started to crackle and pop as a large cloud engulfed Gypsy, Toby, and Pigdor. They floated around, randomly bumping into globs of many different shapes and sizes.

"What are these?" barked Gypsy.

"Oh! I read about these when I was in the waiting room to go to heaven," Pigdor boasted. "These are viruses. They are surrounded by protective waxy membranes called capsids. Inside of them are bits of RNA or DNA. They form clouds of viruses, and bacteria rains down on the earth, sweeping the nasty macromolecules from one continent to the other."

"What?" asked Gypsy.

"Never mind," Pigdor said. "They appear to be friendly. Look, the icosahedron wants to dance with Toby."

The viruses were dancing, drinking, and laughing. While Gypsy, Tobias and Pigdor were still tied together, Gypsy kicked up her heels and danced a jig. Pigdor asked a swine flu virus to dance the flamenco with her. Tobias flipped the long, black hair out of his eyes and started to break dance. The sky boomed with thunder and flashes of lightning surrounded them.

After hours of dancing, Gypsy barked, "I just noticed a change in pressure. Did you?"

Pigdor replied, "I don't know. I'm dead, so I wouldn't feel it either way."

Tobias shivered and whined. The capsids on the viruses congealed, and the blobs stopped dancing. The water particles began to solidify and band together. The dogs and the guinea pig were quickly folded into the crystalline structure of a large snowflake. Then, all at once, they were expelled from the pathogen cloud. Frozen, but together, they lazily drifted down from the troposphere.

The Wave

Rayne navigated three sets of eight-foot waves, bobbing up and down between the fourth and fifth set of breakers like a buoy where the trough was well over her head. Jagger began to swim after his sister, but Rayne dove under the last wave and disappeared. Jagger frantically called for her.

Her head emerged in the calm past the breaking waves, where a group of surfers floated on their boards. Jagger dove under another wave; the sea was frothy and rough. As he came up for air, water splashed his face. Jagger coughed and struggled, but his cries were drowned out by hoots and shouts from the surfers.

Someone cried, "Look! A giant wave!"

The sky darkened. A clap of electric blue lightning snapped and knocked the surfers off their boards. The large wave morphed into a godlike figure. Tendrils of light surrounding the apparition crackled and buzzed. The watery deity raised his hand high, and hurled a lightning bolt at Rayne, who was perched on her surfboard with Excelsior wrapped around her left arm. Rayne stretched out her arms, and the electrical phantasm surrounded her. Thunder boomed and fish fell from the sky. Rayne rode the wave expertly, zipping through the tube and spinning around while flickering in and out of view.

Jagger ducked under the giant wave. As he tumbled in the turbulent water, Rayne's surfboard hit him in the head. The leash ensnared his hand, dragging him along with her as they were sucked into a glimmering tunnel. Rayne grew to about six feet tall. Her hair lengthened and billowed around her head. Her cherubic cheeks remained as youthful as before. Jagger grew taller, too, from about five foot eight to around six foot three, and he also grew a beard in record time.

The world around the siblings became pixelated, and then changed to resemble Impressionist acrylic paintings. Finally, their bodies became amalgams of fractals, like Romanesco broccoli. Rayne's hair flared out in quantum curls. Jagger's hand, still tangled in the leash, bled drops of fire.

Jagger moaned. A gargantuan golden dragon blew its fiery breath onto the cord, searing his tether. Jagger broke free and then lost consciousness.

Back to the Ground

Ember, now in the form of a rainbow, beamed through the sky toward an ocean. Ember knew from Cinder's story that her romance would be fleeting. Was it already over?

Xavier spoke, although she could not see him. "I see you understand that it is time for us to part. Beware my evil twin brother, Damien. This demon has destroyed entire dimensions. I could not bear it if he were to impersonate me and trick you, too. Goodbye, Ember."

Ember landed on the hard deck of a ship. Ember stood up, materializing once again in a humanoid form. Her legs were like jelly. Steam shot up as a glittering haze in front of her and she reached for it, thinking it was Xavier, but the mist slipped through her fingers into a feathery fog and away into the humid air. Before Ember had the chance to utter his name again, he was gone.

Titrate Me

The craziest concoction that could never be
Was you and me
Titrate me . . . with your being.
To quench the fire . . . that burns within
Can you feel . . . the heat . . . when you and me . . . stand together?
I saw you standing there in the door . . . my heart dropped through the floor.
It fell into the mouth of a snake whose thirst it couldn't slake,
That serpent threw my heart from his garden.
It was too sour for him to stomach any longer.
It rolled down the hill to the ocean, to the bottom of the sea; a volcano erupted
Made a new continent; you took the sand
My heart lay in your hand your fingers wrapped around me!

And then you titrated me just to see how caustic I could be!
I want you to take me . . . and drape me . . . all over your body.
Titrate me with your tea drip on me and burn the flames!
Can you feel the heat when you and me stir it up together?
The happiest romance that would never be
Was you and me . . .

Ember was so sad. What had Xavier told her about Damien?

"Oh no!" she exclaimed. "Cinder was with Xavier's evil brother! Like the serpent in my song, had he fooled her into believing that he was worth her heart?"

Beating drums pulled Ember away from her thoughts.

Big Berty

Beauregard and Midnight clawed out of the book into a bright night sky lit up by two large moons. Something above them caused a large shadow. Their tails puffed out. Midnight put his paws over his face and Beauregard prattled on.

"Cover that white spot on your chest, silly tuxedo cat. It gives you away."

A menacing figured circled above the cats. The pusses pawed the air frantically as the giant flying beast cawed overhead. Midnight fainted. A giant bird, bedecked with battle gear, plucked the cats out of the sky.

Beauregard squealed, "It's just that arrogant blue jay, Berty!"

Berty dropped the cats from his talons. The mousers caterwauled and cartwheeled through the atmosphere, the ominous sea looming below them. Before they met their demise, Berty swooped down and caught them with his beak, then stuffed them into an enclosure that was affixed to his back.

Beauregard snapped the latch of the cage shut and strapped the still-unconscious Midnight into a seat. Once Beauregard had buckled himself in, Berty dropped like a bullet directly down to the ocean.

Berty hovered above the water like a helicopter, splashing the water up wildly. Next, he flipped over and dunked the cats into the ocean.

"Sorry, guys. Well, no, I'm not. Is Midnight awake yet?"

As he swooped back up to the sunlit sky, Beauregard mused, "Yes, now he is."

The cats growled and shivered. As if he hadn't noticed, Berty cheerfully observed, "You know if I were to eat you, I'd start by pecking your eyes out like caviar."

"What's your beef with us, Big Berty?" Beauregard screeched.

Midnight sheepishly put his paws up.

Berty cawed, "My beef is with *you*, Beauregard. You tried to kill me when I was a hatchling!"

"That was years ago, and I was so hungry!"

Midnight shrugged, but Berty teased, "You weren't blameless, Midnight. You could have alerted Ember when you saw Beauregard attack me!"

Beauregard defended the black cat. "He's obviously sheepish, so stop pestering him. I'm sorry! I have a problem with my weight, can't you see? Overeating is an addiction, especially for an old eunuch like me, who was once a strong and strapping tiger. It's physically impossible for me to pounce on you now and eat you, for you are a gigantic war bird covered in armor. Plus, you never would have met Ember if I hadn't tried to eat you that day. She saved you and raised you until you were a big, strong, healthy blue jay who could fend for yourself. So stop pestering us. We need to be a team to save Ember."

Berty relented. "Okay, but we have to have a circle of trust here. No more games, cats. You said it yourself; we need to rescue Ember."

Beauregard purred. "I do miss her scratching behind my ears." The grey cat inspected his paws. "Now, with my opposable thumbs, I can do it myself, but it just doesn't feel the same."

Resolved to work with his former attacker, Berty flew higher into the sky. "Hold on tight to my feathers!"

The Brigantine

Ember had a body again, but it looked like a cartoon. She was surrounded by a mesmerizing emerald sea, aboard a ship that had two masts.

"Seems like I'm back on track with Cinder's story, on sort of a schooner perhaps."

A striking girl with dark purple skin and milky white hair, dressed like a pirate, was quick to correct her. "We're on a brigantine, silly. Are you new? I'm Ivory."

Ember recalled that brigantines maneuver easily, but they were only popular from the thirteenth to the eighteenth century. Then she remembered her manners.

"Hi, I'm Ember."

Other women who were also dressed like pirates scurried around the brigantine busily. Some were very tall, some were really short, and some were colors she had never imagined. The ship listed and lurched, causing chaos. The ocean bubbled up, creating a foam. Out of the froth rose a formidable female with iridescent green, leathery skin. She hovered above the waves and vaulted onto the deck with surprising speed. Although there was no wind, her curly crimson hair flew around like it was electrified. The girls on the brigantine were quiet.

The lady from the sea stood high above all the other women and searched their souls with piercing yellow eyes. Ember gasped when she noticed the squid tentacles that were wrapped around the woman's thigh-high boots. With a *swoosh*, the mysterious visitor reduced her relative height as her legs and boots melted into tentacles that then wrapped around her like a dress. One of the squid-like extensions shape-shifted into a dog, which promptly peed on the deck of the ship.

With a booming voice, the woman announced, "I'm Queen Acacia-Lee, queen of the sea 'round these parts. I plucked King Triton—who cheated on me—out of the waters and threw him into a different dimension. Don't mess with me."

The ocean stirred again, and a slimy, scaly, brown, snot-covered, boulder-like head peeped over the edge of the ship. The brigantine rocked, and another head surfaced. This one was even more pimpled, pussy, and barnacle-encrusted than the other. In unison, the awful organisms opened their mouths, baring six rows of razor-sharp teeth each.

Acacia-Lee screamed, obviously incensed with rage. The queen's tentacles attacked one of the ogre's heads. As Acacia-Lee pulled the savage serpent up out of the sea, the other one disappeared, then reappeared at the end of the other beast's body. Ember realized that the heads were connected by one long frame. Finding it hysterical, Ember tugged on Ivory's hand and chuckled, "It's like *CatDog!*"

"What's a catdog?" asked Ivory. "That lower life-form is called the amphisbaena. It, or they, had an affair with Triton when he was engaged to Acacia-Lee."

Ember scratched her head, trying to imagine how Triton and the two-headed sea mistress would make love.

"Is that physically possible?" she inquired with a grimace.

Acacia-Lee bit the amphisbaena's midsection, sending intestines and feces flying all over the ship. Ivory leaned into Ember and puked on her bosom, which caused a chain reaction of vomiting by the other crew members.

The wind whipped up as the angry queen twirled her two-headed foe above her head. The heads of the amphisbaena screeched, "Triton was my lover before you were a sparkle in Zeus's eye!"

Acacia-Lee roared, chomped the amphibious foe in half, and catapulted its remains into the sky. The ship rocked violently as Ember, Ivory, and the other members of the crew slid around the deck, covered in beastly fecal matter.

Enter the Dragon

Excelsior led Rayne into a dark void, and the gecko cackled.

"Queen Rayne, you have entered a forbidden realm where I can regain my full dragon powers instead of being trapped as a stinking lizard! I infiltrated the Air Force compound in Los Angeles and discovered that the shelf off the coast of Santa Cruz hosted a rift in the Earth-Otherworld anti-continuum. This portal will allow me, your Excelsior, to gain back my powers and take over the universe!"

Rayne pressed, "Why were you on Earth? Were you banished?"

Excelsior flew into a rage. "You may be Cleopatra incarnate, but you are still a kid who shouldn't ask useless questions!"

Rayne began to cry, and Excelsior placed her clawed hand on her shoulder. "Dear, dear child. I am sorry. I will save you. I will teach you how to use your powers and talent to influence empires, too! Only I can do this for you, so we must stick together."

Rayne replied, "I've always felt different, like I don't belong on Earth."

Excelsior led Rayne out of the void and into a light. The gecko was no longer a tiny lizard, but a giant, golden dragon.

"Look at you, Excelsior! Wow!"

Excelsior's voice grew deeper as she said, "And you, my dear, are as tall and strong as Wonder Woman! Climb on my back. We will fly together."

The great dragon unfurled her bat-like wings. Black blood visibly pumped through the thin skin covering the skeletal fliers as she soared over a glistening lake, which turned into a great waterfall. A drop of water flew up and stayed suspended in front of Rayne, and the girl peered into the orb in awe.

"There is an entire universe in this one drop of water!"

"Yes, yes, child," nodded Excelsior. "Do you feel your strength?"

Rayne's eyes lit up with greed, but then she frowned. Excelsior flew on until the air grew so humid and thick that the dragon took a sword and cut through it. The pair finally arrived at a door. Excelsior breathed fire onto one of her golden talons. The metal softened and she inserted it in the lock in the door. The dragon then blew cool air onto the lock, waited a moment, and unlocked the door.

Rayne shuddered loudly as Excelsior led them into a meticulously manicured garden. Golden trees with leaves of jade and jeweled fruits stretched out in rows before them. Excelsior looked into Rayne's eyes, and the girl's face lit up.

"Did you just send me a telepathic message? Did you just say that the trees are made of diamonds and sapphires and that the stems are made of living gold that grow from the ground?"

Excelsior cackled. "Climb on my back."

The dragon propelled herself into the air. Rayne's hair flew wildly about as they soared past quartz mountaintops. A marble path amidst peridot fields led to a gaudy, ominous castle.

Excelsior landed on the tallest turret and screamed, "I, Excelsior the Dragon, The Great Daughter of the Golden One, the one who slayed God, have returned from exile with the human Queen Cleopatra reincarnated by my side! My mission will be to take over the universe for those who know how to serve the Greater Good."

Meeting of the Minds

Jagger was awake, soaring through the air on a flying carpet surrounded by a pixelated, tourmaline ocean. The world came into focus, but only for a moment. Jagger's magical rug morphed into a flying saucer, then a large yacht.

He stretched out his arms and said, "Yeah, this is the life." But his ride changed yet again. The luxurious cruiser turned into a tipsy, wooden canoe. "Great," he muttered.

He breathed a sigh of relief when the canoe grew larger and transformed into a pirate ship with four masts, leaving him standing in expansive, opulent sleeping quarters. He looked in a mirror.

"That's not me! I look like I'm almost thirty! And I'm a caricature of myself! In fact, everything looks like a cartoon here." Jagger's frown turned into a smile. "Oh, I get it! This is all a dream. Thank God, that means Rayne is safe."

The newly minted man strode charismatically out of the cabin and onto the deck, where a crew of young pirates plugged away.

A stocky, orange bloke approached Jagger and hollered, "Hail to the captain!"

A platoon of plunderers hurrahed.

Jagger shrugged his shoulders sheepishly. "Remind me, what did I do?"

A tall, lanky pirate with coal-black hair gave Jagger a fist bump. "Dude, you saved us from Fractasia, where the evil dragons and their minions kidnap carbonaceous creatures, transform their matter into blocks to build their castle, and then suck out their souls. Thank you for bringing us into this land of enchantment."

Jagger replied, "This is the craziest, albeit most realistic dream I've ever had. I like it."

Out of the blue, the decapitated head of something belonging to the sea landed on the deck and splintered all over the startled assemblage. The pirates sloshed around in green goo.

A lithe man in the crow's nest, scope in hand, signaled to the horizon and harked, "Set the sails! I see another ship!"

Jagger, hands on his hips, bellowed, "Godspeed, mates."

Chaos Circus

Ember was glad that the two-headed gargoyle was gone, but gagged as beastly entrails dripped down her visage and clothes.

Before she had time to process the mess, a small, sinewy woman with dark curls screamed from atop the mast, "Ahoy, my queen! A pirate ship is sailing toward us! It's a sloop full of men!"

Acacia-Lee extended her tentacles to the eight oars in the galley. The brigantine bucked forward and zoomed across the ocean so fast that water splashed over the deck and the girls, cleaning up the mess. Just before the two vessels collided, Queen Acacia-Lee swirled her tentacles about the pirate ship to stop it from crashing into them.

The queen ordered, "Ready, aim, fire!"

The women began hurling jackfruit, durian, star fruit, papaya, and dragon fruit at the men, blasting meaty fruit all over their deck. Ember rushed over to a free cannon and was both disappointed and confused to see only a few balloons meander out of the end. The next proved more fruitful after she loaded plaid gelatinous balls with fruit bits into the barrel. She squealed with excitement when she drenched an opponent in a stream of bright pink liquid, but then tasted it and grimaced.

"It's fermented Hawaiian Punch!"

The male pirates jumped on the brigantine, screaming and hooting. Ember thought that the queen might do something to stop them, but was puzzled to see that their regal leader was instead kissing a hairy-chested brute of a man.

Ember shook her head. "Well, you won't catch me doing that. First there was Titus, then there was Xavier. No more men!"

A young man jumped on deck in front of Ember. She grudgingly noticed that he was attractive, although he was dripping in red punch that kind of looked like blood.

"So, you're the cozen wench who cannoned me with juice?" he demanded. The man then extended his hand to her. "Hi, I'm Jagger!"

When Ember held Jagger's hand, a strange force flung them both into the sea. Ember had an incandescent mermaid tail. She blinked, but when she opened her eyes again, she was back on the ship.

Read and Repeat

Ember tried to understand what was going on. Had she not just been a mermaid? A sleepy-looking set of dots that looked suspiciously like a repeat sign from sheet music flew by her nose. Ember captured the strange figure.

"What are you doing here? Did you stow away on me from the book?"

The repeat sign squeaked loudly and bit her hand.

"What a nasty beast! I suppose you are going to make me go over the last scene again. Is that why I am standing on this ship again?"

A female approached Ember exuberantly and gave her a high-five. "Hey, Cinder, great shot! You just hit the captain of the ship with a bunch of bananas."

Ember wondered if she could believe her ears. "Ivory, did you just call me Cinder?"

Her pirate friend looked concerned. "Cinder, are you okay? It's me, Jade. Who's Ivory?"

Ember scanned her surroundings. She was no longer in a cartoon land, and Ivory was gone. Jade's eyes glowed green as she looked at Ember quizzically. Was this Cinder's Jade? Had she ended up in intersection of space-time?

"I just got dizzy," Ember finally said. "I need a moment to sit down."

Jade rushed to a cannon. "Okay, but hurry up, because the opposing ship is coming fast!"

Ember plopped down on a burlap sack. That repeat note had certainly screwed things up. Too bad—she had taken a liking to Jagger. Now she would never see him again. What had Hawking said about time travel? If you fly around a black hole for five years at the speed of light, then you'd be five years younger than your friends back on Earth?

"Oh no! When I was in the primordial stew, my DNA replicated. What if Xavier being there with me mutated me somehow? Will I get cancer? We spent who knows how long there, and then traveled faster than the speed of light back. Who knows how many copies of me could be floating around! What if I'm evil somewhere else?"

With a great cacophony of commotion, the pirates jumped onto the deck and snapped Ember out of her thoughts. A male pirate covered in creamed bananas stood before her.

"Are you the cozen wench who doused me with juice?"

Why did Jagger's parallel universe twin say he's drenched in juice when he's really buried in bananas?

Ember grew faint and lost her balance.

Bosom Buddies

Shadows danced like dark ghosts. The undersea world came into focus like a pond settling into a reflection. The ocean's ceiling was a stained-glass window that relentlessly shifted, weaving a story that was never the same, bringing warmth and light to the sea's teeming cauldron.

Dappled shafts of probing sunlight coruscated off the nacreous scales of Ember's fishy tail. Large, abalone-like shells covered the fullness of her bosom, but just barely. Strings of pearls served as straps for her clams. Ember pulled gently at the shells, wondering how they stuck so well. To her surprise, a large mussel reached out and slapped her hand.

"It is daylight; you keep your clothes on, missy! How dare you. Hmph!"

With a squirt of bubbles, the shells clamped down firmly on Ember's chest. A cherubic fish with plump lips lulled Ember into a trance. Ember reached toward the fish when something grabbed her, pulling her away.

"Hey! Let me go!" Ember caterwauled, pummeling her attacker with her fists.

"Are you okay?" a worried voice asked. "That queen angelfish could have killed you! They are venomous."

The angelfish exploded into flames and became a demon wielding a sharp pitchfork. The miscreation spit out a string of expletives that unraveled like toilet paper.

Jade floated into view, kissing a ruddy-faced man with an apple-shaped figure and a remarkably large head.

"Hey, girlfriend! This is my special friend Jack. He's from Atlantica City, and he wants to take us to his favorite sushi restaurant. Who's *your* friend?"

A familiar voice responded, "My name is Jagger."

Ember remarked, "No, it can't be."

Jagger squinted at her. "Haven't I met you before?"

Jack's tail flicked back and forth like an impatient cat. "Let's race to Atlantica City. Follow me!"

Jade replied, "You're challenging me? You're on!"

Ember tried to follow Jade and Jack, but she shot wildly around in a circle so fast that she nearly whipped herself with her own tail. Jagger swam closer to Ember.

"Here, I'll help you. Just feel the rhythm of my body and try to mimic my motions."

"Yeah, I've heard that one before," Ember mumbled.

But Jagger looked sincere. "May I please help you learn how to swim? I'm a surfer."

"Fine," growled Ember.

Jagger put his muscular arms around Ember, making it even more difficult for her to concentrate. Ember smacked Jagger with her tail.

"Ouch!" he yelped. "Dude, relax!"

"Don't call me *dude*. I'm a woman!"

"So, you don't eschew chivalry?" Jagger asked, seeming surprised.

"Well, I am from the South," she teased with an exaggerated drawl.

Jagger laughed. "The Southern Seas in the Land of Enchantment, where cartoon people throw rotting fruit at each other?"

Ember halted. "Wait, why did you say *cartoon*?"

"I don't know. I guess I dreamed that I met you in an animated world. You wouldn't understand, because you're only a figment of my imagination anyway. I'll play along, though. I'm from Santa Cruz, on planet Earth."

Ember's mouth dropped open, letting a fish swim right into her mouth. She coughed it out and sputtered, "That's impossible. I'm from Cullowhee."

"Cullo-what?" questioned Jagger. "See? Exactly. Just a dream."

"No, you dolt! Cullowhee is a Cherokee name for 'Judaculla's place.' He's a big, ugly beast who, as legend tells it, terrorized local Cherokee folk with his long sharp claws."

"Okay, definitely not from Earth."

"Judaculla is a myth. Cullowhee's about an hour west of Asheville, North Carolina."

Jagger's face became serious. "So, you're really not from here. Is this a dream? If it's not, I need to find my sister. She's little and she could be in trouble."

That made Ember feel guilty. "I'd like to find my pets, but they obviously aren't as important as your sister. One of them is dead, anyway, but they can talk and they might be able to help us. Is this all my fault?"

Jagger hugged Ember and cooed, "I'm so glad you're real."

Ember melted into Jagger's warm arms. They descended into a darkening forest. Schools of fish drifted by, reading books and learning lessons. Her hand accidentally grazed Jagger's thigh, and her tail lit up. He brushed her cheek with his hand, but she growled and clawed at him.

Jagger looked angry. "What's wrong with you?"

"I just had the strangest urge to rip into your throat and eat your heart out. Maybe I'm just hungry. Are mermaids cannibals?"

Jagger sniffed the water. "Now that you mention it, I think I can sniff out Jade and Jack's trail."

Ember nodded her head. "It's so weird, but I can, too."

"Let's go find them. Just don't follow me *too* close, please!"

Ember raced after Jagger. Finally, her tail moved in perfect harmony with the water. She caught up with Jagger and passed him, her sudden cannibalistic desire gone. Ember burst into song, once again unable to control her voice. It was almost as if she were in a fairy tale.

Reel Me Out
My days in the school were cool
Always swimming in a pack.
One day this fish swam off
Never ever to look back.

Like a flounder deep in
The Mariana trench,
I was flat and really down.
I was low down on the ground.

Before you reeled me out
(Of the ocean),
I was just another tail
Skinny-dipping around.

Then you reeled me out
(Of the water).
Your cast didn't fail
Now round and round we flail.

It was happenstance.
I was moving along,
Got up from that gulch,
Started bubbling a song.

Morphing fluke my eye moved around,
Then I saw that bait
Dangling down, ate it great.
I grew up and hit the ground.

Before you reel me out
(Of the sea),
I need another reason
To taste that temptation.

Then you reeled me out,
You didn't quite know what to say.
Were looking for a tuna
But got a flounder anyway.

Reel me out of the water
I'll take the bait.
Can't wait to butter you up
And put you on the table.

Jagger gazed at Ember, entranced. "What was that? Is this a musical now? Are birds going to fly to your shoulder and sing, too?"

"Maybe," she answered impertinently.

"Duly noted." He gave her a wink.

Ember and Jagger entered a pair of ionic columns adorned with seaweed and anemone blooms. Clownfish darted in and out, laughing hysterically. Ember composed herself, did a perfect loop-de-loop like a coryphée, and swam into the city alongside Jagger. They followed a luminescent thoroughfare alongside houses and cafes, soaking in the sights until Jade and Jack hailed them from a marble balcony.

"Shall we just swim up there?" Jagger shouted, starting to swim.

"No!" screamed Ruby, swimming over the side of the balcony. "You have to cross the bridge first. The moat monster, Biff, will eat you if you don't pay a toll to cross the bridge."

Ember patted her thighs and laughed, for she had no pockets on her tail. "Well, I don't have any money."

"I think that you have what it takes, Ember. You must pet Biff."

"What?" asked Ember. "But he's so ugly!"

Jade responded, "You must look past his ugliness to enter. If you look inside his soul, you will see the beauty within."

Ember was not convinced. Was this some sort of moral test?

"Okay, whatever."

She inched closer to Biff, who wagged his rusty tail and stuck out his forked tongue. She extended her hand and put it on his crusty, scaly head. When she opened her eyes, she saw that Biff had the most beautiful soul she had ever seen. He had transformed into an angelic unicorn with a mermaid tail. He led Ember and Jagger peacefully over the gate, which lit up with rainbow colors as they swam over the stones.

Undersea, Again

Ember opened her eyes to find that she was in a coral reef smooching a rough sponge. Clown fish, bouncing on their beds of anemones, bellowed out hearty laughter. Jagger, Biff, and the undersea city were gone.

Jade with her long hair floating about her shoulders, was laughing, too. "There you are, Ivory! What in the world are you doing with that sponge? Cleaning your lips? Follow me!"

Ember noticed that another repeat sign was stuck on her tail. She shrugged her shoulders and ate it. She assumed she had slipped into another parallel dimension again. That would mean that this girl probably wasn't Jade.

"I'm sorry, I must have had a bout of amnesia. What is your name again?"

"That's okay, Ivory. It happens to the best of us. My name is Ruby, like my long, ruby locks."

"My name is actually Ember."

"Okay, if you say so," Ruby professed. "My, look at the time. We should get ready for the ball. We can go to my abode and snack on some herring and seaweed salad. I know I'm famished."

"That would be very pleasant," replied Ember, still somewhat confused. "Where do you live?"

"I live in the Enchanted City, capital of the Land of Enchantment. I personally prefer the Enchanted City to the scene in Atlantis. Atlantis has a dismal underground holding facility for humans who end up there. The poor creatures are captured and kept there to preserve the secret of the city. No human has ever made it to the Enchanted City. But obviously you aren't human because you are a mermaid, right?"

Ruby took Ember's hand and led her through a twisting tunnel of rock, after which they came to a dark wall.

"Open, Poppy Seed."

A hidden door opened to a reveal a bustling city inside. Blackjack and poker games, dealers, and elegant, distinguished figures filled the casino. Laughter, drinks, and sand dollars floated through the room. A flounder band played lively background music. Glittering plants hung from the ceiling. Plankton chandeliers radiated eerily.

Ruby clarified: "We just crossed the border. It's known as the Ruby Light District. I live in an enchanted castle down on Anemone Lane, but if we take a manta ray, we will not have to swim."

The girls left the casino and came up to a row of flat cephalo-pods. Ruby produced several sea-dollars and handed them to Ember.

"Here's your fare. All aboard!"

Ember felt like she was Nemo. She tentatively positioned herself on the back of her manta ray, and they sped off to Anemone Lane. Even though the rays swam no faster than she could, it was nice to have a rest. Magnificent mansions and peculiar dwellings lined the streets. Fast-food restaurants with holograms of rotating fish burg-ers tantalized her desire for a quick meal.

While they traveled, Ember told Ruby about her strange adventures.

Ruby replied, "I've had some unbelievable journeys, too."

Ruby led Ember to an enchanting castle with gardens, mazes, and rows of coral that provided a playground for its young inhabi-tants. The girls swam onto the terrace and into Ruby's bedroom.

Ember inquired, "Have you always lived here, Ruby? In the Enchanted City, I mean."

"No, I have not. Would you like to hear about how I came here? I think we have time before the ball."

What was with this mysterious ball? Was Ember stuck in the mind of an author who would never finish and publish a book? She didn't want to relive the same scene over and over again, ad infinitum. She wondered if the author of a story is the only author, for each and every copy of a book exists in the mind of its reader, creating a dif-ferent universe depending on those who have ever read it in the past, present, or future. What if she were really trapped in a book and had never existed except in the minds of readers? Did she even exist at all?

"Do I need a spaceship or a time machine to try and find some real meaning to all of this?"

Ruby felt Ember's forehead. "What are you going on about? You said you wanted to hear about my past, then you just stared off into space."

"Wait. Stop, Jade—I mean, Ivory. I mean, Ruby! Sorry. I already know this story and I already found a boy and I know you have a salamander brother. I'm running out of time."

Ruby's face was red. "Ember, I don't know where you're getting your strange ideas, but I don't have a brother who is a newt. My name was Echo in another life, not Jade. Perhaps if you learn to be a better listener you might resolve your quest."

"I'm sorry, Ruby," Ember conceded. "I'm just tired of this journey. Please, tell me your story."

Ruby's Story

"I was a mountain nymph on Mount Olympus, minding my own business, when one day I spotted an extremely handsome man with bulging thighs, tan skin, and a fantastic pompadour hairdo. His hands were tanned, supple, and strong, with soft glowing skin."

"Oh my," blathered Ember.

"I began to follow this handsome young man who kept peering into the pond to hunt fish, until he became completely entranced with something in the water. The fish must have put a spell on him, because he just kept saying his name over and over. '*Oh, Narcissus!*'"

"Uh-huh. Quite the charmer, I'm sure."

Ruby responded, "You wouldn't believe how handsome he was! Don't judge me. Do you want to hear the rest of the story or not?"

"Please do tell, Ruby—Echo."

"No! Don't call me that!" begged Ruby. "I entered the fairy witness protection program, and now I'm a Ruby fairy in the Land of Enchantment. My duty is to keep everyone's spirits up, even when pending doom awaits."

"Excuse me?" coughed Ember.

"Well, after I tried to embrace Narcissus, to save him from the spell, he spurned me. In a weak, whiny voice, he prattled, 'Leave me alone!' He threw me down and I broke a wing. When I finally made it back home, Aunt Nemesis banished Narcissus to be a flower for the rest of his life. Zeus was furious, so Aunt Nemesis had to change my name and hide me in another dimension."

"Wait a second," Ember interjected. "Even I know this story. Ruby, you mean to tell me that you didn't know that Narcissus was only in love with himself?"

Ruby blinked. "Really? Is that why he was so rude? Aunt Nemesis always told me I needed to pay attention more."

Ember hugged Ruby. "It wasn't your fault that Narcissus rebuffed you. He only cared about himself, and it sounds like your aunt may have been a little narcissistic, too, because you aren't slow. You are wonderful."

Ruby brushed her off her lap, threw back her shoulders, and flipped her luxurious hair. Red ringlets framed her face perfectly, like a doll. Her eyelashes were long and soft like velvet.

"I'm so glad I met you. You made me feel good, and I'm supposed to be the cheery one. But isn't it time to go to the ball? Ember?"

Queen Rayne

Excelsior announced proudly, "This is Castle Clarity in the land of Fractasia. Rayne, you are Cleopatra, Queen Isis. Can you feel the raw power of the universe coursing through your veins?"

As Rayne stepped onto the opaque black panels of the castle floor, a surge of light flowed into her feet. "I feel a deep sadness, but also hope."

Excelsior looked worried for a moment, but then attempted to smile, revealing her sharp teeth.

"What do you mean I'm a queen?" replied Rayne.

"Let me show you around the castle," purred Excelsior as she stroked Rayne's dress. "The fabric is made of nano gold. Each thread is only one atom thick, and they are held together through an electromagnetic field. This magical dress was made by Hephaestus himself, the blacksmith of the Greek gods."

Rayne beamed. "It's magical? Is that why this dress fits me perfectly?"

"You are a very intuitive child. Don't you love the castle?"

"Well, it *is* grand."

Excelsior scratched the air frantically with her front claws. "Rayne, where are you? Queen Rayne?"

The Mystical Magical Tour

Rayne was no longer in the castle. She was running down a rotating tunnel toward a bright light. Her dress lifted her into the cosmos, past a million stars, and into the center of a large sun. In the middle of the sun was a large masculine figure.

In a meek voice she asked, "Who are you?"

"I have so many names. Some say I am a great creator, and that I make matter from the fog."

Rayne giggled. "Can I call you the Fog?"

"That sounds reasonable for someone with more names than the number of floors in the Burj Khalifa."

"What's the Boorj California?"

The voice chuckled. "Do you know what the Tower of Babel is?"

"I think so."

"The Burj Khalifa is the tallest building on record in your time on Earth. It is in a city called Dubai. It's reportedly about 2,717 feet tall, and has 163 floors."

Rayne replied, "Okay, well, I like the Fog. It's easy."

"Funny you say that—I just lifted the fog from your brain. Now, back to why you are here. Your father wasn't human, but the emperor of Planet Apex 279.Z."

Rayne inhaled sharply. "Really? What was his name?"

The Fog expounded, "His name was Mar. Millions of years before your father was born, a race of dragons ruled Planet Apex 279.Z. Most of the dragons were good, but once they developed time-teleportation, a sect of them became so evil and powerful that they threatened to destroy the universe. The dragons began to fold time, thus changing the present, future, and past of many worlds and causing general chaos. When the beasts sought to destroy me, their creator, I sent Zeus to the planet to annihilate them. Unfortunately, Zeus brought along Eris and Pandora. Eris sneakily stole a dragon egg, hid it in Pandora's box—where she thought it would be safe—and stashed it in a forest of the Planet Apex 279.Z. Millions of years later, when Mar was a young man, he traveled to a vast desert that used to be the forest where the dragons roamed. There he uncovered Pandora's box, and the dragon egg within. Mar raised a dragon, which he named Excelsior. Your father and his dragon were inseparable. With Excelsior, he began to explore the universe. One day they warped through time and space to Earth, where he met your mother. Excelsior was crushed. She killed your dear dad and transported herself back to the reign of the dragons, when they were able to alter the future, evade Zeus's wrath, and infiltrate the galaxy again."

Rayne frowned. "But if Excelsior turned back time, why am I alive?"

"Just because dragons can travel through time doesn't mean they can change what's already happened. When you stepped on the surfboard the day Excelsior led you into the ocean, what did you feel?"

Rayne's eyes flickered. "I could feel knowledge bubbling beneath me. When I crossed dimensions, I could *feel* the space in between calling to me, whispering to me."

"The moment before you make a decision, there are one million outcomes that could occur. That space, that moment between the dimensions is so powerful because it can take you anywhere. Most sentient beings don't know how much power they have before they make a choice. Many let the universe take control, which basically means that chaos takes control. If you choose carefully, you can have a say in what happens next."

"The moment I stood up on the surfboard, it was like I peered into the door of the universes," Rayne mused. "I saw worms, strings, and threads going in and out of Excelsior."

The Fog explained, "She was letting anarchy control her. What else did you see?"

"I saw the intention of every dragon."

"Yes, dear child, these evil dragons are telepaths, so you must guard your thoughts, lest all of them know what you do."

"I see. I felt, deep inside my soul, the evil objectives of all the dragons in the universe," she said. "I could sense their hate through the electrolytes in her sweat. I could smell their sulfuric thoughts. The silky strings surrounded Excelsior, wrapping her up and pulling her into a fire. I became tangled in the web, but the acrid fumes burned my eyes, and I felt like I was pulled off the surfboard."

"She was pulling you into chaos, and in that moment, I made up the Land of Fractasia to divert the dragons and save you. They did not know about it until I created it, but since they are ruled by greed they are also blinded by the truth."

"That's pretty weird."

He replied, "Well, I'm the Fog, or whatever else you want to call me, and I'm pretty weird myself. This universe is ruled by chaos, and sometimes I have to work with what I have."

"Okay. What's next? Am I the queen of the dragons?"

"You are not the queen of the dragons, per se, but you have a quantum relation to Excelsior because of her connection with your father. You, and only you, have the power to reach into Excelsior's brain and switch off time for her," the Fog explained. "Since she's connected to the other dragons, you could theoretically reach into all of their minds. Try it now so she doesn't notice you are gone."

Rayne closed her eyes, searching within for her supposed connection. When she opened them again, she said, "Wow, I did see into Excelsior's mind. How very strange!"

"The dragons are evil. You are so powerful because your childlike spirit will always prevail. Because of that, your mind is not limited to the constraints and prejudices of adulthood. Use your powers for good, Rayne, and help me save mankind from itself."

"Why did she call me Cleopatra?"

"Do you remember when you weren't here on Earth?" asked the Fog.

"No!"

"Rayne, you have been reincarnated many times. One of your fathers was the Egyptian god Geb, who was also the father of Osiris.

He was once a small child, too, running through the beginning of time. He grew up on a planet in the far reaches of the galaxy, his mother knitting sweet bibs for him to gnaw, but as soon as he was grown, Human Resources whisked him away to a rural planet with no technology."

"Human Resources?" asked Rayne.

"Yeah, that would have been me. Geb had potential. He needed room to grow. I sent him to Earth to rule over the Egyptians and to teach them how to make pyramids so they could make gold and harness power from the sun for the city. When the humans started to become powerful and had thoughts of exploring space, Zeus became jealous. He started screwing with the humans, injecting them with greed, hate, and lust, thereby stunting them and starting wars.

"Zeus descended from Mount Olympus to fight Geb. On his way to Earth, Zeus met Hera, and he was quickly distracted after she spurned him. Around the same time, Geb became infatuated with the intriguing Ptolemaic ruler Cleopatra. When she became pregnant, she seduced Ptolemy to hide the fact that the Egyptian god was the father. Your royal blood runs thick, as you were once Cleopatra and a great ruler, but that was in the past. This is now. Since matter is neither created nor destroyed, those who inhabit Earth are all part of each other. It's not the bloodline that matters, but your will."

Rayne blinked. "This is all really strange, but I always knew I was different. Why did Excelsior call me Isis?"

"Isis is one of Geb's daughters. She was a caring goddess who loved all, sheltered families, and cured the ill. She was one of the supreme goddesses. Rayne, you are also the goddess Isis. This is so important, because as Isis you can help the dead enter the afterlife. There are many souls wandering around lost in purgatory. The evil dragons want to steal these wandering souls and turn them into jeweled mortar to build the walls of Fractasia. You can save them by bringing them to Hades where they can cross the River Styx and finally rest."

Rayne argued, "It sounds like you are making this up."

"When you were being pulled into a web of chaos, I had to make a decision. In that moment, I created a path to Fractasia. Maybe I diverted the dragons, but the chaos was always there. What does it matter what choice I made now? Castle Clarity in the land of Fractasia on the planet Böse that swirls around the sun is what you have to work with right now. Oh yeah, you should probably see how your brother is faring, too, because right now he is a merman swimming to Atlantica City."

"What? Is he okay?"

"He's fine. He's trying to find his way, too."

"Jesus!"

"And what does Jesus have to do with any of this?" the Fog asked sarcastically. "Now, do you know who Geb's grandfather was?"

"Who?" asked Rayne.

"Atum, or Ra. The Creator." The Fog suddenly bathed Rayne in sunbeams. "You are my precious granddaughter. How else could you walk into the sun?" As the revelation sank in, Rayne shed a large, golden tear that dropped into the hand that emerged from the light. "Off you go to save the world, my little ray of sunshine."

Rayne nodded, stepped back, and flickered back onto the fractal floor of the Castle Clarity in Fractasia. She stood in front of Excelsior, and then snapped her fingers.

Excelsior bowed low to the ground. "What are you thinking, Queen Child? I can no longer read your thoughts."

"Why would you want to read my mind?" Rayne asked.

Excelsior glared at Rayne, backing up and bowing down low again. "The Cleopatra/Isis child grows stronger."

The dragon ran backwards, screaming and spitting sapphire and gold fireballs into the air.

"Come now, Excelsior, calm down. I will help you build your castle with your poor souls. I am on your side. I want to be your Queen. Humans are stupid, fickle fools who are worthless." Satisfied, Excelsior stepped forward to Rayne, allowing her to scratch her behind her ears. Rayne spoke in a soft voice. "You don't need to read my mind, but know that I can indeed read yours, for I *am* Isis."

Rayne threw her head back, and beams of light shot out from her mouth and eyes, overlaying the inside of the castle with gold.

The Doldrums

Ember rolled into a ball and faded away into a listless dream. She found herself sitting at a desk studying abstract equations. Her teacher told her she needed to learn a language called Trillallalee to understand the teacher for the math course. After enrolling in the language course, she became infatuated with the teacher's apprentice, who trilled to her all day, and a dog with the dana-bee moth in the cloth, all whilst wondering whether things really happen at random or for specific reasons. Ember began to wonder about energy and made up a little ditty.

Sleep and Dream
Quasar at the bazaar
Black hole from afar
Wormhole
Brings you near
Dear, like a lily of the valley

Nestled 'round my ear
Burst into fractal infrared
Mendeleev mode virtual
Scatter Rayleigh

Sleep and dream
Sleep and dream

There's no free energy
So let's pedal you and me
Take the breeze
Make energy
From a waterwheel

> *I flew last night*
> *In a dream*
> *Threw out my arms*
> *And careened*
>
> *Wings swept up by wind*
> *Float through a cumulous*
> *Sirius*
> *Fly away*
> *Sleep and dream*
> *Sleep and dream*
>
> *Crawlin' crawdads red*
> *Reach out and claw my hand*
> *Slip, slide down mossy dreams*
> *Blazing sun in swirling skies*
> *In the shade*
> *There's no free energy*
> *Gibbs me free energy*
> *Gibbs me free energy*

After singing the song, Ember danced in a music video. The melody started out folky, then changed to heavy metal. A tiger in a bunny onesie urged her to dance faster and faster until the beats became a techno tune. She started in on an Irish jig when Ruby danced up and slapped her hard in the face, her red curls billowing about her in anger.

"Ember, what the malarkey?"

Ember opened her eyes and said, "OMG. Where have I been? If I could turn back time . . ."

Ruby reached up to slap Ember again, but stopped when a loud song filled the air—the kind that soothed the soul and inspired dreams of peace and harmony. A golden chariot burst into view, bathing their surroundings with a bright, blissful light. Ember squinted against its luminosity.

When her eyes adjusted, she could not help but notice the chariot's handsome young driver and the elegant muse beside him: the mysterious songstress. Ruby laughed aloud.

"Ember, don't you worry your pretty little head. May I introduce you to Helios, the god of the sun, and Aeode, the goddess of music. Helios will speed us backwards around the sun a couple of years so you can get back to when you were before you got lost in a time warp."

"Okay," Ember muttered. "That makes total sense."

Back to the Story

After a very dizzying ride, Ember's brain hurt. She felt chilled. She wanted to see Jagger again. She should have predicted that writer's block would come to get her, just like it had Cinder.

Aeode approached Ember. The songstress's long, curly locks flew about her head like Medusa's snakes.

"Ember, you know better than to think like that. There are no mistakes. You must fight. You must take charge. Either you let this story run around forever in your head, creating chaos for you and all the characters involved, or you sit your butt down and write the darn story."

Ember gushed, "Thank you, Aeode. Can you just tell me what to do next?"

Aeode stood tall before her. "Dammit, Ember. Didn't you hear me just now? It's up to you. I know I'm perfect, but I can't make you perfect like me. Only you can do that. How do you think I got the way I am?"

Helios hailed his glorious goddess. "Aeode, you *are* my muse."

The sun god grabbed Aeode's face and tried to kiss her. She pushed him away coquettishly, knocking Ember and Ruby out of the chariot. Ruby's wild locks swirled all around them as they careened through space.

"Hey, Ruby?"

"Yeah, what's on your mind? What you're going to wear at the ball?" Ruby tousled her hair.

Ember thought about Cinder as they continued to descend. "I've got it! I know what to do! In the original book, Sergio took Cinder to the magic snow kingdom, where he said they were going to prepare for the ball. I'm going to need a snowsuit."

Ruby tilted her head. "What's that?"

Ember said, "A suit to protect you from the cold."

"Okay, whatever. But just in case you haven't noticed, we are mermaids again."

Ember looked down at her fishy tail. "Drat."

Before they could say anything else, they plunged into a frigid ocean.

Land of Ice and Snow

When Ember and Ruby entered the water, they continued to sink. It was as if Ember were in a dream where she couldn't swim no matter how hard she tried. The slow descent was maddening.

Ember sat on a sandy surface. Her head hurt and her eyes were out of focus.

After a moment Ruby nudged Ember enthusiastically. "Ember, what's this? Have you ever seen a door like this?"

Ember knew exactly what the rectangular room in front of them was. "It's called an elevator."

The elevator door had one button that depicted snow-covered mountains and the words "The Snow Realm."

Ember was excited. It felt like she was in control of the story now. "Ruby, if all goes well, our mermaid days will soon be over. Would you kindly press the button for the Snow Realm?"

"Sure, I'm a pro at this." Ruby squinted. "Except I can't decipher those scribbles."

"Press the button that has the snow on it."

"What's snow?" asked Ruby.

Ember said, "Ruby, would you please press the only button?"

"And a button is?"

Ember glared at Ruby. "The round circle.""Of course. I can do this!" Ruby giggled, but still looked befuddled by the task.

Ember finally pushed the button and the elevator door opened. Ember entered and beckoned Ruby forward, who gingerly stepped forward. Once the girls were inside, the elevator was sucked into the ocean floor. Ember felt claustrophobic as they traveled through the layers of the earth so fast that their journey was like a wildly colored moving picture. For a portion of the trip, the backdrop was liquid and so hot that the elevator boiled. Their transport shifted directions and the earth became darker and more difficult to penetrate. Ember wondered if they would be stuck in a portion of the asthenosphere forever.

Ruby obviously had a different opinion than Ember, because she said, "This is fun! How long do we travel in this box?"

On the wall was a circle with an arrow. The arrow traveled around the circle until it came to the words "You are here." The elevator stopped abruptly yet smoothly.

"This is obviously our stop," Ember said.

"If you say so."

They door opened, and water rushed out before unceremoniously dumping them onto a slate floor. At first, Ember wanted to cry, but then she started laughing. Ruby seemed to get infected with her giggle soon after that, and their merriment reverberated around the room like bells, masking the sounds of approaching footsteps.

A shadow loomed before them. It was Jagger. "Hello, there! I thought I might find you here."

Ember looked up. "Jagger! Is that you?"

"It is."

"*The* Jagger?" Ember pressed, squinting suspiciously. "From Santa Cruz?"

Jagger laughed, bending down and caressing Ember's face. "Are you okay, Ember? Is this the Ember I know, from Kullowhitucky?"

"Cullowhee!" Ember cried emphatically.

"Ah, it *is* you!" Jagger handed each mermaid a towel. "Do you need any help unzipping your tails?"

Ruby blushed. "Excuse me?"

Jagger looked earnest. "You must be very, very careful not to move, because apparently if you catch on the zipper, your tail could fuse right to your legs and could get stuck there forever!"

Ember's jaw dropped, for near the hearth, a surly merman swam in a large fish tank.

"That's what happened to Jack," Jagger explained. "He was too eager and blew it."

"I can *hear* you!" the merman yelled, his voice distorted by the glass.

Jagger pointed at him. "That's Jack."

Ember froze. She didn't want to end up like Jack. But she was very distracted by the smell of Jagger's fresh, clean skin.

Ruby feigned distress and drawled, "Why, I'm absolutely trembling. What if I catch a cold, or maybe the consumption? Will you please help me, Jagger?"

Ember felt a twinge of jealousy and gave Ruby the side-eye. "Don't worry about me. I can do it myself because I'm an independent woman."

Jagger glanced at Ember. "I'm sure you can."

It was then that Ember realized that Ruby really didn't know how the zipper worked. After they'd assisted her, both women shed their tails and stood on the stone floor shivering, their long hair serving as ad hoc bikinis.

There was an uncomfortable silence, and then Ember pointed to Jagger's pants. "Uh, can we get some of those?"

Jagger stared down at his thighs, apparently amused. "Excuse me?"

"The clothes!" stated Ember, throwing her hands up in the air.

"Oh, uh, yeah. Check out this 3D machine over here. It even came with instructions. You take this wand, wave it over yourself and say, 'zippity-zoppity-doo.' Then it prints a set of clothes for you, made from stem cells from a single strand of your hair. Cool, huh?"

Ruby squealed in delight. "Oh, do me! Do me now, Jagger!"

Jagger laughed uncomfortably. "Eh, where exactly are you from, Ruby?"

Ember warned with a wink, "Don't ask. It's confidential. I could definitely use a haircut."

After a whirl and a twirl, both girls were wearing stretchy, silky snowsuits.

Ruby rubbed her arms sensuously. "Wow, what a perfect fit."

Ember scolded, "Okay, kids, we are wasting time. We need to get to the ball. Jagger, are we in the Snow Realm now? Do you have a snowcraft to take us to the ball?"

Jagger hurried to reassure her. "We are in the Petrified Palace in the Snow Realm. How did you know? And I do have a snowcraft, but it's more like a flying cigar. After we were separated, I spent the past year learning how to operate it. Every day, I went out into the frigid landscape looking for my sister, and for you."

"I had writer's block for a whole year?" Ember gasped.

"I know!" Ruby added. "That's, like, such a short time."

Jagger looked both confused and amused. "Ember, I don't understand. You keep talking about a book. Are you saying you sucked me into a book you're writing?"

Exasperated, Ember paced the room. "No! I got sucked into a book I was reading. I thought you knew this already. Let's just get to that damn ball. It's all anyone talks about, and I don't even know why."

Jagger placed his hand on Ember's shoulder. "Ember, I don't know why I trust you, but I do. Let's go." The three of them promptly boarded in a silver vehicle that looked like a bullet. "Buckle up!" he said, taking the commander's chair. "Since I departed Earth, I've been a captain of various vessels. You'll just have to trust me on this. The ride is kind of like surfing or snowboarding. All systems go!"

The snowcraft slid down a ramp out of the house and onto a sheet of black ice. They were surrounded by jagged crystals on both sides.

"Oh, it looks like it's made of diamonds!" gushed Ruby.

For a moment, they were enveloped in a feathery fog as the hydraulic lifts blew billows of sheared ice all over the place. Jagger changed the ship to antigravity mode. The powder settled, and when the dust dispersed and blew away from the windshield, Ember's stomach dropped to her toes. They blasted down the side of a tall cliff at lightning speed.

The snowcraft accelerated until it was swept up into a scintillating whirlwind of coruscant crystals. They were suspended in midair.

Jagger pushed various buttons and pulled strange levers with fervor. "We're stuck in a glitch." Panic grabbed Ember by the gut, but Jagger seemed quite composed. "Never mind, I've been through this before. The system will resolve itself in a moment. Enjoy the snowflakes. Every single one is different."

Ember peered out into the snow. "Yeah, I've heard that one before."

Ruby pulled on Ember's arm and yelled, "Holy Zeus! We need to rescue those poor puppies!"

Ember looked and saw Pigdor, Gypsy, and Toby plastered to the window like frozen paper dolls.

"We must do something! Have you ever heard of the kid in *The Christmas Story* who licked the lamppost? The poor pig and the pooches don't have the energy to reach over the activation barrier to get inside. Perhaps if they are particles and they really want to come in, they can tunnel through the glass!"

Ruby shrugged her shoulders. "I wish Apocalypse were here right now. He's smart like you."

"Do you mean Zeus's brother?" Ember gave Ruby a quizzical look, but shook it off to focus on the matter at hand. "Jagger, do you have a quantum mechanical tunneling mode?"

"Yes, I do! Do you want me to activate it?"

Ember huffed impatiently. "Why do you think I asked? Of course!"

Jagger lifted a lever, but nothing happened.

"Something must be missing from the equation," Ember said exasperatedly.

"Oh no! Look, they're melting!" warned Jagger.

And then Ember had an idea. "Call out their names! According to the quantum tunneling equation, since they don't have enough activation energy to overcome the barrier, they need to become excited enough that their particles tunnel through the glass!" They began to call for her pets passionately, and Ember placed her hands against the wall of their vehicle and proclaimed, "Tobias, I can feel your warm fur. I feel your cold wet nose against my palm. Gypsy, remember how you love to chase after big rocks? Pigdor, I love your squeaks and purrs when you eat fresh lettuce."

Tobias's tail began to wag, then Gypsy's. Pigdor opened his eyes and began to purr. In an instant they transported through the glass.

At the same moment, a blue bear with a cloudy tummy whooshed into the sleigh.

Ember was greeted by two licking dogs and a zombie guinea pig. She rushed forward to cuddle her pets.

Ruby tried to pet the blue bear, but he griped, "Hey, why are people always doing that?" A humid haze hovered above his head and it started raining. "Now look what you made me do!"

Ruby backed away and into Jagger. The snow toboggan lurched.

Jagger looked stunned because Ruby had fallen on top of him. Ember felt a twinge of jealousy.

"Wake up, Jagger! You need to drive the ship. And we should secure the pets."

Jagger looked embarrassed as he tried to help the bear buckle into a seat, but the animal zapped him with tiny lightning bolts.

"Leave me alone! I'm not a pet! My name is Grumbles. Don't you know what personal space is?" Grumbles drew a neon rectangle around himself that crackled with static electricity and sent Jagger backing away to his captain's seat.

Ember sat next to Pigdor, whose fur was falling off and exposing his skull. "Pigdor, I'm so sorry you are dead! I didn't mean to leave you out in the sun! I was only a child."

Pigdor nibbled the seat belt. His front tooth hung on its last rotting nerve. He spoke, and the incisor clattered to the flat surface below her feet. "Ember, every time you dwell on what you could have done differently, you relive the trauma of that day. My passing was merely a consequence of a choice you made as a child. Can you tell yourself there are no mistakes? Can you see that we are sitting here now, in the present, having a good time? How will you create the future you seek if you tell yourself you are unworthy?"

Gypsy chimed in, "Ember, are you going to continue to let those pesky mistakes drag you back into the past and control your future? Don't you want to create your own destiny?"

The blue bear looked nonplussed. "You are so depressing, Timber."

Ember retorted, "That's like calling the kettle black. By the way, my name is Ember." Then she had an idea. "I think we need a ray of sunshine in here to balance you."

At a snap of her fingers, a lemon-colored bear with a sunny tummy popped into the seat next to Grumbles. He began to rain again as he groaned, "Oh no! It's Sunbeam."

Meanwhile, Sunbeam radiated light and warmth, which dried up Grumbles's storm. She tickled Grumbles and warbled to him about the sunny weather.

"Now that's more like it." Ember felt like she was in control again, and wriggled her nose like a witch.

Sunbeam's stomach played techno music and produced a trippy laser show. Skittles shot out of her stomach, and everyone except Grumbles danced along merrily. The solemn stuffy tried to make it rain, but Sunbeam's influence overpowered the precipitation and instead created a sauna-like steam.

Wandering Plot

The party in the flying bullet eventually died down. Everyone but Ember and Jagger dozed off. Ember told him all she knew about the ball, which was turning out to be a mysterious but recurring theme with them. Was it just another distraction like the repeat sign? Was it just an abstract idea to derail her train of thought?

"We need a plan. Otherwise random events will keep throwing us off course."

Jagger looked into her eyes. "I have a proposal."

"What's that?"

"Ember, I really like you and I'm glad you found your pets, but I really need to find my little sister. Her name is Rayne. She's only five, or maybe six now. I fear she's lost somewhere in this world. I'm really scared for her."

"I understand your urgency, Jagger. I want to help you find her, but how?"

"If you are the author of this story, you tell me."

"Okay, okay. We will find Rayne soon."

As she spoke, the sky lit up with hundreds of beaming rainbows.

Ember inhaled. "What is this place?"

"I don't know. Somewhere over the rainbow? I've never seen this place."

The two bears evaporated and reappeared outside, sliding on the rainbows.

Ember chuckled. "How predictable. Follow them!"

Jagger pursued the bears up a wide rainbow, which turned into a golden block road.

"Ember, that's not very original. You're not Dorothy from *The Wizard of Oz*."

Ember rolled her eyes. "Look! A mansion in the sky! I see steam and hot springs!"

Jagger steered toward the chateau while Ember gently woke Ruby and her pets. They exited the snowcraft once it was stationary and approached the front door. Ember stepped forward and knocked.

A man with wavy brown hair answered the door. "Ember! You've arrived! It is I, Alexander!"

Ember gaped at him. "Cinder's Alexander?"

Before he could answer, a female with beautiful caramel skin came up behind him. She looked like Ember, yet different.

"Cinder?"

The girl nodded. "In the flesh."

Ember then noticed that Cinder was holding a man's hand and asked, "Sergio?"

A girl with green flashing eyes twirled around behind them. "Yes, and I'm Jade."

After Ember introduced Ruby, Jagger, and her pets, she inquired about Ivory.

Alexander answered, "I've studied your story. Ivory was briefly introduced, but she was a parallel version of both Ruby/Jade as well as yourself. Strange. Maybe it's a glitch?"

Ember shrugged. "Who knows? We have plenty of characters now. I'm confused myself. How did you all get here?"

"Not quite sure," Alexander admitted. "After you emerged from the writer's block, we found ourselves here, together. There's a copy of your book on the coffee table. It's called *Ember*. See? Each day there is a new page, but the end is unfinished. You must be tired after your last set of adventures. Sangria? Have a seat."

Ember sat with her friends on a circle of large, furry couches. Gypsy and Tobias cuddled together at the hearth. Pigdor tried to drink a hot toddy, but it seeped out of a rotting wound in his mouth and spilled on the floor.

"Oh, my goodness. I would love to tipple, but my jaw is about to fall off."

Ember implored, "There must be something we can do for you, Pigdor."

As Ember petted Pigdor, she closed her eyes, concentrated, and felt her energy flow through her hand to him. All at once he transformed into healthy guinea piggy again, fluffy and cute. He sipped his drink.

"This is wonderful! Thank you, Ember."

Ember sat quietly. She had a sneaking suspicion that Alexander was hiding his true identity. She was also worried about Ivory because it was as if she'd ceased to exist. Ember didn't want to lose any more characters because she cared about all of them.

She was distracted from her thoughts when she noticed Ruby flirt with Jagger again. It was as if acidic fumes stung her eyes. The sudden jealousy prompted her to suggest that Jade, Sergio, Cinder, Alexander, and Ruby go back and fetch Jack from the Petrified Palace.

"Jagger and I are going to stay here and figure out a plan." Ember felt a little guilty for sending them off like that, but she also felt very connected to Jagger because he was a real human. After the others departed, Ember took Jagger's hand. "Do you have a moment to talk?"

Jagger laughed nervously. "Sure."

Ember led Jagger into her room. "Sit down, please. Are you anxious?"

"Ember, I know I look like I'm in my twenties, but in the real world I just turned eighteen."

"Oh. Well, I'm only twenty."

"Yes, but you look like you are twenty-five," he remarked with a smirk.

Ember paused for a second to consider that. "I do? Jagger, if you've been here a year, then you're nineteen. What year were you born?"

"1994."

"And I was born in 1998, so you're actually older than me. You'd be twenty-four if we were back on Earth in my time, if that makes any sense at all."

Happy with her conclusions, Ember leaned forward to kiss Jagger, but he backed away.

"But in my time I'm an eighteen-year-old guy who's never had a girlfriend." Jagger stood up. "I'm going to bed, Ember. I'm sorry, I just can't do this."

Ember retired to her own room. She thought all along that Jagger had been giving her signals.

"I'm just as lost as last year's Easter egg."

Dragon Palace

Every time the sun rose in Fractasia, another member of Excelsior's dragon family arrived at the castle. Each scaly beast brought one hundred wandering souls, lost ghosts who could find neither the road to Hades nor a way to heaven. When the sun set, Excelsior chanted, and the poor misplaced specters turned into ornate opal blocks they'd use to fortify Castle Clarity. The castle grew grander and grander by the day.

One night after dinner, Excelsior gathered the dragons together. "Five million and fifty of us! That means it's been five hundred thousand days, the number of days it takes for Böse to encircle our sun. That means it's been a year!" As soon as their cheers died down, Excelsior continued. "Dear family, dear dragons. Now that we have strengthened in number, and our castle is reinforced, what do we need?"

The dragons beat their wings and blew fire. "More! More!"

"Exactly!" cheered Excelsior. "And how can we get more?"

"More souls! Let's trap them!"

Rayne emerged from the shadows. Her golden dress floated about her shoulders, undulating spookily.

The dragons hissed, but Excelsior hushed them. "Let your queen speak!"

Rayne proclaimed, "We shall have a ball. We shall have the party of the millennium. You need the souls of gods to fortify your castle!"

"Hurray! Hurray!" sibilated the dragons.

Rayne continued. "I have a guest list for you. Feel free to include others but do check with me first. Excelsior will direct the planning committee for the party. You will invite Poseidon, Triton, Hermes, Eris, Dionysus, Athena, Aphrodite, Persephone, Napoleon, Thor, Sif, and, last but not least, Zeus. He has historically not been able to contain his lightning bolts, thereby stirring the primordial stew and making beef Wellington out of it."

Excelsior croaked, "Can you explain your last comment, Queen Rayne?"

"Zeus was the king of the Greek gods, married to Hera. However, he was a meddlesome leader and could not contain his passions. When he sewed his seed among men, he created half-breeds, thereby allowing humans to have powers they never should have had. We will make Zeus pay for this! We will kill him, along with his consorts and his crew. Once we have him trapped within our walls, we will harness the power and rule the universe forever!"

The young dragons huddled around Rayne. She leaned down and petted their heads. "Tell us more about Zeus!" they chattered while the youngest of them burped and farted fire.

"Of course, my little ankle biters, I will indeed tell you all about Greek mythology. Sit down around me."

Excelsior's claw tapped Rayne's shoulder. "Queen Rayne, I have a question about the guest list."

"Enough!" bellowed Rayne. "Just get to work. Meet with the committee I established and start planning! We have only one hour before the party starts. Can't you see I'm telling the children a story about their guests? Do you want them underfoot while you are preparing? They will eat all the snacks and burn the decorations."

"What's wrong with that?"

Rayne shook her head. "Because that will scare your guests away." She turned back to the fledglings. "It all began with a beautiful goddess named Rhea, who rode a chariot pulled by lions. Rhea ruled the world with her brother, Cronus, the leader and the youngest of the Titans. They had five wonderful but challenging children: Demeter, Hestia, Hera, Hades, and Poseidon.

One bright spring morning, as the sun shone into her bedroom window, Rhea decided to take a break from motherhood and ride her chariot to Crete, where her fans adored her. While Rhea was gallivanting around the island, Cronus's mother, Gaia—who was jealous of Rhea—told Cronus that his children would castrate him one day and take over his throne. Cronus quickly devoured the offspring he had incestuously begotten with Rhea. Her heart was broken, but she did not show it. She gave Cronus six skins of wine, laid him in the ivy, and then fled to Crete to have her sixth son, Zeus."

"What happened next?" asked a little green dragon.

"Once Zeus was grown, he tricked his father Cronus into drinking an emetic that made him throw up his siblings. After that, they overthrew him and imprisoned him in Tartarus. The siblings all became powerful gods. Zeus himself had many children, including Athena, Hermes, Eris, Dionysus, and Persephone, as well as the half-breeds. His brother Poseidon was a bad-tempered god who ruled over the sea, other waters, earthquakes, and horses. His children were Atlas, Orion, and Triton."

A red dragon tot marveled, "I've heard of Triton. What does he look like?"

Rayne giggled. "Triton was a merman. He has a tail like a fish."

The little dragons laughed, and one whistled before exclaiming, "Why, I'd eat him up! I'd bite off his silly tail and roast it on a stick. I'd show that Triton who was boss!"

Rayne countered, "Come now. How would Triton rule the sea if he had legs like a man? Now, Hermes, the second youngest of the Olympian gods begotten by Zeus, was the messenger of the gods by day, but by night he was a guide to the Underworld."

"I like death!" squeaked a little black dragon with sparkly eyes.

Rayne stared at him solemnly. "Really? Have you ever experienced it?"

"No," stated the drooling fledgling. "But I've eaten people, and they taste really good."

Rayne stroked the dragon's head. "Do you want to know more about Zeus and his family or not? Maybe you'll find his kids more interesting. I know I do. Dionysus, also half-brother to Hermes and Eris, was kind of a silly god who gorged on grapes and had skins of wine hanging from his belt. His lips were purple, always stained from wine, and his eyes drooped because he was always drunk."

A purple dragon jumped up and down. "I ate a guy who was drunk once. It made me feel funny."

"Exactly the reason why youngsters shouldn't drink!" scolded Rayne. "Zeus's daughter Athena was his golden child, and was the goddess of many things, including war. Eris felt jealous that her father favored Athena. Zeus accused Eris of being sensitive and volatile. He told her she would probably end up in purgatory because she didn't deserve to live on Olympus. The mighty Aphrodite took after her father in that she loves the pleasures of the flesh, even human."

The bell to the front door rang, and the smallest dragon ran to open it.

Rayne announced, "It looks like our guests are starting to arrive."

Pool of Deception

Ember felt the urge to gaze upon the stars. She jumped out of her bed and ran to the balcony. The frigid middle of the night air was electrifying.

A pair of warm hands settled on her shoulders. She could sense that it was Jagger, so she did not need to turn to see his face.

He spoke in an apologetic voice. "Ember. You seem tense. May I rub your shoulders?" Ember nodded. "You are what a flame dreams of and cannot live without. You are what mankind needs to thrive. I don't just mean men, either. I am talking about the gender-inclusive mankind. Is there a word for that? You tame the caveperson, yet convince them to thrive at the same time. This is part of the reason why I'm drawn to you."

Ember, still groggy, let him knead her back. She allowed her worries to transfer from her shoulders through his strong grip. Underneath her, perfumed steam rose from a great pool below, soothing her senses. Glasses clinked together as melodious voices discoursed. The owners of the voices splashed merrily in the water.

Jagger hands soothed the knots out of her tense shoulders. "Ember, let's join the others in their gaiety. Forget about your plot for today. Besides, if we don't stop to enjoy the moment occasionally, we'll get so wrapped up that we just might get stuck in your writer's block and be forever gone."

Ember turned to face him. "Jagger, I yearn for you."

"Unfortunately, in this world, none of us were blessed with, uh . . ." Jagger belted out a hearty laugh. "Haven't you noticed you don't have to go to the bathroom here?"

He disrobed, and Ember was stunned to find that he did not have any defining male anatomy.

"Jeez, I hadn't noticed. Even more reason for me to take off all of my clothes, eh?" Ember undressed, leaping off and over the balcony into the enchanting hot springs beneath. Jagger jumped in after her.

In the pool, Cinder and Sergio stood together, kissing, bodies intertwined. Their auras melted together in trippy swirls. Ruby and Alexander were on the edge of the pool, leaning on one another and watching the others. Jade's head popped up from below, followed by the merman Jack.

Thick laughter wove through the crowd, taking on strange shapes and infecting others. Ember watched as a rope of laughter fed from her mouth into Jagger's.

They spent minutes, hours, days, or maybe just seconds doing whatever they wanted. The troupe dined on luxurious appetizers of manna, honey, pomegranate, figs, dates, and ginger tea. Salvers of food kept mysteriously refilling themselves by the side of the pool. Ember felt that everything was in its divine, raw, heavenly form, like something out of the Garden of Eden.

Ember munched on vegan grains that tasted like lobster while Jagger laughed. "Is this ambrosia or divinity? Is this the food of the gods?"

Ruby gulped some wine, turning to Ember with flushed cheeks. Her words gushed out of her mouth like gumdrops. "I really like Jade and Alexander. It's like I've known Jade all my life! I think that you really like Jagger, too. I know that Jagger told me he was a little younger than you? But we've been here for years now, maybe two, fifteen, one hundred fifty, I don't know. What is a year's difference when you've lived thousands?"

Ember guffawed. "One hundred fifty years? That's so funny! Ruby, Cinder—all of you—I love you. Man, I really love all of you. I want to stay here forever. I just want to sing."

A lyre floated by and Ember and Cinder began singing in perfect harmony while Jagger and Sergio brought up the chorus. Ruby and Alexander held hands, watching, while Jade petted Jack's mermaid tail.

Horatia

Horatia, you are my lover
Horatia, there will ne'er be another.

I'll take you to the moon one thousand times tonight
Step into my time machine and let's take flight.

We flew to the east and we traveled to the west,
When one thousand dragons
Came flaming o'er a crest.
With fiery breath they charred our tattered rags
We shouldn't have been at a toga party when we took flight.

Horatia, you are my lover
Horatia, I've never known another.
A million sighs I've sighed waiting for your love.
Please don't go down in flames (from the dragon) without
your safety gloves!

Make love in Machu Picchu,
Have sex in Bombay.
At the ancient Parthenon,
In B.C. Pompeii,
We'll go live in Otherland; we'll go there "hand in hand."

Horatia, lying in the clover
Horatia, I wanna turn you over.
I'll fold time so we can play in spaceships made of clay

Horatia, you are my lover
Horatia, I only need five others.
Along the way we'll shout and say,
We all love each other!

Grand Entrance

In Fractasia, a fire ripped across the sky and crash-landed in the gardens in front of Castle Clarity. When the flames dissipated, a very smoky Zeus stood up and dusted off his skin with a frown.

"I hereby decree that the ball may begin! Lay out the red carpet. No flash photography, please." Zeus looked around, but no one was to be seen. "Where is everyone? Shoot, am I early?"

Looking flustered, the deity snapped his fingers and disappeared, all but for the tip of an ornate lightning bolt that stuck out of his pocket. Excelsior, who stood at the entrance of the castle with Rayne, laughed.

"Look, Zeus thinks he's hiding from us. I sent him an invitation with an earlier arrival time so he would be unfashionably early."

Rayne tilted her head. "Excelsior, do you know the great Zeus?"

Excelsior sneered. "I was once his favorite pet dragon. He coddled and petted me all day long. One romantic evening, I declared my love to the ruler of Mount Olympus. I was sure that once I professed my love for him, he would return my feelings. After all, he'd bedded all of the maidens. I was wrong. Zeus guffawed so loudly that the extremities of the marble statues in gardens all across Greece broke away from their bodies. I was mortified. Static electricity crackled in his cheeks as he tried to keep from laughing. He jested, 'You thought that I would like a dragon? When I said I liked curves, I didn't mean *reptilian* curves! To tell you the truth, I wasn't even sure if you were a girl or a boy! I said you steamed me up, but that was when you nearly singed me with your dragon breath! I'll have to stop peeing in the garden next to you if that's all you think about.'" Excelsior made a fist with her claws. "I was crushed. I just wanted his arms wrapped around me again. Maybe I didn't really love him like a woman loves a man, or like a goddess loves a god, but never mind!"

Excelsior looked like she was going to cry, when suddenly she stiffened instead. Eris strutted toward them with a smirk on her face and a platter in her hands.

The goddess asked Excelsior, "Are you the one who ordered the hors d'oeuvres?" The dragon greedily grabbed the appetizers and devoured them. Eris remarked, "Well, it looks like someone shares my love of chaos. This should be an interesting party."

The ground rumbled. Eris rolled her eyes. "And it sounds like Poseidon's here. As usual, each god's entrance will try to best the others."

A huge horse carrying the god of the sea galloped toward the castle. Poseidon pointed his trident toward the earth, sending a tsunami of dirt toward the semi-invisible Zeus and knocking a chunk of lightning off his bolt. The electrical fragment zapped Poseidon's trident out of his hand. He jumped off his horse and fumbled in the dirt to find it.

A grapevine sprouted out of the dirt, and Dionysus's head popped up out of the ground. Hermes, who was trotting up the road wearing only spandex pants and a pair of Nikes, tripped over Dionysus's head and landed headfirst in a muddy puddle.

Athena and Aphrodite flew down from the sky in a chariot, bickering about who was more desirable.

The earth cracked open with a puff of sulfurous smoke, and a large pomegranate flower unveiled Persephone, who observed, "I *am* the most beautiful of them all!"

A Bugatti spun out, showering the gods with dirt and debris. Napoleon carefully stepped out of the car, wearing sixteen-inch heels. Before he could present himself properly, a Tesla dropped out of the sky and landed next to the famous military leader, showering him with dust. Napoleon cursed in French as he frantically brushed the dirt off his coat.

The driver of the electric vehicle opened his door and stepped out of the car, but was promptly knocked back by a leather-clad woman with rippling raven locks, who was zooming by on a cannonball.

The man in the Tesla, who was no worse for wear, swore. "Crikey! What did you do that for?"

The beguiling woman glared at the man with surprise. "Conor, what are you doing here?"

The man called Conor responded defiantly, "Hey, Camila, I was invited, too! Do you think really think the world revolves around our failed relationship?" He surveyed his surroundings suspiciously. "Anyway, I think that's the least of our concerns right now. Don't you think this party is odd? I thought I was driving to a party in Laurel Canyon, but then a tornado swirled me away. I blacked out and landed here. Did something similar happen to you?"

Napoleon suddenly rushed Conor and knocked him to the ground. Camila threw her head back and laughed hysterically. "Is that Napoleon?"

Rayne sprinted towards the melee, Excelsior at her heels. She exclaimed, "Oh no! Is that the famous couple Camila Clark and Conor Knick, otherwise known as 'Camilick'?"

Excelsior answered, "Who? That man fighting with Napoleon is Thor. The woman with the Medusa-like hair is his plus-one, Sif."

Camila's face twisted with rage as she approached Rayne and Excelsior, hands on her hips. "Excuse me? I am nobody's plus-one!"

Rayne looked exasperated, but then her face relaxed into a smooth mask. She asked Excelsior to help Napoleon out of the dirt and extend her apologies while she led Conor and Camila away from the others. Rayne's golden dress shimmered in the wind, catching Camila's eye.

"Please, excuse my manners. I love your dress. Who's your designer?"

Rayne responded, "Camila, Conor, I am so sorry, but someone screwed up the guest list. Thor and his wife Sif were invited. I'm sorry for the confusion."

Conor argued, "I'm not my brother, the most famous thoracic surgeon on Instagram who calls himself Thor. I am the famous Broadway dancer who built an empire of gingerbread cookies that resemble world-renowned Broadway characters. I make more money than he does, even though he has more followers. And I look nothing like him."

Rayne smirked. "Some would beg to differ, but that's not the point. This is a dragon's palace in a magical land. The gods are real. If these fire-breathing beasts smell that you are hominids, they will eat you. What if you utilized your awesome Broadway acting skills and pretended to be Thor and Sif?"

A red-faced Conor looked flustered. "Do you think I am more handsome than Thor?"

Rayne shook her head, composed herself, and said, "Let's start over, shall we? Hello, I'm Rayne, hostess of the party. Welcome to Castle Clarity in the land of Fractasia. I'm so glad you and your fiancée could make the party."

Camila laughed. "Whoa, whoa. Looks like you didn't get the memo. Conor and I divorced in 2020. Actually, it's refreshing to hear you don't know that."

Rayne inhaled sharply. "2020? Isn't it still 2018?"

"Not unless you went through a time warp. You're funny. By the way, great castle! How did your special effects department rig up that cannonball? It was so realistic!"

Rayne stepped back and muttered, "I wonder where the time went? I guess it's all relative anyway."

They were interrupted when Dionysus bumped into Camila and Conor. "Oh, excuse me! Who are you? And where are my manners? Would you like to partake of a Hellenic deity's alchemy wine? It's made of lead, so when you go to the bathroom, your movement is made of gold!"

Rayne stumbled and knocked the glasses out of Camila's and Conor's hands just as Poseidon arrived in a great to-do in his chariot, pulled by four hippocamps. The mythical seahorses issued high-pitched shrieks as their tails flapped wildly in the wind.

Zeus, who was still invisible, mumbled grumpily, "My inferior brother looks so ridiculous with those silly mermaid-horses. He could have built his chariot with any type of gold, but he chose a living thing, a tree. How weak!"

Aphrodite conversed with Persephone, who leaned on Dionysus. "And that's how I came to be the firstborn of the second generation of the Titans. I was pulled straight from Uranus."

Persephone, already visibly tipsy, slurred, "That's absolutely ridiculous!"

Aphrodite continued, "It's true! And then Granddad sliced open Cronus's testicles and threw them in the sea, and that's how I was born."

Persephone giggled so hard that she collapsed while Dionysus blurted out, "I thought Zeus was your dad!"

Aphrodite riposted, "Duh, that's my parallel universe self from *The Iliad*."

Dionysus rubbed his chin. "Interesting."

Persephone clutched a skin of wine hanging from Dionysus's shoulder to pull herself up from the ground. Eris, with a gleam in her eyes, stepped on Aphrodite's dress and the goddesses began to bicker.

Athena was visibly irritated. "Order, order! I have a bad feeling about partying with the dragons. Don't any of you remember the crush that strange female dragon Excelsior had on Zeus? A senseless dragon is no match for a goddess or a human when it comes to bedding handsome Greek gods."

Aphrodite quickly composed herself and said sarcastically, "I see you came prepared, fully clad in your armor, as usual. Chill out! These dragons just want to show us a good time."

Napoleon interrupted everyone with a shout. "Tidal wave! It's Triton!"

In the distance, Triton road along on a great wave, but the swell dispersed about a football field away from the castle door. The disgraced god awkwardly propelled himself forward by flapping his fish-like tail along the desert sand.

Eventually, all of the gods and the guests entered the castle. Excelsior announced, "The Dragon Ball of the Millennium is officially beginning. It's party time!"

Labyrinth

Ember opened her eyes and found that she was traveling through a labyrinth. She was dressed up in a maid's outfit and had the body of a Minotaur. Ms. Minotaur was her name, and her husband Felix hadn't been home in weeks. She began to sing the sad, lonely, yearning song of a poor Minotaur trapped in a labyrinth with an alcoholic, verbally abusive cat-husband named Felix.

Ms. Minotaur's Sad Song
Plumes of plural
Glittering gadgets
Conceal the carnage
The beast beneath
Lies in wait
To snatch the sweet date
Enrobed by the palms

Weathered fronds
Brush her bosom

Worn by the babes
Since forgotten
Slightly aged
So Gouda
Still sweet
To the prey

He lay prostrate
As the vixen feasts
Famished and parched
She panted like a dog

Fearing a full stomach
Will not quench her thirst

For once that occurs
He will call her a Hur
When she leaves him naked in the dirt
The mind cannot fling far away
Whether she really did . . .

Nothing is sweeter
Than those salty tears of success
That erupt from an electric earthquake
Of bliss
Better by far
Because fewer are attained than claimed

Bewitched by the tresses
The buck falls to the floor
Heart punctured by piercing
Lifeblood drains dry

He awakens to find
The peacock plucked his heart blind
Of fear, love and pain

So bloodlust he gains
And will ne'er again
That single moment reclaim

The song angered Felix terribly, so he stuffed Ember into a smoky, stinky Volkswagen bus. Her Minotaur ankles did not fit and had to stick out the windows. The bus began to roll forward, and Ember felt sick. She no longer felt the desire to live. She did not want to die; she just wanted to sleep. If only she could get another hour of slumber, or just ten more minutes. Ember drifted into a delirium.

Sitting in a dark corner of the same dingy apartment she was stuck in before, she felt like she had to vomit. Pages flew out of her mouth, blowing away.

"No!" she screamed, trying to chase after the pages, which had started burning up. "All my work! All my characters, gone! I'm lost forever, stuck in this hell."

Ember slumped her shoulders are cried. She heard a kitten meow. She looked around, trying to find it. At the end of a hallway, she found a basket of kittens. She picked them up and cuddled the adorable felines.

A piece of paper flew into her hand. On it was a poem.

Gone
I didn't shed a tear for you
It rained the whole damn week
Today a slight chill I get
But this sadness just can't keep
I'll go running down the road again
This time to stop to slow down time
Perhaps I'll pick a path anew
One apart from the one we grew.

Ember wondered what the poem meant. Perhaps it was telling her that she had to let go of her desperation, her sadness, and the past in order to build a new and greater beginning. She smiled, sat down, and fell asleep as she listened to the kittens purring in her ear.

The Mad Moggies

Ember awoke in a seedy gentlemen's club where the dancers were humanoid cats.

She wailed, "Oh no! Am I a cat now? I hope that the poem I found doesn't mean I have to spend the rest of my life as a feline."

Dance music, or rather, R&B with a heavy beat pumped through the speakers. A pretty, long-haired, pure white cat with a beautiful face and smile gyrated on her leg to the beats of the music.

She whispered in Ember's ear, "Hi, I'm Tasha. You're beautiful! Are you a stripper, too? Felix said you needed a lap dance. Can I kiss you? You can't kiss me back, though."

Tasha held a dragon fruit to Ember's lips and poured a sweet liquid into her mouth. Ember felt exhilarated. All inhibitions and cares gone, she focused on the beat.

Tasha was mostly human, but she had very soft fur all over her body. The fur was longer at her wrists, feet and cheeks, and she had cat ears. She pressed her body into Ember's with each beat of the music. It felt like a massage. The perfume, the music, the darkness—Ember just sat, mesmerized, drinking it all in, and feeling like she was a part of a special group. These were her new friends. She would be safe in the club, especially if she never left. She could stay in the club all day, all night, drinking the yummy drinks that made her feel good.

Just then, Tasha handed Ember a couple of bright pink mushrooms. "Eat these."

Ember devoured the funky fungi. They tingled until her mouth almost hurt, but eventually she felt numb and couldn't move.

"Here, breathe this in," purred Tasha, blowing pink smoke in Ember's face before handing her a hookah. "Smoke some more. There you go."

Ember was transfixed. She could barely move, so she sank into a soft, furry pillow behind her. The pillow moved, and a fluffy rabbit jumped out from behind her back. She watched, both transfixed and horrified, as Tasha attacked the bunny and consumed it.

Her husband, Felix the cat, the king of the cats and head pimp, strolled along and kissed each cat passionately.

Ember sang a silly song.

The Kangaroo and the Girl
Some Sallies they do
Ride a red kangaroo
To get to Rocket Top Tower
They hop up High Hill
Covered in krill
That came from precipitation power
Salty tears, oh dear
Who lost his cracked crayon
Though he had nothing to write on
So Sally was summoned
Lest come the snow and cold winds blow
From the start of the year
Till the end of December
A freeze so frigid
And worse than remembered
So Sally she did
With a quo and a quid
Let the kangaroo ride
Her to the green goblin store
Filled with trinkets and more
Grape gilded goo and galore
And an eight-pack of crayons
And paper to write on
Sally paid with a sixpence
For those latter two
And packaged them up
With love and a bow

The face on the cloud
When he opened the box slow!
The air lit up and with static it filled
And what do you know
You won't believe this
That out of the sky
Rained tree frogs and fish

Ember began to feel quite drunk, and not in a pleasant way. Felix drank so much that his feet faltered. She sang another song, which only served to enrage her intoxicated feline husband.

Flowing With the Booze
When I said, "I do"
I never thought it
Would be for worse not better
My soul is all
Black and blue
Charred chipped and cheddar
You can walk away from me
But stay when your son says
Papa please don't you go
Down the road that runs
From the barrel
Scraping up what's left
When it's not
Flowing with the booze yeah
He'll be rolling with the booze, babe
Till the day that river stops
Before it gets to the ocean
Cause you drank it dry
If you're gone come the morning
Don't come back in on the sly
Oh boy your moves are so smooth

They could frost a wedding pie
Won't you stop running away?
Just sit on down
I'll leave on the train tomorrow
If you say you will
Quit all-night roaming round
Soulless eyes
Solstice skies
You are a fright!
Get away ye demons flight!
Flying with the booze yeah
He'll be spinning with the booze, babe

Felix finally left Ember alone after she began to vomit. And after a very long time, Ember no longer knew who she was, or who she had become. Her former self was gone. She had had dreams of aliens and rainbows and dragons and donkeys—wait, no. That was in *Shrek*.

How *shrecklich*, the German word for "horrible," all had become. Ember giggled as she wondered if Shrek was called Shrek because he was *shrecklich*. Ember's head rolled from side to side. She could no longer see the whole picture. It was as if her words had been printed out on a huge piece of paper, which she could now see and digest. But it was no longer that. Was she just broken pieces of chemicals and distant memories, and many jumbles of her current occupation? Who could help her rein in these thoughts?

"God, are you there?"

To her surprise, a booming voice responded, "Yea, verily I say unto you, your peace lies within, yet the demons will always try to steal your soul. There is the one, but it is not who you think."

"I'm lost," Ember confessed. "I feel I'll be wandering without purpose forever."

Lost
Cover your tracks and don't look back
Or you'll be salt and dissolve to the sea
Or get chopped up into a gourmet treat
Boiled blessed and kosher-ized
Only to end up in someone else's salty tears
Oh my.

Awakening

Somewhere over the rainbows, Sergio, Cinder, Alexander, Ruby, Jade, and Jack lounged in the mystical pool. Pigdor, Tobias, and Gypsy lay in the grass. Unexpectedly, the party was disrupted when an old Volkswagen bus careened past them and crashed into Jagger's bedroom, where he was sleeping.

A pink-haired cat leaned out the window and howled, "You are dead meat, roadkill!"

Jagger sprang from the bed. Ruby, Jade, Cinder, and Alexander ran through the opening into Jagger's bedroom.

Ruby coquettishly winked. "What happened in here last night? Is that Ember hiding under your blanket?"

A frenzied Jagger moaned, "No, I haven't seen Ember in . . . in I don't know how long! Didn't you guys just see that Volkswagen bus filled with cats crash through my room? I thought Ember was with you guys, partying and doing who knows what!"

Alexander leaned over and picked up an empty liquor bottle. "Aha! Those were the party animals! They think they're cool cats. They must have taken Ember to the party world. It's a scary place. It is said that there is no escape. Once you have been invited, you can't leave until the party ends. But the party never ends. It lasts until the break of dawn, and then it starts again."

Jagger clenched his fists. "That feels exactly like this world! There must be a way to save ourselves and Ember! What if you haven't been invited? Can we crash the party?"

"That's quite an abstract idea," replied Ruby.

"Yes, it might work," agreed Alexander. "If I'm not mistaken, this gaping hole in front of us is now a portal. Only one can enter, however, or we will come out the other end as one mixed mass of people. The systems in this world are not yet advanced enough to allow two-party travel. Jagger, you alone can crash the party."

Jagger fumed. "I cannot allow Ember to spend the rest of eternity with a bunch of stupid, partying felines. Can you imagine what will happen if she imbibes too much? Cat copulation is barbaric! She doesn't have claws to defend herself. I must save her!"

Alexander nodded. "We'll be waiting for you right here. It's a shame I couldn't be of more help in this story. My character was uncomplicated and short-lived. Even the stupid guinea pig has a larger role than I do."

Pigdor grunted in his sleep.

"Yes," replied Jagger, "but you provided key elements for the resolution, and perhaps you, Ruby, Jade, and Jack can be part of other, more developed plots. And what about Cinder and Sergio? Ember told me that they are parallel universe versions of me and her. Surely there is more to the story!"

The portal started to blink, and Jagger ran forward to dive into the light, but then he tripped over a repeat sign and did it again. He repeated himself until Sergio stomped on the note over and over and it finally stopped squeaking.

The portal flickered. Jagger clawed his way into it, and it swept him away.

Dance, Dance, Dance

Inside the ballroom at Castle Clarity, an electric orchestra played. The dragons swayed and bobbed their heads up and down as the gods danced wildly. Napoleon danced on the bar, slashing a sword back and forth and kicking his heels high like a Rockette. Eris, Athena, Aphrodite, and Persephone danced together in a circle, chattering about who might bed Thor that night.

Hermes approached the group of goddesses. A portly rooster was perched on his left hand, and in his right hand he held a pair of copulating serpents.

He smirked. "Would any of you like to hold my large cockerel, or perhaps get gripped by my writhing snake?"

Excelsior stepped out of the shadows, blasted fire on the animals in Hermes's hands, and laughed. "Hermes, is that *all* the game you have, or would you like me to roast up some *small* hors d'oeuvres, too? Perhaps roasted nuts?"

Hermes backed away nervously. "Barbecue, anyone?"

The goddesses erupted in laughter and clapped Excelsior on her back.

Triton, who was playing with a conch shell in a small wading pool next to Poseidon, whined, "When can I get a place of my own, Dad?"

"When are you going to grow up and get a pair of legs?"

They began to wrestle furiously, tails flapping wildly in the pool.

Dionysus tried to breakdance, but was obviously inebriated. He slipped in the water that had splashed out of the wading pool and dumped wine all over the floor. The fledgling dragons lapped up the spilled spirits and stumbled around.

Aphrodite approached Camila, who was dancing with a large iguana in a gilded robe. The buxom goddess put her arms around Camila and ran her fingers down the fabric of her gown.

"Dear Sif, would you please introduce me to your husband?"

Camila sputtered, "We're divorced!"

Aphrodite furrowed her thick, perfectly manicured brows. "Really? How peculiar! I thought only humans did that!"

Camila reached forward to braid Aphrodite's hair. "Your locks look like spun gold. They feel like silk." Then Camila leaned over to Conor, who was slow dancing with Eris and whispered, "Hey, I think this actress playing Aphrodite wants to meet you. By the way, isn't this party a gag! Everyone stays in character all the time!"

Something crashed into the front door of the castle. Excelsior opened the door to reveal a small cyclone of dust. When the twister crossed the threshold of the castle, it dispersed, revealing Zeus, who kept twirling around in circles. "I'm a tornado! Observe my awesome powers!"

Excelsior smoldered. "Zeus, you are unfashionably late to the ball, and you are not a twister anymore. You are just a man spinning around in circles and you're going to get dizzy and fall. Stop this nonsense and join the party."

He looked up frantically at the dragon. "What have you done with my powers?"

Excelsior raised her eyebrows. "The rules of this party are to leave your weapons at the door, dolt."

Zeus scoffed, "I would never agree to relinquish my weapons. What have you done? Never have I seen magic so strong. I must go the others out and warn them!"

Excelsior wheezed, "Zeus, you are dirty from all that spinning in the soil. I suggest you freshen up in the men's room. Do you really want the others to know you don't have powers so they can overtake your throne?"

Zeus shuffled down the hall and muttered, "Where is the bathroom? I have to go."

Excelsior called, "To the left! To the left! To the left!"

Quantum Tunneling

Jagger's body spun around and around in the portal. "I have to crash the party, but how? Do I pretend that I am a cat? Do I sidle up, knock on the door, and say, 'Pizza delivery?' No! I'm going to fly into the party like Superman and save Ember. It's theoretically possible if I can imagine it, right?"

Jagger's body unraveled. Chemical and mathematical equations, theorems, and question marks flew out of his head and zoomed into the distance. Suddenly, the theories snapped back together, forming a dense sphere. Hovering in the center was a double-helix strand consisting of phosphates, sugars, and proteins linked together to form a lattice.

Jagger was gone. In his stead was a pulsating globe of information that hurled through a flickering tunnel. The ball careened through twists and turns in a wavelike fashion until it was stopped by a looming barrier. The ball bounced at the obstacle over and over, unable to move past it. Finally, the sphere leaned into the great wall, pressing into its side. After a time, the orb split apart into particles, which were promptly sucked into the barrier.

Strike

Ember floated in a lake of her own vomit. She tried to sink herself but was unable to. She burped. A tabby cat with red-gold stripes floated by on a raft and poured liquor into her mouth.

"Get on the boat, you bloated fool. Felix sent me to fetch you. He wants to dance with you."

The cat dug its claws into Ember's hands and pulled her up onto the makeshift dinghy. Ember peered up at the dark sky, which always seemed to be dark as night with brief periods of dawn, then darkness. She had a fleeting memory of something—a pair of eyes, intense as the night yet as warm as the sun. She tried to speak, but no words came out of her mouth.

The tabby slapped Ember's face, but she was too drunk to feel the pain. "Okay, time for a shot of adrenaline."

Ember felt a twinge on her arm and jolted upright. "Jagger!"

Felix stood on the shore of her pond of puke, enraged. "Huh? Who's Jagger?" He pulled her by her bleeding hands onto land. Felix took hold of Ember and then began to lick the blood dripping from her digits. With a wild look in his eyes, he bit her.

A bright light flashed in the sky, chasing away the darkness. The cats scampered about, covering their eyes, hissing, and spitting. Particles rained from the sky and coalesced into a humanoid form. The cats brandished their claws and bared their teeth, when a shadow from the sky sent them scattering.

Ember looked up to see a gigantic armored blue jay flying down from the heavens.

"Berty!"

Berty swooped down, took Felix in his talons, and decapitated him. The other cats ran away. Blood started to pool beneath Ember's feet. A condensed group of glowing particles metamorphosed into Jagger. She reached toward him, but quickly dissolved into another dimension.

Asleep

Ember was awake in her dream, lost in her regrets. Was she ready to move on, finish the story?

Clean up
If you think my poetry is bad you should see my dreams
I can PC up my blog but those thoughts I cannot clean
For the while I'll brighten up . . .
Not slight you up . . .

Butterflies and fluffies brighten my bitter day
Life is really good, is really good
But in an alternate reality I fly away

Vampires red, red dawn, and reindeer
Chase me through the sands of Egypt
As I drink blue smoke through my ears

The aliens surround my house
I crawl through the ceiling and slide
Hiding the babies

I wake up cold not quite alone
But will any ever understand where I stand?
Because I truly stand on my hands

Can I corral that horse that trots and bucks?
When she's told to conform
I've never understood the norm

In this unjust world where I live like a queen
Food and shelter and a shoulder on which to lean
Sometimes . . .

I've had one potato and savored its flavor
Glad to have a job and some leftovers for later
From the sweat of my brow and the tip of my pencil
I'll sit down with you and share my lentils

We are all only human, or so I think.

Zeus

Zeus washed his hands in the bathroom at Castle Clarity. The handsome god gazed at his face in the mirror and encouraged himself.

"Humans and their tragic flaws! I'm not like them. I have powers. Zeus is potent."

Smoke billowed into the bathroom. Zeus darted out the door. Lightning bolt in hand, he burst into the ballroom just as the dragons dropped a metallic cage encrusted in jewels over the dancing guests. The dragons hovered around the enclosure spitting fireballs on their prisoners. Triton wet his pants, which caused him to revert to his merman form. He looked fearful as he sat powerless on the floor, fishtail flapping.

Poseidon, Triton, Hermes, Eris, Dionysus, Athena, Aphrodite, and Persephone tried using their powers. They flailed their arms around wildly, gesticulating futile spells. This prompted Napoleon, Conor, and Camila to strike similar poses.

The dragons laughed as Excelsior ululated, "You have no abilities within these walls!"

Poseidon looked defeated, and Eris admitted, "I usually thrive on chaos, but this is a bit much!"

Persephone pouted. "Well, the worst that can happen to me is that I'll go back to Hades where I belong."

Excelsior shrieked, "Eh, wrong answer! Your soul will be trapped in a block to fortify Castle Clarity!"

Camila attempted to lift the cannonball, but it would not budge. It was as if it were made of lead. Conor flexed his muscles.

"Stand aside, Camila!" He seemed surprised when he couldn't move it either and whispered, "This isn't a prop. It's the real thing. How were you bloody riding on it before?"

"I don't know. Why are we even here?"

Triton and Poseidon began to argue again, and when Triton's tail smacked into Hermes, Hermes threw a punch, which connected with Dionysus's head. Dionysus stumbled back into Aphrodite, who grabbed Athena's hair as she fell. The dragons snickered as they watched the trapped gods and goddesses fight each other.

Excelsior announced, "We might not even have to kill them!"

Zeus, the only god outside the cage, crept up behind Excelsior and tapped her on the shoulder.

"Darling, look at how beautiful your scales are today. They're so nice and shiny. Are they made of gold?" Excelsior's head swung around and locked eyes with his as he continued, caressing her face with the back of his hand. "Oh my, what beautiful teeth you have."

The dragon smiled for a moment, but then frowned. "You idiot! You think that that old line is going to work on me? The least you could have done was say, 'Oh, how iridescent and titillating are your eyes, Excelsior.' This is just another reason for me to take your powers away forever. You have no idea how to treat women!"

"You're a female?" Zeus quipped.

Excelsior screamed, and fire flew out of her mouth to singe and burn the cage. The ceiling broke apart, and Berty flew down. He landed on the cage and cut the bars apart with his basalt talons. Jagger jumped from Berty's back, landed on the ground, and helped the gods out of the cage.

Eris darted over to the orchestra and urged them to play a techno song, after which she began dancing wildly. Pandemonium ensued.

Excelsior stood up tall on her hind legs, mouth wide open. Berty swooped down and pecked at the dragon's dress, but Excelsior puffed out her wings, clawed Berty away, and let out a terrifying scream.

"This is war!"

Rayne approached the gods calmly, hands on her hips. "Fools. Fighting with your family makes you weaker. It makes you softer than humans, who have saved you. Zeus, assemble your crew outside where your powers work so we stand a chance at defeating the dragons."

Zeus cried, "The girl is right! It's time to put our differences aside. Let's go."

En masse, the gods and goddesses exited the castle.

Camila looked at Conor. "Dude, this is the best party, ever!"

Intruder

In the Great Smoky Mountains of North Carolina, a chorus of crickets chirped outside the window of Ember's room. Their rhythmic reverberations were interrupted by someone banging angrily on her door.

A deep voice bellowed, "Ember, you didn't come down for supper!" A middle-aged man stood in front of her door. His face was red with rage as he wrinkled his nose and sniffed the air. "What's that skunky smell? Is that marijuana?"

Ember's father forced her door open. He looked around her room, then picked up a book that lay on her desk near her computer.

He opened it and read part of a page before throwing it to the ground and grumbled, "Stupid fantasy book. Her head is in the clouds, just like her mother."

Music began to play, and a ghostly voice whispered a song.

Black Hole
Quasar at the bazaar
Black hole from afar
Wormhole
Brings you near
Dear, like a lily of the valley

Nestled 'round my ear
Burst into fractal infrared
Mendeleev mode virtual
Scatter Rayleigh

Sleep and dream
Sleep and dream

There's no free energy
So let's pedal you and me
Take the breeze
Make energy
From a waterwheel

I flew last night
In a dream
Threw out my arms
And careened

Wings swept up by wind
Float through a cumulous
Sirius

Fly away
Sleep and dream
Sleep and dream

Crawlin' crawdads red
Reach out and claw my hand
Slip slide down mossy dreams
Blazing sun in painted skies
In the shade

There's no free energy
Gibbs me free energy
Gibbs me free energy

His face contorted. "Is that awful noise coming from her computer? She must be on drugs. What stupid music. I should have sent her to an all-girls school."

No Place Like Home

Ember was in freefall. She cartwheeled round and round in space until she crashed through the ceiling of her room on Earth. She landed on someone.

Oh no. It was her father. She was half naked, partially covered in cat fur, and crying hysterically.

He threw her off of him. "You absolutely reek of marijuana and alcohol!" He grabbed her arms. "Track marks! I knew it. You're cooking meth, aren't you? I knew it. You are nothing but a worthless junkie."

After all that had happened, Ember could only listen helplessly as her father ranted on. "I'm head deacon of the local church and the county's chief police officer. If anyone finds out that you're doing drugs, I will lose my reputation, my status, my job!

Ember lay on the floor, flailing her arms. "Just you wait, Beau and Berty will save me!"

Her father called 911 and diverted Ember to a psych ward for a week, after which she was taken to jail where she was to await trial on several charges: assault, drug manufacturing, and illicit drug use. Ember's parents would not answer her calls from jail. She sat in her cell, alone. She used a plastic fork to poke at a piece of toast covered in cold gravy on a thin Styrofoam plate.

Later that afternoon, a probation officer worker came in to talk to her. "Hi, honey," she said with a saccharine smile. "I work with your daddy."

"Really?" Ember snarked back, eyeing her suspiciously. "Are you sleeping with my dad, too, just like all the other women he cheats on my mother with?"

The social worker leaned forward and got in Ember's face to whisper, "Now listen here, you little hussy. I'm not the high-schooler and druggie that got pregnant, got drunk, tore her clothes off, and assaulted her father!"

Ember couldn't believe it. She had been a college student when she left Earth last. She fell through the space-time continuum and landed on her father. She definitely hadn't assaulted him. And anyway, the crazy cats were the ones who forced her to drink, threatening to sever her jugular vein if she didn't comply.

"What? High school? That's impossible. What year is it?"

The probation officer spoke with acid in her voice. "Ember, cut the crap. You know damn well it's 2016, and you've gotten your butt in a deep, deep load of manure. Now, your dad sent me down here to talk some sense into you, but I see that you aren't willing to take responsibility for your actions, just like he said. Let's talk about this baby. Do you know who the father is?"

Ember gasped, "Pregnant? But I wasn't with anyone!"

The social worker then spewed a litany of other veiled threats, all masked with false concern for Ember's future. "Now, normally in a case like yours, I would recommend an abortion and sterilization so that you don't pass this kind of mental illness down."

Ember's father stepped around the corner saying, "Will this kill her sex drive? This, uh, sterilization? I mean, I'm an upstanding, responsible citizen, and I normally wouldn't condone this, but for her health's sake, did you check first to see if she's anemic? She'd surely need an abortion then, right?"

Ember screamed at her father. After being restrained and drugged, she was transferred to a mental institution in Salem for the duration of her pregnancy. Because she was short, she gained a lot of weight and looked like a plump mushroom waddling about. She was quite happy not being around her parents during that time.

On April 30, 2017, Ember gave birth to a beautiful baby girl she named Elderberry. Her parents forced her to move back in with them, and her father was disappointed that Elderberry was born on Walpurgisnacht, a Satanic holiday.

Her father soon announced that he was looking for a suitor for her. "Ember, you are still a smart, beautiful girl. You should get married so your little girl has a father. It's the right thing to do. An assertive man will be able to control you, keep you out of trouble. I've narrowed the candidates down to a lawyer, a psychiatrist, and if all else fails, a logger."

Ember didn't even answer her dad. She longed to be worlds away, but now had a baby to care for. She gazed into Elderberry's eyes, and her little girl gave her a mysterious grin.

Distracted

The sun shone on the oasis in the sky above the rainbows. Cinder ground coffee beans with a mortar and pistol. A teakettle whistled with boiling water.

"Isn't this just the best? Hmm, that reminds me. Has anyone seen Ember or Jagger lately?"

Sergio, Alexander, Jade, and Ruby rushed up to Cinder excitedly. Sergio grinned from ear to ear.

"Cinder, we are going kayaking! Jack said he'd go, too. The river comes right out of the hot springs. It's warm. When we're done, we can go skiing at the ski resort on Mount Blank. It hardly has any trees, just long, open fields of the freshly fallen snow."

Cinder clapped her hands. "Let's do it!"

The assemblage gathered by a row of brightly colored kayaks at the end of the pool, where it cascaded off into a crystal clear river.

"This is such a perfect world," Alexander said. "We can do whatever we want, whenever we want, all day long."

Sergio declared, "Look at this boat! It's named *Master Jedi*! I want it! It's long, and I'm tall."

Alexander chose an open deck canoe. "This one looks like it will fit my feet!" Then he turned to Cinder. "You know how to kayak. Why does mine have half a paddle, but yours has a double blade?"

"Leverage, man. You need leverage because you sit on your knees in a canoe."

Jade and Ruby considered a double kayak, but settled on fiberglass squirt boats.

"A squirt boat is thin like a surfboard," Cinder informed them. "It will slice through the water elegantly. You will look like two beautiful dancing ballerinas."

"What's Jack going to do?" inquired Alexander, eyeing his merman tail.

"Dude, what do you think? I *am* my own boat."

Cinder showed Sergio, Ruby, and Jade how to don their neoprene spray skirts, which connect a kayaker to the boat, preventing leaks. One by one, they dropped from the pool, off the cascade, and into the rushing river below. Jack adjusted his helmet and dove in after the others.

The first section of the river wove between tricky boulders. Then it dumped over a hundred-foot rockslide that cascaded into a wide pool. Ruby and Jade's squirt boats sank under the water, then reemerged hundreds of feet away.

"There are fairies under the water, and one tried to kiss me!" Jade trilled.

Jack dove into the river. After a few moments, his head rose back out of the water and he smiled coquettishly.

Sergio winked at the others. "What happened, Jack?"

Jack was jovial. "Those are some very friendly fairies."

Cinder led the group out of the calm water and into a series of waterfalls, each higher than the next. The water rushed over a vertical drop and into a hydraulic, where they all began cartwheeling about in their boats—except for Alexander, whose boat sank when it filled with water.

Finally, they arrived at a serene lake filled with gargantuan sea dragonflies.

The friendly dragonflies began to beat their wings, and the waters from the lake swirled up and whisked them away to the ski slopes of Mount Blank.

Elderberry Pie

Ember settled into life on Earth, thinking less and less about the abstract ball of equations that had dumped her back in her room.

"So that was the ball? What a letdown."

She stopped trying to explain to her parents and friends that she had traveled through space and time and had experienced an immaculate conception, except when her father introduced her to potential suitors. The last thing she cared about was partnering up with a man of her father's choosing. Besides, she still had feelings for Jagger, whom she assumed was somehow Elderberry's father. Had she quantum mechanically willed Jagger's DNA into her?

Ember tried to convince her parents, who had conservatorship over her, to allow her to go to college to study science. She figured that a college education would be the only way to free herself from her parents forever. They told her she couldn't afford it and that she would never be accepted. She secretly applied for student aid and was also granted a scholarship at the University of North Carolina at Chapel Hill.

Ember spent the next eight years in college and obtained a master's degree in law, as well as a PhD particle physics.

By the time Ember graduated, Elderberry was eight years old. One day, Ember took her daughter on a hike on the Blue Ridge Parkway. Hand in hand, they walked through the emerald forest.

Elderberry took Ember's hand. "Mom?"

Ember bent down to her daughter's level, "Yes, dear?"

"I know I'm not supposed to ask about my father, but I feel in my heart that someday he will come and rescue us both from the dull monotony of Earth."

Ember laughed. "Those are big words for a little girl. Who told you not to ask about your dad?"

Elderberry looked down at the trail. "Oh, a little birdie told me."

Ember hugged her daughter. "A bird like a blue jay? It's okay, sweetie, you can ask me anything you want, anytime."

"Yes, it was a giant blue jay who visited me in my dreams. Do you know him? He takes me to distant planets and tells me that I can step through the fabric of space and time if I can figure out how to rip it. Does that make sense?"

"Totally," Ember agreed. "Tell me more."

Ember listened to Elderberry for the entire duration of the hike. That evening, Elderberry asked Ember to teach her how to sew her own quilt. Ember showed her daughter how to pair fabric and stitch the pieces together. Ember watched in fascination as Elderberry quickly assembled scraps of fabric into the form of a dragon, all while singing a song.

To Know
Never quite knowing
Where the next step is going
Or how will your tread
Fare the way

Out of the factory
Step on a toad
Stool drop
Please take your coat
When it's cold

Strive for success
Nothing less than the best
Don't slump on your rump
And sleep all day long

When it's gone
It's away
Build your house

For to stay through the storm
High up on a hill

Take the day
For your own
So you'll know
You can do it if you try

Midnight to moonshine
Light the way
Keeps you warm
Till the dawn
Out of the wild
Out of lone cold silence
I looked for you to find only
A stone

As flashes of Jagger, the Snow Realm, and mermaids rolled through Ember's head, she could not contain her sadness.

"Mom, I didn't mean to make you cry. I won't sing again."

"Oh, sweetie. Sing as much as you want. Your voice is beautiful."

Elderberry showed Ember her scene for the quilt. To her amazement, her daughter had pieced together an elaborate scene that depicted a group of young men and women at a castle fighting a group of dragons.

"Now I'm going to add the Greek gods. We can't forget Zeus!"

Ember laughed. "You're right, Zeus is unforgettable. Do you want me to make a lightning bolt?"

After a few more hours, Ember glanced at the clock. "Honey, it's way past midnight. Is your story complete?"

"Mom, we need to stay up until the witching hour."

Ember tickled her daughter. "Okay, okay, but just this one time."

Elderberry toiled away with her creations as Ember followed behind her, stitching the quilt together.

About an hour and a half later, she announced, "Mom, here are your valiant pets!"

She produced a grey cat, a black cat with a white bowtie, a guinea pig, and a giant blue jay. Ember froze. She had never spoken of her adventures to her daughter.

Unaware of her mother's preoccupation, Elderberry clapped her hands together excitedly. "Berty's my favorite!"

A bell tolled one time, two times, and then a third. Ember looked around. "Where's that coming from?"

Elderberry pointed to the center of the quilt. "It's coming from the tower, see? Come on, Mom, it's time to go meet Daddy and save your pets."

The light flickered, and Ember took Elderberry's hand. "You're right, honey, you did it. Hold on to me tight. Don't let go!"

The thread Ember was holding pulled her and Elderberry through the eye of the needle, along the long thread, and into the fabric of the quilt.

The Moth in the Cloth

Ember and Elderberry tumbled along the thread, through a giant sewing machine, and were finally deposited on a green field by a castle. Ember inspected her hands.

"Dear me, our bodies are made of fabric. If this is really your battle scenario, we need to take cover now!"

Ember picked up Elderberry and ran to the edge of a field by the woods and ducked into the underbrush. Ember rolled onto her back and sighed with relief.

Elderberry tugged her shirt and inquired, "Mommy, who is that?"

A brown-haired man lay on his back, his arms folded behind his head.

"Hi, I'm Damien."

"Holy cannoli! You *are* the devil!"

Ember contemplated running, but was afraid of the battle depicted in Elderberry's quilt.

"I know what you're thinking, Ember. Xavier told me all about you."

Ember remembered the night she unshielded her electrons with Xavier. She covered Elderberry's ears.

"Damien, Xavier said you were his evil twin!"

"I knew he might say that, but he's really the wicked one. I mean, he did kiss and tell, didn't he?"

"You are pestering me. I'd like you to leave."

"No worries, I'm used to it: Xavier being my evil twin and all. He's quite the trickster. Say, who is the little girl?" he inquired, pointing at Elderberry.

Ember hugged her daughter closer. "She is NONE of your business!"

"Did you use protection with Xavier?" he asked, as the first loud shots of the battle were fired.

"Watch your language. She's only eight!"

Damien laughed, "Eight human years? Sounds about right. Seriously, Ember, I'm you're only hope. Only I can get you back to the ball."

"What do you mean?" demanded Ember. "I thought that damn sphere of abstract equations *was* the ball, and it nearly killed me!"

Damien explained, "Your friends are at the Dragon Ball of the Millennium, and they could use your help because they haven't been able to resolve their mission without you. Ember, don't you want your daughter to grow up with her father?"

Tears ran down Ember's face. She wanted to punch Damien, but she dug her fist into the ground until her cloth hand started to unravel.

"Ember," Damien said. "Look at you! You're coming apart."

"Darn it!"

"Mom, I hate to see you unraveling at the seams like this."

Damien produced a sewing kit, and Ember allowed him to stitch her back together. What else was she to do?

Battle On!

Outside Castle Clarity, the gods and goddesses regained their powers and quickly built a small fortress. Rayne gathered them in the main hall and spoke to the group. "Gods and goddesses, have you forgotten who you are? You are the mighty Olympians."

Poseidon yelled, "I object!"

Rayne cleared her throat, adding, "Excuse me—and a Titan."

Athena remarked snidely, "Triton, Persephone, Eris, Hermes, and Aphrodite are technically demigods, not *real* Olympians."

Aphrodite argued, "You can't prove I'm not an Olympian!"

Eris roared, "I am the daughter of night, an entity that existed before the Titans! I am the most important."

Persephone screamed, "My husband is Hades, so you can all go to hell!"

Rayne folded her arms. "Enough! This is exactly what I was talking about. To defeat the evil, soul-sucking dragons, you are going to have to stop clashing and band together. Generation after generation you fight, trying to assert your power over each other. Zeus, you should forgive Cronus. Throwing him in prison is eating a hole in your heart."

Zeus looked reflective, almost as if he was going to cry. He leaned over to Poseidon and hugged him. Poseidon extended his hand to Triton.

"Group hug?"

The Greek Gods linked hands, and Camila made a pitch. "Can we join?"

Napoleon stated, "*Oui, oui.*"

Aphrodite stroked Napoleon's head. "We know you are a little man."

Napoleon retorted, "That's a myth. I'm five foot nine in American inches. That's an average height for a male. Gods are taller than humans. And '*oui*' means 'yes' in French."

Rayne rolled her eyes. "Napoleon, I invited you so that you could lead us into battle. You are our new commander."

Zeus glared at Rayne. "This is no little girl. Reveal yourself!"

Poseidon asked, "What do you mean?"

Rayne admitted, "I am a reincarnation of the goddess Isis. My father is Geb, and my great-grandfather is Ra. Yes, I am the offspring of the sun, and I am here to help save you. The evil dragons unsuspectingly trapped you, their guests, in a viscous deception, but they knew your weaknesses: narcissism, sex, and gluttony."

Camila interjected, "Ha! Finally, someone breaks character. The joke is on you! You're mixing Egyptology and Greek mythology!"

Rayne countered, "So you're saying we are not all connected?"

Zeus paused for a moment. "She's right; we are all linked together through space-time continuums. If it has been written, it is so."

"Zeus, have you ever been forced to face a challenge you didn't think you would surmount?" Rayne asked.

Aphrodite laughed. "Do you mean a challenge he would never *mount*?"

Poseidon poked Zeus in the ribs. "Come on, guys. Let's get serious and form a game plan, together."

Zeus scoffed at his son when Hermes nodded. "Okay, Herpes, what do you do?"

Hermes begged, "Dad, it's *Hermes*! If you don't even know my name, I'm not surprised you don't know my power. Lame!"

"Of course I do, son! You give people boils, right?"

"That's herpes, a disease that affects humans. I guide souls to the afterlife."

"Sound riveting." Zeus turned away from Hermes. "So, Napoleon, what's the plan?"

The gods and humans huddled together as Napoleon scribbled in the dirt. Berty flew around Castle Clarity to monitor the dragons.

Jagger quietly backed out of the circle. Rayne approached him.

"Brother, you look sad."

"How can they call themselves gods if they are just a bunch of meddlesome, narcissistic ninnies who fight among each other? No wonder we humans are the way we are. I'm a failure."

"You've been instrumental to this quest," Rayne assured him. "You warped through worlds on a gigantic blue jay and saved Ember from certain demise."

Jagger shifted his feet in the sand. "But I lost you, and then let Ember slip away again. It was all my fault. I'm worthless."

Jagger started to turn away, but Rayne grabbed his shoulder. "Jagger, you *are* worthy. If you go through life looking backward, you can't move forwards. What would happen if you told yourself there are no mistakes, just choices and consequences?"

Jagger's eyes widened and he sank to his knees in front of Rayne. "But I was supposed to save *you*."

"You have always been there for me, but you have to take care of yourself before you can help others. If you open your eyes, you will see that you have all that you need to keep on going. It's up to you to decide whether you want to thrive. Ember is okay. She was pulled away because she was not yet ready to fight. She hadn't yet found herself. Now, she's ready to finish her story."

As Jagger stood tall and joined the others to discuss battle plans, Hermes puffed out his chest. "I have a great idea. Thor, where's your hammer?"

Conor looked annoyed. "I am *not* Thor."

"Then you're Loki? Do you think we could borrow your brother's hammer? Perhaps it will shatter the blocks of the Castle Clarity. They look fragile."

Conor threw up his hands in exasperation. "I give up. Hermes, try Camila's—I mean *Sif's* cannonball."

"You mean that big flail without a tail?" Hermes asked. He produced a chain and hooked it to the ball.

"No, *Thor*. I will hurl the flail." Camila confidently wrapped the chain of the ball around her hand and whirled it around above her head. When she let it fly, she knocked out Napoleon.

Rayne winced. "Oops. He'll be okay. With a little practice you'll be a lean, mean fighting machine."

Camila's eyes gleamed. "I already am one."

She ran outside with the others at her heels. This time, she expertly hurled her weapon toward Castle Clarity and struck a corner of the massive structure. A block exploded, and a flurry of screeching souls flitted out from the dust. They then blended together in a mournful, dissonant chord.

"That sounds worse than *some* people without auto-tune."

The souls spun around in a flurry toward them and hovered above Hermes, who groaned, "It looks like I won the lottery, because now I need to take these spirits to Hades before the dragons trap them again. I'll be back."

Berty flew down from the sky. "The dragons doubled over in pain when the brick broke!"

Camila laughed maniacally as she swung her weapon over her head. "I never thought that I'd actually do something constructive with this. I'll use it to tear something down so something new and better can be built. Profound." She gave Conor a wry glance.

He replied, "Yeah, good point."

Strangely, Berty's back began to meow. "Oh my goodness. I forgot all about Beauregard and Midnight. They must have been taking cat naps in the cage on my back all this time."

Camila climbed onto Berty's back to help the cats down. "Poor kitties."

The cats sprung out of the cage, hissing, and immediately squatted to pee.

Beauregard meowed, "Don't look at me!"

Once the cats had relieved themselves, they scampered to and fro. Finding no bushes or stones to take cover under, they soon began to pant in the hot sun.

"Why don't you take shelter in the fortress, where it's cooler?" Rayne offered.

Conor tried to pull Beauregard's tail. "How did the special effects department manage this one?"

Beauregard growled, "And who do you think you are?"

Unperturbed, Conor pulled on Beauregard's fur. "I should be asking you the same. Who are you under that makeup? Leo? Brad? Pete Davidson?"

The grey feline furrowed his brows. "I am a talking cat. At least I have my dignity. You, however, look like a weak human bumbling around in the wrong world."

Camila pointed at Midnight and hollered, "What's wrong with the black cat?"

Midnight was retching, his body bulging and convulsing with the effort. His fur turned black and curly. Before anyone could react, he was a sheep. Beauregard shrieked as Midnight bleated and hastened into a field, where he munched on a patch of grass.

"He never was much of a conversationalist anyway. He always seemed so dark, so introverted," Beauregard mused. "Fine, let me in your fortress before I wilt in this sweltering heat."

Seduced

The sun glistened off the scintillating, prismatic snow of Mount Blank. Jack surfed expertly down a powdery slope using his merman tail as a snowboard. Jade followed on a snow bike. Alexander swooshed along on a snowboard, doing a triple spin. Sergio bounced down a hill of bumpy moguls on telemark skis. Cinder zoomed along on a bobsled. Ruby grew a pair of wings and flew into the air.

Day after day Cinder, Sergio, Jade, Ruby, Alexander, and Jack had grand adventures. Every morning, new delicacies were spread out on the table for them. Each evening, carafes of wine mysteriously filled. Pigdor munched on a patch of grass that regrew almost automatically, and freshly cut slabs of meat were always available for the dogs.

As the sun set that evening, an ember-colored petal fluttered into Cinder's hair. Tobias nudged her leg.

"What's up, boy?"

Gypsy looked side to side at the frolicking humans. "Have you all forgotten about Ember? Each day, you humans do something for fun. It's totally hedonistic. You think only for your own random wants and whims. Pigdor, look at yourself. You eat so much that you are as giant as a horse."

Alexander remarked, "Gypsy, you are a wise dog. I always wanted to help this story move along, but I've become just another character who doesn't add anything to the plot."

"You're right. We are not helping Ember's story move forward," Sergio agreed. "This land that is full of peace and void of excitement. Even the most daring adventures make me yawn. I hate to say this, but I think I miss chaos. Plus, the lack of testosterone is totally affecting my brain!"

Tobias barked and Gypsy translated for the others. "He agrees with your last statement. Ember's parents sent him to the vet to get fixed after he chased down a Chow Chow that was going to attack her, which caused her to wreck her bike. He says he's just a shell of his former self."

Ruby and Jade rushed to console Tobias. "You were castrated because you tried to save Ember? How awful!"

Cinder chided, "Guys, there you go getting off track again! I have a bad feeling about Ember. It's been nagging me for days, but we just kept on having so much fun. It's almost like we are being distracted just so that we couldn't help her, just so the story would be stuck in limbo."

Sergio added, "So procrastination is the antagonist of the story. Or is it just the author's tragic flaw? Let's do something for Ember! After all, we wouldn't exist without her."

"Speak for yourself, Sergio!" Cinder protested. "I existed before Ember did. Did the chicken come before the egg?"

Gypsy barked. "Stop! Stop! It doesn't matter! We all exist. Does it matter how or why? I am an old dog, and I have lived a long life. I do *not* want my uterus back. You must go and save Ember. Tell her I love her, but I'm staying here."

Sergio picked a flower out of Cinder's hair. "Huh, it's a lotus flower."

"We are lotus-eaters!" Alexander pronounced. "The food we are eating contains lotus, which makes us apathetic. We have to get out of this place, pronto!"

Cinder, Sergio, Alexander, Ruby, Jade, Tobias, and Pigdor rushed to the snowcraft, piled in, and executed the quantum tunneling function.

The Tangled Forest

At the entrance of the fortress, Eris leaned against Berty's perch. She watched, amused as he squawked in his sleep.

"No, no, Mommy! That big, grey cat was watching me, he was! I'm falling from my nest Mommy. The cat has me! Oh no, a giant human hand! A human hand has taken me and put me in a bowl! Mommy? Mommy! Ember, are you my mommy now? Can I have more food? Oh, I'm sick. Ember, thank you for giving me medicine to save my life. No, please don't put me back in the cage with your guinea pig. Ah! The cat is clawing at my cage! Ember, I must go back to the woods with the other blue jays. Farewell."

Eris pulled on one of Berty's tail feathers.

The giant jay opened his eyes and blurted out, "Why is gravity such a weak force?" Then he plummeted from his perch to the ground.

Eris chuckled. "If gravity is weak, how did it slay the giant war bird?"

"Gravity isn't a weak force if it's strong on the Planck scale, the energy scale that catalogues minimum limits. Does the moon not make the waves?" Rayne remarked.

Berty chimed in, "Then I, a blue jay, can dominate a strong force such as gravity?"

"You must get down to an elemental, atomic level to see gravity's strength," Rayne informed him. "That reminds me. Zeus, where is your brother, Apocalypse? We could certainly use the god of gravity now. We need his knowledge. Do you know where he is?"

The corners of her mouth turned up with suspicion when Zeus looked around nervously. "Rayne, I am not Zeus. I think you know this. Around four thousand years ago, the three judges—Rhadamnathus, Aeacus and Minos—sent Zeus to Tartarus after he gave antibiotic-resistant syphilis to Sodom and Gomorrah. Since the courts didn't want any forces, like the Norse gods, to challenge the Greek gods, I have been pretending to be Zeus since then. I am the great Apocalypse, the god that can manipulate the universal force of gravity. If Ember can get down to an atomic level, she can travel faster than the speed of light through a pathway that connects the subatomic particle in her body to its twin, which resides in Jagger."

"Would you like to explain what brought Ember and Jagger together through space and time? Did the particles exist in them before they met?" Rayne asked.

Apocalypse said, "You're catching on. Twenty-five years ago, Jagger's father and Ember's mother were both at a Grateful Dead show at Chicago's Soldier Field. During the song 'Box of Rain,' I slipped a cosmic joint into the crowd. I fooled them, because it was just oregano, and it contained twin particles. Jagger's father inhaled one of the particles, and Ember's mother inhaled its mirror image. When Jagger and Ember were born, respectively, the particles were passed to them, linking them forever."

"Wow, so that's why we are connected!" Jagger exclaimed. "It's all about quantum physics, not love! Thank goodness."

Camila lifted her hand to her mouth. "Dude, that's spooky and twisted."

Apocalypse nodded. "Girl, you don't know how right you are!"

Gravitokinesis

In the cloth world, Ember, Elderberry, and Damien hid under the bushes at the edge of a felted forest of conifers. A fluttering flock of silky moths flooded the sky, then descended and began to attack the villagers. Children screamed and writhed in pain as the moths chewed them threadbare. Elderberry darted out from the underbrush and went after the moths.

"Crumpets!" Damien cursed. "We were just ready to teleport to Fractasia!"

Ember hurried over to Elderberry. She picked a stick off the ground and swung it at a giant moth. The winged warrior crumpled to the ground, feelers flailing. Ember and her daughter started hurling stones at the fearsome flyers. Damien soon joined. In no time, they managed to conquer all the vermin. The cloth children cheered around them.

Ember embraced Elderberry, but the girl started screaming just a moment later. A hefty, furry caterpillar was chewing on her darling's foot. Ember tried to stomp on the loathsome larva, only to have it sting her before she could do much damage.

"Quick, take my hand!" Damien pleaded with her.

"What?" Ember screamed. "Her foot is falling off, and we still have to save the others!"

"Ember, snap out of it! Look, the villagers are already gone, safe and hidden. They were just another distraction to pull you away. You must trust me. I am here to help."

Ember glared at Damien, picked up her wounded daughter, and began to run. She tried to shield her dear Elderberry in her arms as caterpillars surrounded them. Damien tackled Ember, and they all folded in between dimensions.

Once they were whisked away, Ember was both mad at herself for not believing Damien and glad that he had saved her and Elderberry, anyway. She closed her eyes as they warped through time and space, praying that their next landing would be safe.

When Ember opened her eyes, she was inside a strange fortress, surrounded by people who looked like Greek gods. Jagger was there, standing right in front of her. Surprisingly, he hugged her. At the contact, Ember felt something like liquid lightning course through her body.

"Ember, I'm so glad you are safe." Jagger looked down at Elderberry. "Who's this?"

Ember brushed a wayward strand of Elderberry's behind her ear. "She's your daughter." She caught Damien giving her a suspicious look and wondered what was eating his goat. "Damien, can you give us a moment alone?"

Jagger pulled Ember aside. "I don't understand. First, we never, uh, did anything. And second, you were gone for two days. How do you expect me to believe we have a five-year-old together?"

Ember snapped, "She's eight!"

At that moment, Jagger aged and grew a long beard. He shrugged his shoulders, bent down and hugged Elderberry, and then picked her up and held her in his arms.

Apocalypse laughed. "Eerie, indeed, but I'm afraid we don't have any more time. Rayne, Jagger, Ember, and Elderberry: go find Hermes and ask him to release Zeus and Cronus from Tartarus. Together, the Titans and the Olympians will help the humanoids defeat the evil, soul-sucking, foul-mouthed dragons so we can save the universe together."

Rayne hoisted Elderberry into Berty's basket, after which Jagger and Rayne followed. Berty soared up into the air, high above Castle Clarity. Jagger turned to Elderberry.

"This world is called Fractasia. To get in and out of it, you have to be converted into fractals."

Elderberry grew excited. "I know what those are! Mommy told me all about fractals! They are like a Romanesco broccoli. Are fractals infinite? Do they ever stop?"

"I don't know the answer to that." Ember giggled and allowed the cool air to wash the worry off her face as they twisted and twirled around the atmospheric fractals until they found a flashing space worm that burrowed its way into the sky and transported them to Tartarus.

The darkness was cold, so Ember and Jagger snuggled with Elderberry to keep her warm. Rayne removed her golden cloak and draped it over all of them, explaining that it would keep them hidden from evil spirits on their journey to the prison of the gods.

The Fortress

In a burst of light, Cinder, Alexander, Ruby, Jade, Jack, and Sergio arrived in Fractasia. Their ship landed on a dragon and squished green goo all over Conor, Camila, the gods, and the pets. At first, Apocalypse wanted to kill the humans, partially because *he* was trying to slay the dragon and his pride was wounded, and partly because he didn't know who the humans were. Eventually they had a long, confusing discussion about the dragons and Ember. Everyone was trying to talk at once.

"So these evil, soul-sucking, foul-mouthed dragons are going to destroy the universe?" Cinder posed to the group.

"You're telling me that this human named Ember is responsible for this madness?" Eris vociferated. "Starting chaos is *my* job!"

"No, the author of my story—I mean, the author of *this* story . . ." Cinder started, then gave up on that train of thought. "Now I'm confused, too. I'm a parallel universe version of Ember, I guess."

"Everybody calm down!" Apocalypse thundered over the din. "We need to work together! Greeks, humanoids, mermen, *and* pets."

Jack broke the ice by leaping into the kiddie pool with Triton. "I really felt like a fish out of water."

The goddesses were quickly distracted by Alexander and his striking Roman features. Aphrodite gave the other girls the side-eye. She then surreptitiously removed her famous love belt, slipped it around Alexander's waist, and led him inside the fortress to "show him around," while flipping off the other goddesses behind her back.

Midnight napped in the sun next to Beauregard, and then the black cat abruptly morphed back into a black sheep. Midnight scurried over to a field of grass, where Pigdor, now the size of a hippopotamus, greedily grazed.

Sergio helped Persephone gather lost souls and group them together so they could be transported to Hades upon Hermes's return.

Dionysus sang and threw seeds on the ground, and moments later, grapevines grew high above their fortress. With a wave of his hands, Apocalypse petrified the wood and boasted, "Now our stronghold won't burn if those evil, soul-sucking dragons come to attack us."

The grey-eyed Athena wove tapestries that had actual moving stories on them. From those tapestries, Dionysus cut flying carpets, which he gave to Camila and Conor. "At least these will make you feel like you have powers like us gods."

Extended Sunset

After the humans left Gypsy alone at the pool, groups of fairies and angelic cherubs fed her blackberries and lotus flowers from the garden. Her fur was still partially golden, but her whiskers were grey. She spoke to her friends, recounting the days she used to chase cars, and the times the cars got too close to her wards. She told them about how she had gotten her human, Ember, through the years during many trials and tribulations.

The fairies flitted around the old dog's head as she told them stories, between barks, about rattlesnakes, yellow-bellied black snakes, copperheads, black bears, and yellow jackets.

"One time, when Ember was only eight years old, I was too late, and the poor thing had run away from home. She got caught in a thicket so dense that she could not move. She sat on a log, and even Tobias abandoned her because she was sitting on a yellow jacket's nest. When I saw little Ember, she was running, literally flying out of the woods and down the mountain, despite the underbrush and the briars." Gypsy laughed. "I remember the daily walks around the mountains, sometimes for miles, watching over Ember. I was a happy dog. Was I a good dog? I think so, even though I barked a lot. I was fiercely protective of that silly girl, who always seemed to be in trouble because her parents just didn't seem to care about her."

Day after day, Gypsy sat by the pool. "I wonder if someone will pass by?" she asked a cherub who lounged beside her.

The cherub chirped, "Gypsy, good things will come to pass. Even if you never see Ember again, you will one day be visited by another traveler to care for."

To Tartarus

The space worm that Ember, Jagger, Elderberry, and Berty rode on their quest to reach the Underworld chewed its way to the front gate. Ember was shocked that Hermes was selling wares in front of a food cart. Ember gently nudged Elderberry awake.

Hermes stood by the River Styx, shouting, "Elote, chocolate eggs filled with toys, kale chips, kombucha! Last chance for a taste of Earth before you go on to eternity!"

Berty bent down and gobbled up all the Mexican corn in a couple of bites. He glared at Hermes and wrapped his talons around his neck. "How many licks does it take to get to the center of a Hermes pop?"

Jagger gave Berty a strange look. "What does that mean?"

Berty opened his beak menacingly. "Haven't you ever seen that old commercial for Tootsie Pops? It takes more than three hundred licks to get to the center of the lolly, but I bet I can penetrate Hermes's skull with only three pecks of my beak."

Jagger threw up his hands. "Settle down, killer. I don't think you want to murder Hermes. Without him, we'll never reach Hades to save Zeus and Cronus. But seriously, Hermes, what are you doing wasting time like this?" Jagger scolded. "Shouldn't you be saving more souls from Fractasia?"

"Your ideas of time, space, and value are totally warped. You have no idea what you're talking about," Hermes lectured. "I'm here to soothe and save souls with whatever methods I choose! Don't you think these weary souls are hungry, too? Plus, what are they going to do with their money once they are in Hades?"

Rayne patted Berty softly on the back of the neck until the bird released Hermes.

Ember asked sweetly, "How much is passage to and fro for six?"

Hermes had a distant look in his eyes. "I keep a resting place for weary men. The cool spring gushes."

Jagger snorted. "Okay, buddy, I don't think the lady cares about your, uh, sprouting spring."

"Near the hoary grey coast—"

Before he could go on, Jagger punched his shoulder. "Now you've gone too far."

Hermes looked Jagger squarely in the eye. "Obviously, you don't know your Greek mythology."

Jagger flexed his arms. "Are you going to take us to Tartarus or are we going to have to commandeer your raft?"

Hermes scoffed, "You really think you could do that?"

"Obviously this conversation has digressed," Ember interjected. "How much is the fare?"

Elderberry offered Hermes a quarter. "Please, Mr. Psychopomp, will you take us across the River Styx?"

Hermes took the payment and stuffed it in a bag of coins tied around his waist.

Jagger looked perplexed, so Elderberry clarified, "A psychopomp carries people to the afterlife. Anubis is an Egyptian psychopomp. Humans used to bury their loved ones with coins so they could pay to be ferried across the River Styx. Even Christians did it."

Hermes looked at Elderberry with mild admiration. "I'm impressed. Who are you?"

Ember beamed. "She's my daughter," she said at the same time that Jagger chimed in with, "She's our daughter."

Hermes looked confused and slowly swung his head from side to side. "Okay, never mind, I shouldn't have asked. Don't touch anything, and I mean *anything*! If you do, you will go straight back to Earth. If you drink from the River Lethe, then you will forget your earthly life. Above all, do not eat anything, or you will stay here forever!"

Elderberry wrinkled her nose. "As if I would want to eat anything here. It smells like old Camembert here!"

"Sorry—all that corn gave me indigestion," Berty apologized.

Ember giggled. "It's sulfur, Elderberry. It smells bad in Hades because of all the hot minerals."

Hermes inspected Berty closely. "I see that you've been indulging in more of the Underworld. Female fowl? Food? Welcome to the dark side, knight rider."

Elderberry perked up at that. "Hermes, how do you know about *Star Wars*?"

"Are you kidding? Darth Vader is so evil that he is locked up in Tartarus for eternity," he said with a laugh. "What? Did you think I lived under a rock?"

Jagger scoffed. "You kind of do."

"I think I've been around the block a time or two more than you. You probably don't even know what the KITT is."

Ember chuckled, for her mother used to show her reruns of *Knight Rider*, a show in the '80s about a talking car. "KITT's old news. Now we have Elon Musk to deliver us to the future."

"Ha! And the human race hasn't even invented teleportation yet. You are literally millions of years behind us gods," Hermes chortled. "Never mind. Let's return to your quest before we get lost in this abysmal argument for eons, for there is no try!" He helped each of the humanoids step onto a rickety ferry on the banks of the River Styx. He handed Charon, the ferryman, a few pennies.

"If you touch the water, you will experience the greatest pain you could ever feel." Charon stuck his finger in the river and winced, but Ember thought he looked like he was in ecstasy rather than in agony.

Hermes slapped his assistant on the back. "Just get on with it."

Throughout the journey, Rayne and Hermes murmured secretly together, which Ember found odd, but she tried to focus on her daughter instead. She and Jagger swung Elderberry between their arms.

"Will I disappear if I hold my parents' hands?" she asked. "I guess not, because we are all still in Hades!"

Jagger pointed at a wandering soul who was playing the song from *Deliverance* on the banjo. His jaw dropped, and he let go of Elderberry's hand for a moment. She rolled to the edge of the raft, nearly falling off.

"What the Hades?" demanded Ember and huddled over Elderberry protectively.

Jagger hugged Elderberry. "Sorry, I guess I've seen too many thriller movies. Locals playing banjos while we wander through actual hell scare the bejesus out of me."

Hermes warned, "Stick together and don't do anything stupid. This is especially important after we've crossed the River Styx."

Ember felt a sense of dread as soon as they stepped onto the ground of the Underworld. Minutes turned into hours, and hours turned into a day. Jagger carried little Elderberry in his arms, and she whimpered in her sleep. Ember's feet were sore. They talked and talked and talked, until at last they were silent.

Hermes said, "Finally."

"Are we there yet?" said Ember, losing her typically polite tone.

Rayne held her hands wide apart, "Tartarus is as far from Earth as Hades is from heaven."

Ember was too tired to wait. "There must be a way to get there faster."

Hermes said, "If we use the Jochre Coaster it will be much faster."

"What?" Jagger, Ember, and Rayne asked in unison.

"Why didn't you say anything before?" demanded Jagger.

Hermes point to Berty. "Well, the bird wouldn't fit."

"You're blaming this on me? I can fly *and* I'm a gigantic, basaltic, fireproof bird who now belongs to Hades. I'll meet you in Tartarus." Berty flapped his wings, stirring up a cloud of dust in the process, and flew up high into the burning sky.

Hermes snapped his fingers, and a string of purple cars with gleaming yellow teeth rolled up, cackling maniacally. "All aboard the Jochre Coaster!"

Elderberry giggled. "The Joker is in Batman!"

"True, child, but this is spelled J-O-C-H-R-E and pronounced *Joe-kra*, like *okra* with a *Joe* in front of it."

Ember was pleasantly surprised that even in the Underworld, people had a sense of humor. She climbed into a hot seat that shone silver and black like hematite, placing Elderberry betwixt her and Jagger. Rayne sat in the front, while Hermes climbed into the back. Claw-like harnesses coiled over their bodies, securing them, and they sped off into the darkness.

"Watch your head, for you don't want it to be lost in wonderland," Hermes warned.

The Jochre Coaster sped off with a sinister swoosh. First, they passed a spooky forest, where black figures flew through the trees. As they descended deeper into the trenches of the Underworld, the temperature grew hotter and hotter. The air was thick and sticky, and the stench was even worse. Lava flowed as a river alongside the coaster's track, and nearly singed the humans.

"Don't worry!" Hermes assured his human companions. "Because there is no oxygen in Hades, you won't burn."

Elderberry piped up, "I know about the fire triangle! It takes heat, oxygen, and fuel to start a fire."

Ember held Elderberry tightly as they came to a wide, slow flow of lava spilling over a ledge. "It looks like this flaming inferno goes down to infinity and beyond."

"Mom, that's not possible," Elderberry said. "Infinity is infinite."

Hermes eyed her from his seat. "Really? So you don't believe in *Toy Story*?"

The coaster crept to the edge of the lava, its laughter growing more menacing with every inch, and then slowed to a stop. Ember could feel Jagger shaking, but Elderberry didn't seem scared.

"This is the Flow of Relativity. Be careful! Things are not what they seem here."

Hermes then snapped his fingers and the entire vehicle pitched over the ledge. They descended so fast that Ember felt like her heart was pounding in her head. She clutched Elderberry to her, but realized that the little girl was giggling and having fun.

Ember relaxed and looked around. The stream of lava cooled and crystallized into an amazing array of gems, geodes, and precious metals that cascaded far below. Hermes whistled and the coaster slowed down, whilst the crystals moved even slower. Hermes clapped, and the Jochre sped down all the faster while showers of gems reversed and went back up through the lava, where they were then reabsorbed by the molten river.

A dark shadow covered them. Ember looked up, but it was just Berty, who was also descending into the abyss. Ember mused that although she was in Hades, she was happier than ever. She was with her darling Elderberry, and far away from her hell on Earth with her parents. The theory of relativity was more meaningful than she thought.

After what seemed like weeks, great mountains of jagged jewels rose from below. Sapphires and rubies stuck out like swords from the mounds. Ember wondered if they were at all close to Tartarus, when their ride suddenly halted.

The coaster sputtered and unceremoniously dumped them like piles of discarded dirt in front of an entrance that led to a slide as it cackled, "Get out!"

It backed away, leaving a trail of haunting laughter behind.

Ember tried to brush the dust from Elderberry, but the soot was stubborn.

"Keep your hands to yourself!" Hermes warned again as he led Ember, Elderberry, and Jagger to the obsidian slide.

With her daughter in her arms, Ember zoomed down after the others and tried to hide the hideous ghosts and ghouls lining the walls from Elderberry's view. As they descended, the slide narrowed so that she lay flat on her back. The terrifying spirits hovered inches away from their faces and had rancid, sulfuric breath. The apparitions became more sinister and gruesome, and turned into demonic pigs that squealed and grabbed at them as they passed. Finally, when the screams and the smells and the sights were just too much for Ember to handle, they were deposited onto a pile of dusty bones.

Discordia

The pastel wisps in Fractasia's sky swirled around like freshly spun cotton candy. They piled up quickly and blocked out the sun. While Napoleon discussed battle tactics, Eris grabbed a flying carpet and snuck into Castle Clarity. Eris crouched in a corner and watched as Excelsior paced back and forth, angrily wringing her hands. The other dragons screamed, panted, and clucked at each other like chickens.

Eris had a gleam in her eyes as she wrung her hands. "Such chaos!"

Apocalypse was by her side in an instant. "What are you doing?"

Eris whispered, "I'm going to make sure the author never finishes the story."

"Why?"

"The author began writing this stupid story over twenty years ago. I infiltrated her Hotmail account and deleted the file. Like an idiot, she started the story again," Eris replied. "I allowed her to find a hard copy of the old story, hoping that she would be so confused she would stop. Then she merged the stories, creating parallel universes! I'm going to keep throwing writer's block at her until she goes crazy, so this stupid story will never be published!"

Apocalypse frowned. "Eris, how are two alternate narratives about Ember's story any different than the conflicting origins of your parentage? Is Zeus really Aphrodite's dad, as stated in *The Iliad*, or did she come from Uranus?"

"Aphrodite did not come from my nether regions!"

Apocalypse clicked his tongue. "Eris, I didn't literally mean *your* anus, I meant the god described in Hesiod's *Theogony*. My point is that we exist in this story now. The evil, soul-sucking dragons must be defeated so that we can once again go home to Mount Olympus, or we may remain stuck here forever, ad infinitum. No resolution might mean we cease to exist."

Eris picked at her nails. "Screw you, Apocalypse. Your opinions don't matter. Don't you want to see all humans suffer their weak, emotional pain?"

"I care about the humans. Besides, what fun would we have without them?"

Eris grunted, "I *need* this story to crumble because the author makes us look weak, while the stupid humans are uplifted. Apocalypse, we need a narrative in which only the gods are exalted!"

Eris reached into her pocket and produced a golden apple. Apocalypse became agitated.

"No, not another fruit of discord! Where do you get those?"

"Duh—from the Tree of Discord. Where do you think?"

"You fool! Dragons love gold!" Apocalypse reminded her. "They will kill themselves fighting for it, and they might take us with them! Don't you remember we have no powers within these walls?"

Eris rolled the apple across the marble floor into the dragon's den.

Excelsior was the first to spy the apple and greedily cried, "Gold!"

At once, all of the dragons lunged for the golden apple. The reptilians attacked one another with their claws, teeth, and wings. They quickly formed a pile of spilled intestines and charred bits. It was anarchy at its worst.

As the dragons fought amongst themselves, one of them kicked the apple out of the fray. Apocalypse grabbed it and fled the castle. Eris ran after him, tackling him as he exited the main entrance. The gilded fruit flew up into the air and landed directly in the mouth of Midnight, the black sheep.

Eris laughed maniacally. "You really let the cat out of the bag, Apocalypse."

Apocalypse cradled his head in his hands. "What have you done now?"

Eris jutted out her chin defiantly. "Oops, did I do it again? Would you expect anything less from the goddess of strife and discord?"

"Touché. Did you forget that humans are incredibly resilient and often flourish in the face of chaos? You may have just given them a gift."

Eris huffed and strode away.

Many Hands

The gates of Tartarus were hundreds of feet tall. Cords of molten metal writhed around in intricate patterns of skulls and crossbones, scythes, and demons. Ember held Elderberry, who was shivering as they approached the ominous gates. The entrance was blocked by a large stone stalwart. Unexpectedly, the pillar shifted. Stones and pebbles rained down, exposing three gargantuan monsters, each with multiple ugly heads and many sets of arms.

Ember shuddered. "What are those beasts?"

Hermes muttered, "The Centimanes. The beast protects the gate to Tartarus."

Jagger nodded. "Makes sense. How many limbs and heads do they have?"

"Each beast has a hundred hands and fifty heads. Their Greek name is the Hecatoncheires. Centimanes, or the Latin name, seems to be easier for English speakers to say."

"Centimanes makes more sense to me," Ember agreed. "A hundred hands. Do they have individual names?"

Hermes replied, "The ugly one is Cottus, the uglier one is Briareus, and the ugliest is Gyges."

Ember wanted to vomit at the sight of them. "I don't know how you tell them apart!"

In a single voice, the heads of the Centimanes roared, "Who dares approach Tartarus?"

"It's me, Hermes, and I am here for a concert."

The Centimanes' many mouths chorused, "Well, then, are you ready to *rooock*?"

The beasts stomped on the ground in spiked black boots, each holding different electric musical instruments in their hands. Each instrument was plugged into an enormous Marshall stack. Ember thought they looked like scary marionettes. When the Centimanes burst into song, Ember was blown away, for each head sang a different note, and each was louder than the first.

Hermes took Ember aside. "At the end of the song, they fire up the pyrotechnics, which will probably roast you feeble humans. Take the child and hide behind the piles of bones by the slide. Jagger, stay nearby. I might need your help."

Ember scooped up Elderberry and hurried to the bones. They were nearly knocked over by Berty, who swooshed down the chute with a loud cry.

"Are you okay?" She inspected his feathers and added, "You look different."

Berty lowered his head. "Ember, not only did I eat the food in Hades, but I also met a girl."

Elderberry said, "Berty, you didn't touch her, did you?"

Berty looked ashamed as he recounted his brief diversion from the group's journey. "I saw a beautiful swan, as dark as the night. She seduced me. When I awoke, I was in a coffin, and I was riddled with worms. Hades picked my body out of the dirt and turned it into real basalt, a fireproof fiber. In return, I must forever be his servant."

Ember hugged Berty. "Take heart. I always knew you were destined for greater things. If you won't burn, perhaps you can help Jagger and Hermes get past those pyromaniac beasts."

"Never fear," boasted Berty, puffing out his chest proudly as he marched toward the music.

Ember watched Berty strut over to the Centimanes, who were in the throes of an enthralling percussion solo. Lasers shot out of the beasts' three hundred eyes, depicting hellish scenes of tortured souls.

"Elderberry, isn't this amazing?" When there was no answer, Ember glanced over where her daughter had been just moments before. "Berry?"

But Elderberry did not respond. She was gone.

Touché

Elderberry followed a tunnel until she arrived at a playground made of skeletons. One of the swings swayed back and forth in a nonexistent breeze.

The voice of a young girl sweetly called, "Come here."

Elderberry pointed at her chest and asked, "Me?"

A girl materialized on the swing. She had skin like crepe paper and faint, wispy hair. Elderberry tiptoed over, crunching over a rib cage.

The girl hung her head and cried. "Will you play with me? I'm so lonely."

Elderberry stepped timidly over to the girl. "Hi, I'm Elderberry. I'm seven. How old are you?"

The girl scuffed her feet in the dust. "I think I'm seven, too."

"What's your name?"

"I can't remember my real name, but the others call me Sorrow."

"What others?" Elderberry inquired.

The girl motioned to the slide. "The people who come down that drop call me Sorrow. Then they go in the door where the big ghoul with the hands stands, but he won't let me inside. I try to climb up the slide, but the ghouls frighten me. One time I closed my eyes and crawled up high, but someone slid down right on top of me. Every time I try, I fail. See my bruises?"

Sorrow held up her arms for Elderberry's inspection, but she saw none. "I don't see any bruises. Maybe you are a ghost?"

Sorrow looked surprised. "What do you mean? I can't be a ghost, but if I were, he wouldn't find me again."

"Who is he?"

"I was sleeping at home and a creature from under my bed attacked me." Sorrow shuddered. "I screamed. Daddy opened my door and fought the monster, but then I came here."

Sorrow leaned forward and whispered in Elderberry's ear.

Elderberry's eyes grew wide. She hugged Sorrow, closed her eyes, and vanished.

Alone again, Sorrow wailed.

Searching

Ember inspected the area around the pile of bones. There were paths to the left, to the right, and even up in the air. Her airway constricted and she felt dizzy. She heard sobbing and rushed down a path to find the source. Ember came to a playground, where she found a lone, ghostly figure of a girl. Whilst Ember had sympathy for her, she was more worried about Elderberry.

"Who are you? What have you done with my daughter?"

The girl wept so loudly that the bone playground vibrated and shattered to dust. Ember rushed forward and dug the little girl from the rubble, taking care not to touch her lest she be sent back to Earth.

When Ember saw the child's face, she recognized her and stammered, "Tanzanite? Tanzanite Chrysalis?"

"Yes, yes, that's my real name! Everyone calls me Sorrow here. You know me?"

Ember replied, "I'm Ember. We went to the same church together when we were little girls. Do you remember?"

Sorrow buried her face in her hands and wept even harder than before. "Oh no, I *am* a ghost because you have grown and I am still a child! I must have died on Earth! I thought Daddy saved me. Yes, I think I remember dying . . ."

Ember pondered. When Tanzanite Chrysalis was seven years old, she disappeared, never to be found. "Do you mean to tell you that you were murdered, and that your father knew who did it? Why?"

Sorrow sobbed again.

Ember hurried to console her. "I think that you might be in purgatory, and that's the reason you can't go to Hades. Tartarus is a prison, so you don't belong there. The only solution is to see that your murder is avenged, so you can finally rest in peace. In any case, I must find my Elderberry. How do I trace her?"

Sorrow cried, "I don't know! When Elderberry embraced me, she vanished."

"Oh no! If Elderberry touched you, she may have gone back to Earth. I know what to do. Take my hand."

Ember closed her eyes, hoping she would be transported to the same place as Elderberry.

Head Hopping

Athena and Cinder stood watch outside the grapevine fortress. Midnight bounded past her and nearly knocked her down. Out of his head sprouted six horns—black with white stripes. His fleece shone like gold in the sun.

Cinder shuddered. "What happened to Ember's sheepish cat?"

Athena straightened her posture and claimed, "I, the goddess of wisdom, happen to know that this is not a shy cat, but a fierce Jacob sheep with many horns. When Eris fed it a golden apple, it turned into a golden sheep. Beware, for it has a poisonous bite."

Midnight lowered his head, pawed the ground, and charged at Cinder and Athena. Pigdor, now as large as an elephant, tackled the vicious sheep, who bleated and ran toward the dragon's palace instead. The giant guinea pig raised his head and squealed so shrilly the dragons patrolling Castle Clarity began to fall out of the sky. Camila, who was hurling her flail round, became distracted and knocked Napoleon out cold again.

Athena screamed, "Did Eris steal Pandora's box and open it? What's going on? Enough of this chaos! It's time to regroup and plan our first attack. Everyone inside!"

Athena threw Napoleon over her shoulders and took him inside to the grapevine fortress before throwing him aside on the planning table. Dionysus opened his skin of wine and dumped it on Napoleon's face. Napoleon sat straight up and began cursing in Corsican.

Athena laid a scroll down on the table. "Attention, everyone!"

Rather than settling down, they all began shouting simultaneously.

Pigdor stood up on his hind legs and knocked over the table. "Excuse me," he muttered, spitting seeds all over the room.

Athena grabbed Triton's conch shell and blew it, calling the group to attention. "Hermes, Jagger and Rayne have traveled to Tartarus with Ember and her daughter, Elderberry, to rescue Zeus and Cronus."

Rayne floated down from the ceiling, her golden cape fluttering around her.

Triton brandished his trident and pointed it at her. "How can she be here *and* in the Underworld at the same time? What is this farce?"

Rayne's eyes glowed and flickered, "By combining my powers with Apocalypse's, I am able to travel through space and time. Do you really think that it is the same time in Tartarus right now? Now *that* would be a paradox!"

Triton flipped his tail and pointed his trident at Conor instead. "What do you mean when you say you can combine your powers with Apocalypse?"

"Oh, the head-hopping hasn't happened yet?" Rayne asked. "Wow, time travel can be baffling. Just you wait."

Triton roared, "Are you daft or a demon? And what of these humans who have been posing as gods? They are fake, useless. We should destroy them, then their souls can go to Hades and remain there forever."

Rayne waved her hands and a gentle wind blew through the room. "The first order of business is to save the Titans and release them from Tartarus. They will help us defeat the dragons. In the meantime, we can begin the demolition of Castle Clarity to release the rest of the souls that were forced into the castle walls. Because the blocks were made with fragile hearts and mortared with hate, they are brittle."

"I'd like to talk about the keystone. There is a very important lost soul named Sorrow, who was murdered on Earth when she was a little girl. Until Sorrow's murder is solved, she will wander in purgatory. If her murder is forgotten, she may be a lost soul indefinitely, never able to rest. If that happens, she might join the dragons. With her sadness that has been fueled by countless years of tortuous loneliness, she could help them destroy the universe as we know it."

Eris chortled, "Who cares?"

Rayne pursed her lips together. "What if I told you that our existence depends on the keystone?" Before anyone could answer, the sky rumbled with the screeches of dragons and the flapping of their wings. Rayne warned, "They are feeding off the chaos of our thoughts. If we fight amongst ourselves we will become weak, and they will become stronger."

Suddenly, a great silver dragon soared into the fortress and spit balls of fire around the room. Apocalypse minimized most of the group of humans and gods, sans Rayne, by swinging their gravitational field out of Fractasia and then rolled himself around them like a casing around a cyst.

"Oh no! I've mixed our particles together!" he screamed. "I'm not sure what will happen now! Hold on!"

And then Apocalypse was a young child. His mother, Rhea, hid him in a basket, but then his father, Cronus, swallowed his siblings.

Tobias was a puppy again. He tried to wriggle past thousands of other pups to feed on the mother, but he was the runt of the litter and was pushed away. A giant gathered up the other pups to make giblets. Tobias was so tiny that he could hide in a crack in the floor. A squirrel saved him, and he tried to live off of acorns.

Napoleon was a child at school, constantly teased and tormented for his quirkiness. He turned into a giant egg and rolled down a hill to find a woman who lived in a shoe.

Jade was a blue lobster with a salamander tail. She kept slicing off that tail, which regrew again and again.

Aphrodite was a butterfly in a field of daisies. She came to a pond, and a gigantic toad smoking a cigar shot its sticky tongue out at her. She was reborn as a giant sow dressed in leather attire that was best suited for S&M bondage. She had one hundred teats, which were bulging with milk. All the other characters wore diapers and fought for the milk. A mob of dancing bears with butter churns butted in to take some, too.

Baby Conor wore a bonnet and suckled on a binky. Camila stole his pacifier and bumped into Mama Aphrodite. Milk squirted everywhere, covering all of the babies. The liquid reverted Poseidon and Triton to their tadpole forms. As Napoleon sought the biggest teat, he pushed the others off. Pigdor, now as large as a Tyrannosaurus rex, pushed Napoleon off Camila's teat.

When that happened, Mama Camila uttered a bloodcurdling cry. "Bad babies!"

The gods, humans, and animals blended together like molten lava while Eris flew through and around all of them, cackling like a witch. In a single blob, they warped back to the dragon's castle. The group was entangled in one goopy mass, but then they separated into their singular forms again.

Ruby had a sheep's head. Triton's crab claw arm protruded from Conor's chest, which pinched Napoleon's nose. Aphrodite barked because she had Toby's head. Athena's noggin was stuck on Dionysus's lion/bull body. All at once, they warped back to normal and collectively rose out of the cinders, raising their heads one by one to the sky to clear soot and slime from their faces.

"Sorry, that didn't work out as well as I thought," Apocalypse said to the group. "Invariably, I've mixed up some of our particles. It could be that now the gods have human in them, and some of the humans are part god."

Poseidon screamed, "Where's Eris?"

In his anger, he summoned a great storm, complete with thunder and lighting. The dragons, being pelted with fierce rain, retreated. The deluge continued and quickly filled the moat in front of the castle. Poseidon, Triton, and Jack dove into the water to investigate.

Aphrodite couldn't stop staring at Conor's chest. "Wow look at your muscles! They're huge like Thor's!"

Camila flicked goop from her hands. "Man, I don't think we are in Kansas anymore."

Rayne brushed Camila's and Conor's heads one after the other with her palm. "Do you feel different? Each of the gods has a little less power now."

Camila beamed. "Do I have superpowers now? What's my goddess name going to be?"

Rayne's body started to glimmer, and then she evanesced.

Back to Earth

Ember was in her room on Earth again. Something moved in the corner of the room. Ember sighed with relief as the light of the moon revealed her darling daughter. They embraced and cried silent tears of joy.

Suddenly, Elderberry broke the hug and scurried over to try and to pull off the HVAC vent next to Ember's bookshelf.

Ember scolded her. "Shh! What are you doing? You're going to wake my parents!"

Elderberry just kept scraping at the vent with her fingers. "We have to find it!"

"Honey, what on Earth are you doing? Find what?"

Ember heard her a door open and footsteps approach from down the hall. "Who's there?" her father bellowed as his steps grew closer. "I have a gun, I'll shoot. I'm calling 911."

"Dad, it's me and Elderberry! You don't need a gun!"

His tone was harsh and uncaring. "Ember, just send Elderberry out here, and don't do anything stupid!" When her mother wailed frantically, her father whispered just loudly enough for Ember to hear. "She could be on drugs. She could be dangerous. Did you get ahold of the police? Call our neighbors. Call Stan Chrysalis!"

Ember locked the door. "Elderberry, help me push my dresser in front of the door!"

Together, they pushed the drawers in front of the door, which knocked the air conditioning vent loose.

"Rip it off!" cried Elderberry.

Ember's dad barked, "Stand back, I'm going to knock down the door!"

Ember stuck her head in the duct, but she was too big to reach very far. "What are you looking for, Elderberry?"

Rather than verbally respond, Elderberry pushed Ember away and crawled into the duct and soon said, "Ah ha!"

When she backed out again, Ember heard Stan Chrysalis, Sorrow's father, in the hallway. He sounded angry as he spoke with Ember's father. As she pressed her ear to the door, she recalled that Stan was the owner of an HVAC company. Not long after the disappearance of his daughter, he installed a system in Ember's house. Since it was a retrofit, he had supposedly *creatively* installed it.

Ember's nose started to bleed as she had a vision. Tanzanite was in her bedroom alone, playing. Jameson, a longtime friend of the family, crept into her room while she was sleeping. Jameson put his hand over Tanzanite's face and accidentally killed her while he stifled her screams. Stan Chrysalis walked in the room to see him hovering over his daughter's dead body. Instead of calling the police, Stan helped Jameson cover up the murder. They then incinerated Tanzanite's body in a furnace. Ember watched as Stan gathered his daughter's remains, shaking, and placed them in the HVAC pipes in her bedroom.

Reality came crashing back in when Elderberry yelped, "Mom! Mom!"

Ember heard Stan's voice and started trembling. "If you want your granddaughter to live, I'm afraid we're going to have to take Ember down. You don't want her hurting Elderberry, do you? You said she's mentally ill, a liar, angry, and on drugs."

Elderberry pulled a pillowcase out of the vent. She tilted the sack, and charred bones tumbled onto the floor. He had hidden evidence of his daughter's murder in her room!

Ember's father and Stan broke her door's lock. The dresser began to scoot toward them, and Ember could see her mother standing in the hallway.

She sobbed into the phone, "And then she jumped from the ceiling in her bedroom room and attacked her father. To top that off, she was pregnant, and she doesn't even know who the father is!"

Despite the gravity of the situation, Ember's jaw dropped. "Really, Mom?"

Her mother screamed, "She is suicidal! She's threatening to kill her child! Shoot!"

Ember froze. Police sirens grew louder and louder. Ember's father raised his gun and pointed it at her.

"What are you doing? Are you crazy?" Ember called out, "Apocalypse, NOW!"

Stan seized the gun from Ember's father and pulled the trigger just as Ember and Elderberry began a journey of transtemporal travel. This time, they warped through time and space with the help of spooky vines. Ember winced when she saw a bullet fly past them. She covered Elderberry's head, hoping that Apocalypse's powers would keep them safe until they got to wherever they were going. Fractasia, Tartarus—anywhere but Earth!

Well, hopefully not the cloth world, either.

Enter Cyclopes

Rayne reappeared inside Tartarus, shining like a golden deity and with her long, dark hair hanging in animated tendrils like Medusa's. The residents of Tartarus instinctively bowed as she spoke without opening her mouth.

"Heed, prisoners. I am Queen Rayne, the supreme benevolent ruler of the universe. Zeus, step forward. Cronus, come hither, but remember not to fight with your son, for he sent me here to fetch you. Together, we will take the Centimanes and the Cyclopes to Fractasia, where dragons are threatening to take over the universe by making blocks out of the souls of the universe. Without energy feeding into Hades, nothing new with be reborn. The only thing that will exist will be the dragons and their castle. Great Titans and grand Olympians: put away your past and work together, else none of us will have a future." Rayne put her hands down. "I will stop time here once we leave so that you do not escape until the time that the Centimanes can come back to guard the gates."

All of the prisoners except for Zeus, Cronus, and the Cyclopes froze. Rayne then lured the three Cyclopes—Arges, Brontes, and Steropes—into playing Red Rover. As Brontes barreled toward her, she stepped aside. Brontes hurled through the exit of Tartarus. The one-eyed brute rolled into Centimanes, who were finishing their demonic song with gusto. The Cyclopes banged their heads together and cheered in gravelly voices.

"Whoa! Cool!"

Zeus and Cronus tried to flee Tartarus, but the pyrotechnics from the finale of the Centimanes's concert ended in an explosion, effectively castrating the gods. Zeus and Cronus lifted what remained of their clothes, revealing smoking, singed nether regions. Jagger tried to blow out the sparks, but that just fueled the fire. Brontes and Gyges burst into flames and then wafted away as dark smoke.

Cottus, evidently irritated, spit with each of his fifty heads and covered the gods in slimy saliva that successfully put out the flames.

Zeus and Cronus rolled around on the ground, clutching their pelvises. Cottus and the Cyclopes brothers rolled around on the ground, laughing at the castrated gods.

"At least we are like salamanders. They will grow back," Cronus groaned. "Now I kind of feel sorry about that time I castrated Uranus."

Zeus was instantly enraged. "You did nothing of the sort to my anus! I would have gotten you back somehow."

Cronus snapped, "Zeus, you idiot, Uranus is my father. You know, your grandfather?"

"Shut up about my arse!" said Zeus, grabbing a stick he found on the ground and whacking Cronus in the crotch.

Cottus laughed. "Hey, that's mine! I must have dropped it. It's Uranus's petrified penile appendage. I found it in the sea and have been carrying it around with me for thousands of years."

"Zeus, the joke's on you! You can't even hit me without fooling around with Ur-anus!" Cronus howled with laughter at his own joke.

"Shut up, Dad!" argued Zeus, shoving Cronus's petrified package down his father's throat and killing him instantly.

Hermes and Zeus laughed so hard that their guts started pouring out of their charred testicles, which caused them to fall over dead, too.

"What's happening?" Jagger asked as he helplessly watched it all unfold. "I thought gods didn't die. Weren't they supposed to help save us from the soul-sucking dragons?"

Rayne looked surprised. "Hmm. Maybe the narrative is changing. What I knew of the future appears to be no more. Perhaps another deviation in the time continuum?"

"What do you mean?" he asked.

"Keep going and we'll soon find out. You might just have to return to Fractasia without me."

Rayne ran back to the pile of bones where Sorrow lived and found her sobbing. She reached for the ghostly girl, only for her to shriek and flinch away.

"No, don't touch me! Everyone who does disappears and leaves me all alone in this dismal world."

A tear came to Rayne's eye. "I'm going to take you out of this world, sweetie. You don't belong in Hades, and heaven doesn't deserve you."

Sorrow stopped crying. "But how?"

"First, we have to fight for it. Let's go. Everything will get better from here. Your killer on Earth has been found and your death is avenged. If you choose, you may come with me, to start a new city in a new world that will soon blossom. But you will never be able to return to your old life."

"But that's all I've been thinking of as I sat here playing with a pile of bones. Anything is better than that. I mean, I met a lot of people here, and I helped show them the way to the door . . ." Sorrow shook her head. "Forget it; you're right. I don't ever want to go back. I want to be called Sparrow instead of Sorrow, because I want to fly away."

Rayne took the girl in her arms and they disintegrated in a flash of light as Jagger strapped himself into Berty's cage and beckoned Cottus and the Cyclopes to follow. They then swooshed up the slide in a flash to find their way back to Fractasia.

The More the Merrier

When Ember awoke, she was in a dimly lit cave. Somehow, the natural surroundings provided enough light for her to see. She panicked for a moment and realized that Elderberry was snuggled in her arms, asleep. They were lying together on a smooth rock. Water dripped in the distance.

Ember heard a scuffling noise and whispered, "Who's there?"

A child's voice cried, "She's awake!"

A group of six children, each of whom looked to be between six and eight years old, scurried into view.

"Who are you?"

The tallest child, a girl, bravely stepped forward. "I'm September, and that's River, Chance, April, Jason, and Porter."

Porter sat down by Ember's side. "I'm so glad you are finally here, Mom! We found you!"

Ember was bewildered, but she didn't want to alarm the boy. So, she adopted what she hoped was a pleasant smile. "Hello. So, your name is Porter?"

September explained, "I know you must be confused. When we were babies, a mysterious stranger left us in in the land of the lotus with Gypsy."

Ember grew excited at the mention of a familiar name. "My dog?"

"Yes, she raised us from babies," Jason chimed in. "She told us all about you and said that one day we would join you for a great battle in a land called Fractasia."

Chance said, "Now we are here to help you defeat the soul-sucking dragons so we can save the universe!"

Elderberry awoke and looked bewildered. After introductions, she joined her siblings in their merriment. "Mommy, they are seven, too! We are the same age!"

Ember was overcome by the situation. "That's interesting. Now, let's explore where we are so we can go and defeat the dragons."

The Reunion

Ember and her brood emerged from the cavern. Once outside, she encountered a very bewildered Cinder, who pointed at her charges and asked, "Where did they come from?"

Ember hugged Cinder. "I'm so glad to see you! I've had quite the adventure. And these are my other younglings."

Cinder made a ticking sound with her tongue. "I see *you've* been busy."

The world rumbled. Dirt and rocks exploded as a hundred hands clawed their way up from the ground. Ember stood protectively in front of her cubs. A giant head emerged from the earth. All the hands belonged to it. The kids giggled, and three more beasts arose, each with one with one giant eye.

"The Cyclopes!" Ember muttered.

Elderberry cried, "Look, it's Berty!"

Berty looked different, sleeker—like a machine. His feathers steamed and stunk of sulfur. The giant bird bent his head low to the ground. Jagger stumbled out of the cage on Berty's back and helped Rayne descend.

He eyed Ember and the children suspiciously as she said, "Jagger, these are your other little lambs: September, River, Jason, Chance, and Porter. They are here to help us."

Jagger and the kids sized each other up.

September finally sighed, "He's not quite what I expected."

River remarked, "Me neither. Who is the big guy with all the hands? Cool."

Rather than comment on becoming a father—again—Jagger pointed at the beasts. "Meet Cottus and the Cyclopes brothers. They are also here to aid us in our quest to save the souls from Castle Clarity. Let's hurry back to the fortress to join the others."

Ember felt happy and strong as she strode through the fields with her friends and family.

"For such a long time I mired in my own selfish thoughts. This story is about all of us. This adventure is about overcoming hardship, getting stronger, standing up, and creating success instead of letting life walk all over you. Once we've freed the souls trapped in the blocks of Castle Clarity, we can turn Fractasia into our own universe. Maybe that's why this story ended up with so many characters. Humans, gods, whatever: we all have similar tragic flaws, yet we are unique. We will repopulate this brave new world with our people, setting the stage for another book of journeys."

Apocalypse stood in front of the fortress, with Dionysus at his side. Rayne hovered in a cloud of shimmering smoke, which Apocalypse squinted at.

"How did you do that?"

Rayne lowered herself back to the ground. "Something happened when we were all mixed up, and now I have great powers. I think I absorbed Eris, because I can hear her speaking in my thoughts. I've just returned from Hades. Zeus, Cronus, and Hermes are all dead."

Apocalypse looked flustered. "Impossible!

Dionysus burped and said, "Everyone knows that gods can't die."

When he lunged forward to attack Rayne, a couple of tendrils of ivy sprouted from the ground and started to grow up around him. Green liquid spurted from his head as the vines grew up and covered him, until the drunken god disappeared completely.

Aphrodite screamed, "He's gone!" She panicked, then ran into the wall and keeled over.

Cottus peeked in the door. When he saw Aphrodite, all one hundred of his hands clenched and unclenched. He reached in, grabbed her with several of his arms, and ran into a forest beyond the fortress, dropping his instruments along the way.

Forbidden Love

Cottus ran for miles until he came to a glistening lake. Aphrodite woke up in his hands. His mouths were upturned with mirth and his tongues wagged. "Aphrodite, I have been in love with you for centuries. Though I understand that I am ugly, and I respect your right to deny me."

Aphrodite fanned her face with her hand. "Thank you for saving me, kind beast. I'm flattered by your attentions."

"I implore you, my sweet queen. I will present pleasures to you that you've never known, that you've never imagined. Aphrodite, all of my hands are going to be devoted to loving you, all at once."

"Oh my, Cottus . . ."

His eyes grew wide. "Ha! You do know who I am. Say my name again—in Greek this time."

Aphrodite cooed, "Hecatoncheires—you have so many hands."

Cottus grinned from ear to ear as Aphrodite blushed. Her aura unfolded around him like the soft edge of a wave, moving ashore as the tide heightens. Her quintessence framed his cheeks as the forest whispered around them.

"Say it," he whispered.

"I am the mighty Aphrodite. I tell *you* what to do, not the other way around."

Cottus folded his many arms together all at once. "I want your consent."

"Cottus?"

"Yes, Aphrodite?"

"Will you please massage me? With your hands and whatever else you need to fulfill my need for constant love and affection? I want you to caress my whole body all at once." Aphrodite disrobed, revealing a hundred sets of breasts. "Now, will you reveal your mysteries to me as well?"

Excelsior's Last Stand

Ember rushed out of the smoldering stronghold. She sighed in relief once she saw Pigdor was safe and happily munching on a patch of grass.

A large dragon descended from the sky, and Pigdor squealed, "Excelsior!"

Ember watched in disbelief as the wretched dragon launched a vicious assault on her dear guinea pig friend. Excelsior cackled sinisterly as she spilled Pigdor's guts all over the ground, then picked at a piece of his small intestine.

"Guinea pigs haven't existed in the wild for more than five hundred years. Do you believe they can survive on their own anywhere? Did you really think you could save the guinea pig you killed? Fool, just like all other humans. We will make sure we end your entire race!"

Ember thrust her fist in the air. "I will avenge Pigdor's death!" She turned to rally the others. "Excelsior is eating Pigdor. He's dead."

Jagger grabbed Ember and pulled her aside. "Ember, why are your characters dying? I thought we needed them."

Ember was flummoxed. She didn't know why things were unraveling when she thought she had solved the plot.

"Too many characters," she murmured, sheepishly picking at her nails.

Poseidon started another storm. Triton was sporting a dolphin tail and crab claws, frolicking in a wave, seemingly oblivious to the others. Camila and Conor began busting the blocks of the castle as quickly as they could, freeing a flurry of souls. Napoleon, Athena, and Apocalypse rushed the dragon, but a swarm of fledglings attacked with a wall of flames, effectively barbecuing them all.

"Ember, what will you do without Apocalypse to manipulate gravity in and out of dimensions?" Rayne scolded. "Is there something you can do to stop the slaughter?"

Things were spinning totally out of control. She didn't want any more of her friends to die, even the pesky gods. Her brain felt like it was full of mud.

"What am I supposed to do?"

Rayne shrugged. "That's for you to decide."

But Ember was distracted by the Cyclopes brothers. They crouched together, mumbling about how the storyline built them up to be heroes, and how this is not how Greek tales were supposed to end.

Rayne comforted the Cyclopes brothers, telling them a story about a crème-filled cookie.

"The cookie really wanted to be a potted ficus, and was able to convince a mad scientist to transplant its mind into the plant. The scientist harnessed a jolt lightning from the sky to do it. The cookie became the fig tree, and the ficus became the snack. The scientist's wife ate the cookie, however, and the soul of the ficus was recycled— just like that. Thereafter, the soul of the cookie lived a long life as a tree. I have a twig of that ficus right here. If you plant the scions, then you will be planting the cookie, too. You will be a hero."

The Cyclopes brothers were mesmerized, but then a stray bolt of lightning plummeted from the sky and knocked them all dead.

Ember wanted to tear out her hair. This was worse than writer's block.

Elderberry tugged on her arm. "Mommy, that man named Alexander gave me your book. Here's a pen. Perhaps you should write?"

Ember embraced her children protectively. "Go and hide in the caves so you'll be safe!"

As soon as they did as she'd asked, Ember opened the book and began to write.

The Author

Excelsior crouched over the guinea pig. Blood dripped down her chin as she crunched on the rodent's bones. The greedy hatchlings gorged themselves on the roasted gods. They were so immersed in their feeding that they didn't notice the congregation of spirits hovering above them. Out of Dionysus's corpse sprouted a patch of vibrant red poppies. The dragons all began to stumble and eventually fell.

Apocalypse's ghost wrapped around Excelsior. She began to shrink, becoming smaller and smaller until she was the size of a door mouse. Beauregard bounded by and pounced on the diminutive dragon. The portly cat hurled his catch into the air, and Excelsior landed directly in Tobias's slobbery mouth before he trotted away into a field. The other dragons had also grown much tinier, but they still fled en masse after the dog.

The Great Gaslight

In Ember's room on Earth, smoke from the gunshots hung in the air. Her parents and Stan stood aghast.

"How are we going to explain all this to the police? You saw Ember and her daughter disintegrate into thin air, right? The authorities will never believe that story, and we've unlawfully discharged firearms in my house," Ember's father raged. "My reputation will be ruined!"

Stan looked smug and grabbed the bag of bones. "We can fix this. First of all, though, you've never had a granddaughter. I have no idea who that little girl was."

Ember's mother wrung her hands. "I don't want anyone to think I'm crazy!"

The men told the cops that Jameson, their old friend, abducted Ember and they fired warning shots only because they didn't want to hurt her. Jameson was arrested later that night at his home, where he was found drinking beer. He was later implicated in a string of murders throughout the tri-state area.

Ember's parents and Stan were hailed as heroes. They were even featured in the *New York Post*. Ember's mother shuddered, insisting she always knew something was suspicious about Jameson and that she'd never trusted him. She had apparently been like a second mother to Tanzanite. A GoFundMe account was set up for Ember. Several churches and community organizations held special events in her honor, where her parents gave teary-eyed speeches.

The Great Bash

Ember and her friends cheered as the dragons scurried away. She was hopeful, but only a few blocks from Castle Clarity had been demolished by that point. The castle still stood tall. Many more souls still needed to be freed.

Her hands were tired. The blazing sun made it difficult to concentrate on writing. She decided that she no longer needed a pen; she would take control of the narrative using only her mind.

Camila whipped her hair around her head and rocked out to her own theme music. "I am Positron, the goddess of passion, smiling and generosity, defeating my foes with this golden anti-matter flail I created. It defies the laws of chemistry and physics because it both creates and destroys matter."

Conor held up a scythe. "And I will be known as Cornitropus the Lepton, the god of harvesting particles. On my arm will be a shining sickle, with which I will outwit evil foes. I will cut them down with my wit, and I will weave a fierce fabric capable of withstanding bullets, harsh temperatures, and fear. One perk of being a lepton, especially a charged lepton such as I, is that I can bond with other particles to form various composite particles such as atoms."

Camila and Conor attacked separate sides of the castle. With one hundred souls flying up each time a block was smashed, the air quickly grew thick with spirits flying free.

Rayne approached Ember during the assault on the castle. "What are we going to do without Hermes to take the souls to Hades?"

"I'll take some, but I can only handle one thousand at a time," Persephone offered.

An angry mob of ghosts cried, "That's not enough! We are tired of this turmoil."

Meanwhile, Camila and Conor kept smashing and sickling the

castle away. Some of the more malevolent ghosts began to start mischief in their impatience.

Persephone told Ember, "I really don't care that the rest of the gods have disappeared, but I'm getting nervous. I will take these souls to straight away, if Hades allows it."

Rayne said, "Persephone, your selflessness might just save you from the fate of the other gods."

Cave Camp

The kiddies hopped and skipped on their way to the caves, but Elderberry tripped on something. "What the—?"

September picked up a brass horn and put it to her lips. "Look! It's a trumpet."

Chase picked up an electric guitar and strummed a few chords. Music resonated through the air even though the instrument wasn't hooked up to an amp. "Cool, man! I didn't know I could play!"

River grabbed a bongo drum. Porter scurried over to an electric bass. Elderberry found an acoustic guitar, and Jason found a harp tangled in a tuft of gold fleece; April threw a keyboard over her shoulder. The children gathered a few more instruments and rushed into the safety of the caverns. With little to do but wait, they formed a band and began to play.

The Kids
This is the ballad of the kids
Who were rescued from the skids
In a great hailstorm
Where we were souls in the unknown
Undone we were flying
Until Mom plucked us from the sky
From the Master who sews
Strings from discord
Trying to fold time
Right the wrongs of the past
Who are you, who am I
Why are we here,
Why do we die?
Why don't I remember when I was not on this world?
Why do we fall when we fail due to hue of our thin skins?

We are only children; we are young.
You can't un-have us; the till was rung.
We are here now, we are strong
Hear our song!

Dum, dum dumditty do
Masters of all the wrong chords
Are kids and it's true
Dum, dum littleedeee doo
But we're strong and we're smart and we wash our hands
more than you!
Dum, do, deepa-lickamaroo
I have hands of butter because I baked you some corn
Sham, bam, boomaramoo
But at the end of the day we'll save the future for you!
Kids rock, kids rock!

Letting Go

The sky turned from blue to plum. Ember needed a break. So much had happened in one day. The dragons were not a concern anymore, but the souls were growing insane with impatience and most of the castle was still standing. What would happen when all the bricks had been demolished? Would Fractasia become a kind of purgatory? Everyone was exhausted.

The fortress was damaged and smelled like fire from the dragons' assault. Ember and her remaining friends decided to retire to the underground abode where the children had fled. Camila, still full of energy, heartily offered to stand watch at the entrance.

As they got ready to depart, Ember queried, "What will we eat? I have to feed the kids, you know."

Cornitropus harvested a wheat-like grain from the fields and baked bread. Rayne gathered grapes from the recently deceased Dionysus and prepared grape juice and wine. Ember begrudgingly considered taking strips of Pigdor's roasted flesh when Triton approached her with at least a dozen bright blue, crustaceans.

"These are sure to feed hungry tummies! And there are plenty more."

That evening, they had a great feast on the bounties of Fractasia. Ember had a few gulps of wine and danced around a fire. After many moments of merriment, she saw Elderberry yawning.

"Mommy, I'm sleepy."

Jason spread the gold fleece on the ground to make a great bed. Ember then tucked her tots in between the fluffs of the fleece and kissed each of her darlings on the forehead. Tobias sat at their feet and Berty perched himself on a rock nearby as she told them a tale about a strange planet called Earth.

"Of course, Elderberry's been there."

"Boring!" her firstborn interjected.

Ember was too excited to sleep and thought that maybe she was heady from the wine. So much had happened since she had decided to take charge of her life. In the blink of an eye, she had seven moppets.

And I didn't even get to have physical relationship with Jagger.

She tried to imagine what it would be like lying next to Jagger, kissing him, but she had this nagging suspicion that he would never care for her romantically. She started to feel sad.

Was there something wrong with her? Was she not good enough for him? Her father used to say, "You'll never be a trophy wife. You're just not that kind of girl." But why the heck would she want to be someone's prize, only to never measure up?

Ember pulled her thoughts together. She was is charge now.

She tiptoed over to the far side of the cave, where Jagger slept on a bed of straw, and tenderly touched his hand.

He instantly recoiled and pulled his blanket over himself, putting his thumb in his mouth as he mumbled, "Mommy?"

"Shards." Ember exited the main cavern quietly before things could get even more awkward. It dawned on her that Jagger was not ready to be a father. He was just a teen. It was selfish of her to put that responsibility on his shoulders. Ember resolved to take care of the kids on her own if need be. "Ha! Seven wonderful children who have a cave band on an alien world."

A sphere of light the size of a firefly shot out of her skin. It bounced in front of Ember, taunting her to follow it. The strange ball bounced further away, leading her deeper into the cave through gloomy twists and turns. Maybe she should have stopped, turned around, or even hesitated, but her feet kept moving forward. As her confidence rose, her senses awakened.

Ember yearned for something. As she walked slowly down the path, she thought about Xavier. Ember wanted affection, but the fact that kiddos kept popping up out of nowhere tempered her desires.

Unrequited
Unrequited is more than nothing
My love, nevertheless, is nevermore
Never was

Unrequited,
Nonetheless
Is more than less

Unrequited
As it be, it is still something,
Something in which I can believe

Unrequited is something
At least it cannot fail
As do the rest

Until you my cheek carefully or carelessly caress

Brush my cheeks
Brush my thigh
Alas it's naught
And I

Fare thee well!
Fade into night
Falling fast
Flailing flight

Unrequited, this time I'd thought you'd pass
But then he kissed me, crazed me, and promptly left.

"Oh Zeus!" she cried. "The plot is wandering again because I can't control my thoughts!"

After several more minutes, Ember walked through a jungle of luminescent fibers that led to a beautiful room styled with columns and gilding, adorned with tapestries woven in vibrant colors. A heavy perfume intoxicated her. The fabric of the nightdress that Cornitropus wove for her from the long, silky fibers hanging from the golden-leaved trees swaying in the fields above the cliffs felt sensual against her skin.

There was no denying it. Ember was hungry for love. She had spent what felt like eons without romance while she found herself. She had waited long enough.

A pair of hands materialized before her. A voice she thought she recognized said, "Ember, I have been waiting for you. It is time."

Ember's lips locked with his, and she melted into him. Ember became lost in lust for her suitor as his lips met hers over and over. His molecules entered her body through her saliva, causing her lips to warm and her body to tingle.

After it was all over, the kiss of love lingered on her. Ember untangled her body from his and walked to an opening in the cave. She stood beneath a bright night sky on the edge of a cliff. For the first time in this entire journey, she was able to pause and reflect. As she did, the light from the shining forty-two moons in the sky shone on her visage.

A herd of shooting stars galloped across the sky, their fractal tails whipping wildly in the cosmos. One young charger broke loose and ran down the horizon, holding his head high as he neighed and pawed at the shadows of the stars, the dark matter. It then galloped further down, landing in the valley and running until it flickered out.

She burst into song, the first of many long days, trying to make sense of her senseless inclinations.

Canton of Quasi
Canton of quasi, chaos and candor
Drop-tops of bunny-lops, quixotic and clever
Cantaloupe mangos and strawberry shakes

Are you ready for the party to place?
Where you know you need no mace?
For if you so choose to sit on a log
You may find yourself in a dinosaur bog
Tar pit from my armpit would have killed you sooner
So let's go jump on a Mediterranean schooner.

The fresh night air snapped Ember back to reality. She ran back inside, only to find that she was alone in the dark. The lavish room was gone. Had her kiss only been a dream? She impetuously decided that she didn't care anymore. Ember had conquered so many quests. She no longer needed to be saved. She now had the confidence to take on the world, or the universe, on her own.

"Well, it's nice to have a little help from some friends," she chided herself as he made her way back through the caverns to her children.

Chaos Chowder

Elderberry, Porter, Chance, River, September, April, and Jason woke to find their mother missing. They tiptoed out of the main cavern, where they found an *elevator*, according to Elderberry.

Porter challenged her, "So it takes you somewhere different? Prove it."

"Okay, the bet is on!"

River, the closest to the elevator, was sucked into it before the door closed. Chance banged on the elevator furiously, but it simply opened and whisked him away, too. One by one, the youngsters departed in the mischievous machinery.

A River Runs Through It

River was whisked away on a flight to Dismayland, soaring through an ocean in the sky from the east to the west. Pink smog hung over the city. A lighted sign that decorated a row of mountains read, "City of Demons."

A flight attendant with a mile-long smile bent down to River and said, "I bet you can't you wait to see Roudy and Randy Rat at Dismayland, can you, little boy?"

When the other passengers on the plane debarked, Chase followed the crowds to the front gates. He tried to enter, but an angry man approached him.

"I am Waldo Dismay. Obviously, you have no money to buy a ticket into the park, so you will become my slave—forever!"

Last Chance

Chance sat in a cage at a zoo deep beneath the ocean of Atlantis. Tourists with upper bodies like humans and lower bodies like fish passed by and pointed at him.

He was then forced to board a submarine, which deposited him in Zuredon, a folky land of clockmakers and performers. He gazed around with wide eyes as he strolled the streets, until he tried to take a pretzel from a vendor. The proprietor of the stand caught him and took him away.

September Rain

September boarded a small plane and ended up in the Columbus Isles of Britannia, where the people said "eh" all of the time and skied down steep slopes covered in corn kernels. She grabbed a pair of skis and took a lift up to the top of the tallest berg.

April's Fool

April stepped off the elevator and directly into a helicopter. It flew over mystical waterfalls to Tropticopus, a lush island of talking orchids that handed her berries as she passed them by.

She trotted along the beaches until she came to a group of people feasting by a pool. She meandered through the crowds and sampled the foods, her eyes full of wonder.

Jason the Go-naut

Jason refused to exit the elevator. It even tried to push him out, but he covered himself in his golden fleece and hunkered down on the floor. The elevator was still unable to expel him, his determination winning out.

Walking Like an Elderberry

Elderberry boarded a plane to a world of sandy strips of land surrounded by deep blue, coral-filled oceans. The land was called Aguptus.

The searing sun beat down on her shoulders. She found a thicket of squat palm trees, ate a few fruits off of them, and took a nap.

Jagger Joins the Journey

Jagger awoke. He looked around for the children and shouted frantically, "They're gone!" He peered out into the darkness. "Is that a light outside? Maybe they are over there. I better hurry and follow them."

When he came to the elevator, he stepped into it and then directly onto an airplane. He looked flummoxed. A flight attendant in the form of a large black poodle offered Jagger a cordial, and he accepted. He had another, then began to giggle. He asked the attendant, "Where am I going?"

The steward replied, "Good question, sir! I feel that you will be very pleased to find that you are going to the tropical land called Flourdough, where you will learn how to bake."

Jagger clutched his belly and guffawed. "Perfect! I love to eat fresh bread, pastries, cakes, and pies. Can I have another cordial, please?"

Ember's Ignorance

Ember was elated. She could still feel the mystery man's lips on her skin. She meandered through the caverns until she came to the entrance. The sun was beginning to rise.

Tobias nudged her hand. "Where is Camila? Are you standing guard now?"

She picked up a spyglass and peered through it. Positron and Cornitropus were already hard at work, destroying the castle block by block. Ember was amazed at the godlike actors. Positron wore only a tool belt, utility shoes, and reflectors over her nipples like pasties. Her bulging, yet sinewy thighs glistened as she bashed the bricks with her flail. Cornitropus wore a pair of shorts that looked like a cross between a fig leaf and Speedos. He scythed away, slashing and splintering the castle blocks. As the castle shattered, hordes of ghouls escaped from the splintering wreckage.

Something grunted and groaned nearby. Midnight charged her and then veered away. Two demonic horns protruded from his head. Ember was wary of the sheep-cat, for he was acting even stranger. It was then that she noticed a group of dark souls swirling above his head.

Rayne and Berty appeared out of nowhere, startling Ember. The regal Rayne spoke in a concerned tone.

"Ember, the souls are reaching a critical mass, flying around wildly, causing mischief." She pointed to the sky. "Look! Some are trying to leave the planet, and they are getting vaporized in the process."

Ember asked Rayne, "Where are my parallel universe sidekicks and friends? I haven't seen them in ages."

Rayne furrowed her brows. "No idea. Ember, where have *you* been? You were gone for more than a day. Your kids and Jagger are gone. Ruby, Cinder, Alexander, Jade, Sergio and Jack won't wake up."

Ember felt horrible for neglecting them all. "My cherubs are gone?"

Rayne nodded, then asked, "What are you going to do? I have powers, but I can only do so much. You must devise a plan to save them yourself."

Ember's brain whirred like the fractals. Why hadn't she kept a closer eye on her kids? Had the mystery man of her dreams addled her mind?

Persephone rose out of the dirt, looking tired. "I have just returned from taking my tenth load of souls to Hades. It sure would help to have Napoleon, Eris, Cronus, Apocalypse, Dionysus, Hermes, Athena, Cyclopes, Beauregard, and Cottus around to help. I even miss that character Napoleon and the funny rodent. By the way, where are the humanoids?" A tiny tornado of ghosts knocked her over before she got an answer. "Jeez, it's starting to look like the Underworld around here."

"The souls of the gods are causing the most mischief of the bunch," Rayne observed. "They are starting fires, pulling pranks, et cetera."

Ember wrung her hands. "Maybe Jagger will help. Do you know where he is?"

Rayne pointed to the sky. "Jagger has gone to learn how to bake in Flourdough. Ember, do you really feel you need to rely on someone to save you?"

"Queen Rayne, I beg you. Please help. All has descended into chaos."

Rayne looked exasperated, but consented anyway. "Okay, Berty and I will go to Flourdough to search for my brother. You watch over the fortress."

Right after Rayne and Berty blasted off into the sky, Midnight crept into the mouth of a cave. Ember definitely did not like the way he was acting, so she followed him into the cavern.

Jagger's Journey

Jagger made his way to an organic bakery in the lowlands of Flourdough, in the Rolling Pin state. With almost religious dedication, he planted a seed, which grew a plant, which yielded more seeds. He then took the seeds and planted a field. Out of the ground crawled little green tendrils. On the first day, he saw one peeking above the soil like a slimy green snail. The next day it stretched higher, and on the third day the plants were tall and had flowers. On the fourth, the petals of the flowers blew off in the wind as Jagger painstakingly gathered the seeds. On the fifth day, he dried the seeds, and on the sixth he ground them into flour. On the seventh day, he rested.

During his day of leisure, Jagger skateboarded to the beach and surfed the rolling green waves. A perfect wave crested, and he swam to catch it. Just then, a dolphin with a nose like a rolling pin stole his wave. To avoid being speared, Jagger tumbled off the wave and into the water. The waves pushed him into the coral, cutting him. After attempting to catch a few more waves, he decided to turn in and went home to prepare his sourdough starter for the next day.

After finishing his preparations, Jagger added compost tea to his garden. Finally, he was able to set down and sip on a glass of Malbec. After that, he took a bubble bath infused with lavender oils and then retired to his downy bed. He pulled the covers up to his chin, pored over a recipe, and scribbled notes. He yawned, but nearly jumped off the mattress when Berty crashed through the window. He spilled his wine on the comforter. Rayne hopped off the gigantic jay's back.

"Really, Rayne?"

"You're just sitting here, relaxing? What about Ember and the children?"

Jagger snorted. "I'm working hard. Can't you see? I'm too young to be a father. How could those adolescents possibly be mine?"

Rayne stared him down. "Like it or not, you are technically an adult. Even if these aren't your kids, don't you feel an obligation to protect them?"

"But I never even kissed Ember. I just liked the idea of having an older girlfriend. I thought it would make me look cool. I'm not ready for this."

"I understand that you may have these feelings, and it wasn't fair for you to be saddled with so much responsibility. The fact of the matter is, we need you. Those kids are the future for the new world. The entropy of Fractasia is becoming more and more disordered. The ghosts are increasing the amount of unusable energy in Fractasia, pulling resources away from the plants and animals on the planet. Energy is escaping with the spirits, thereby defying the second law of thermodynamics. Positron is doing all she can to grab the energy back from the other dimensions. Disobeying the fundamental laws of chemistry and physics, however, could cause an explosion."

"Explosion?"

"All in good time, big brother. Thankfully, I can bend time. How about sharing some of those baked goods you have in the kitchen?"

"Yum," chirped Berty. "Got any poppy seeds?"

In the Fog

Inside the cave, Ruby, Cinder, Alexander, Jade, and Sergio were sound asleep in a tangled mass. Their bodies began to grow fur as they metamorphosed into brightly colored bears. Ruby and Jade were cuddled together in the center of the pile, while the males flanked them. Although the top half of Jack was a fluffy purple bear, his bottom half was still a mermaid tail. In his sleep, Sergio sniffed Jack's tail and tried to bite it. Jack's tail smacked Sergio square in the face, but he did not wake.

The girls snuggled and giggled. Their dreams floated like holograms above them. They were eating blueberries, dancing with the Bumbleberry People at a Warlocks show in the Blue Riggle Mountains. They giggled with a young version of Ember, who danced as she passed around a hat for tips.

Midnight entered the cavern. The hologram dreams reflected off of his glossy black horns. In a burst of fire, Damien appeared. Midnight bowed to the sinister man, but he returned the gesture by kicking the sheep.

"Someone might see you, you fool!" he rasped.

Midnight bowed his head. "Master."

Damien's voice held a demonic undertone. "You may approach me."

A torch appeared in Damien's hand, which he then placed it in Midnight's mouth. "Go and set fire to those sleeping hedonists. If we kill their parallel universe versions, they will be weakened. My twin brother, Xavier, will be devastated if anything happens to that weakling human, Ember. Why should he be capable of love when I am only destined to be evil forever?"

Twist and Shout

Ember followed Midnight at a distance. Thankfully, luminescent snails lining the walls allowed her to see the way.

Something rustled next to her and a voice whispered in her ear, "Who's there?"

A group of souls playing guitars surrounded Ember. She couldn't believe her eyes; Kurt Cobain, Jim Morrison, Janis Joplin, and Jimi Hendrix had all appeared. Jimi's eyes were on fire as he flipped upside down. She laughed, because the guitar actually stayed right side up. But her laughter angered the musicians, and they began to swirl around her in a vortex. Janis's hair tangled around Ember and began to suffocate her.

Ember was scared, but also furious. After everything she'd been through, she would not be taken down by icons. A memory of Xavier entered her mind. He told her that he would be there for her if she ever needed him. She called out, "Xavier! Save me!"

The cave lit up as Xavier appeared. He was there! With a swipe of his hands, he swiftly banished the souls. Then he grabbed Ember and kissed her deeply. As her lips melted into his, she realized something. Xavier was her mystery lover from the night before. She went limp. She had fallen for this mysterious man before, and yet he had abandoned her.

Ember pummeled her fists on Xavier's chest and growled, "Go away! I don't need you!"

Xavier took Ember's hands in his and embraced her. His body was warm and made her tingle. He caressed her face tenderly, but Ember was too exasperated to surrender to it.

"Why?"

Xavier opened his mouth to speak, but was torn from her arms. "Brother! How did you get here?"

Damien said snarkily, "I used your little *girlfriend* to find you."

Xavier sucker punched his brother, which cast him further into the cavern. He followed Damien, sending him deeper into the shadows. A flock of bats swarmed Ember, and she covered her face as she crouched in the cold, damp darkness.

A plume of thick smoke entered the cavern, followed by the sounds of frantic growls. Ember couldn't decide if she wanted to go further in, or all of the way out of the cave. While she paced and considered her options, she tripped on something and picked it up. A ringed horn: was it Triton's? She put the relic to her lips and blew as hard as she could, hoping help would come charging in on its heels.

The blast deafened her ears and reverberated through the cavern. She heard water rushing toward her, and a wet, furry body bumped into her.

Riding the wave, Triton held a wand with a glowing crystal above his head as he announced, "Never fear, Ember, for Poseidon and I are here to save you!"

She then saw that she was surrounded by a comical group of colorful bears. One of the bears swam toward her, and she panicked. But it reached out to her and said, "It's me—Jack. See? I still have my glorious tail!"

He flapped his fishy appendage proudly, and Ember giggled because he just looked so funny. As Jack held her close, his torso turned into a human form again. Poseidon swam by and gathered Sergio, Jade, and Alexander in his arms, while Triton saved Ruby and Cinder.

The tidal wave carried all of them out of the cave and quickly disappeared. Ember hugged her friends, but the moment was soon disrupted by a swarm of souls. Xavier dashed out of the cave and shooed them away. Ember ran over to hug him, too.

"Is Damien dead?"

"Ember, you cannot kill your quirky counterpart. He is evil, but if he dies, so do I."

Ember nodded. "I feel like you are *my* quirky counterpart."

Xavier kissed Ember again. "Since we met, I have been watching over you. I know that I said I could never be with you, but maybe there is a way that we can be together. I think that because of our close encounters, we now share many of the same subatomic particle pairs, allowing us to exist in the same dimensions for longer periods of time."

"I don't know whether to think that you are super creepy or my soul mate." In her heart, Ember knew that she had willed this reality to be.

She leaned forward and cupped his face with her hands, pulling it down to her so their lips could meet. This kiss felt right. She allowed herself to feel pleasure and drowned in the moment. When she finally let herself breathe again, she sucked oxygen in hungrily, then let out a sigh. Like picking a fresh blueberry from a bush, she let the juice soak her lips, savoring it. The simple brush of a hand across her thigh let the energy loose, which tipped the scales and caused Fractasia itself to roar.

The sky swirled with dark, screaming souls. The moat in front of Castle Clarity began to bubble. A large tentacle stretched over the side. Persephone rushed up to Ember, breathless.

"Why did you release the Kraken?"

"What? I didn't mean to!"

One of the Kraken's tentacles landed in front of her with a plop, and Positron smashed it with her flail. A glass elevator rose out of the dirt, and Xavier pulled Ember toward it.

"Let's go save the kiddos."

Ember knew that her group of friends and the gods were strong enough to prevail. So, she let Xavier pulled her onto the elevator and they disappeared.

Keystone

Fractasia was dark and damp. Poseidon, Triton, and Jack leapt into the moat around Castle Clarity. Alexander flew around the Kraken's head on a flying carpet, slicing off bits of the Kraken's sucker pads with a sword. Ruby sprouted a pair of wings and joined Alexander in the sky. Persephone ran around frantically, snatching souls and stuffing them in a large bottle.

Positron and Cornitropus stood together in front of the main entrance of castle with puzzled looks on their faces. Positron whipped her flail at it, but it bounced off.

"I can't break the big stone on the arch."

Cornitropus's face lit up. "That must be the keystone." He leapt up and ran his hands over the stone. "It's made of some sort of unknown metal composition. It feels evil. The keystone holds the castle together. If we can break it, the whole castle will fall."

"I wonder what poor soul is locked inside that stone," Positron pondered. "And hey—why is that ram over there staring at us with demonic eyes? Where did it come from?"

"Isn't that the cat? Midnight?"

Positron looked like she wanted to pet the sheep, but decided against it. "Shoo, go away!"

The ram stood, unmoving. Cornitropus raised his sickle. Smoke blew from Midnight's nostrils and he stood up and raised his cloven hooves in the air, pawing wildly.

Positron whirled her flail above her head. "I think we need to kill it."

"Oh well," replied Cornitropus as he raised his scythe above his head. Before he could make a move, dark spirits churned around his head and rapidly rotated into a cyclone. They lifted him up and dumped him right in the midst of the Kraken's tentacles.

Midnight charged Positron and knocked her weapon from her hands, smashing it into pieces with his horns. Positron screamed as one of the Kraken's appendages seized her and dunked her into the moat.

The Kraken then had Alexander, Jack, Triton, Poseidon, Cornitropus, Ruby, and Positron in its clutches. It crushed Ruby's wings and she howled. The loathsome lurker squeezed Alexander and his sword, slicing his left arm off, then bit off the end of Jack's tail. The moat turned red with blood.

Plane Surfing

Ember and Xavier stepped into the glass elevator. They found Jason sleeping on his fleece, reading a book.

"Mommy! I have been waiting here for you."

Ember embraced Jason. "Are you okay?" She felt his forehead.

"Yes, Mommy. The glass elevator was better than the Abyss, and I wasn't that lonely because others are using this elevator all the time. You just can't see the others like I can." Jason waved at a blank space next to Ember. "A werewolf is standing next to you. He's a lawyer. Don't worry, though. He's made of a different type of matter, so he can't hurt you."

Ember clutched Jason's head close to her heart. "This time I'm not letting you go. Jason, meet Xavier."

Xavier embraced both Ember and Jason. "Who wants to go to Dismayland?"

Ember replied, "Xavier, why would you want to go to Disneyland when we need to save the other siblings?"

A sad and weary expression colored Xavier's features. "River is stuck in *Dismay*land. He's being forced to work there."

"If you know this, why haven't you already saved him?!"

"Ember, I am able to see the future, but only so far ahead. We need to go now."

The elevator stopped, and they boarded a plane. An angry flight attendant accused Ember, Xavier, and Jason of not booking their tickets soon enough, so they had to sit in different seats. The attendant then scolded Ember for wearing inappropriate attire. She tried to argue, but he told her she needed to shut up or he would bring out the guillotine.

He pulled his phone out of his pocket, snapped a picture of Ember, and threatened, "Off with her head!"

The phone app showed her head rolling down a hill. Ember laughed nervously, and the attendant laughed maniacally.

Ember noticed there was no first-class section on the plane. The pilot announced that he would be depriving the passengers of oxygen so they wouldn't ask for any service dinner or to use the bathrooms. She felt groggy when she came to and the plane had landed. The person in the next row started clapping and the attendant brought his guillotine phone app out, pointing at it, then the passenger.

"The no noise light is still ON! Now, if you will all remain in your seats until we land, the shark on the tail of the plane thanks you for flying."

Ember peered at the plane's tail and the shark laughed maniacally, pointing right at her. She recognized the grin; it looked a lot like the Jochre Coaster.

Ember, Xavier, and Jason deplaned, and since none of them had checked a bag, they ran straight to the taxi area. A town car was available and took them to the very gates of Dismayland. At the gate, the fare for a family was one small toe.

Xavier removed his shoe. "Take mine."

The gatekeeper chopped Xavier's toe off. When he didn't wince, Ember stared, her mouth agape.

Xavier whispered, "Remember, silly, I'm made of water and air."

Ember looked down and his toe had already reappeared. "Oh yeah, I forgot about that."

Xavier paused to use his ability to peer ahead into the future and then informed them that River was locked in a jail within the Haunted Shed, a log ride full of terrifying ghosts and ghouls. Ember, Xavier, and Jason stood in line for hours waiting in the hot sun to enter the ride. Jason wiggled his way through the crowd and returned with good news.

"Mom, I found a door!"

Xavier took Ember's hand and they surreptitiously wisped through the crowd. The door would not open, so they all linked hands and misted through the keyhole. Behind the door the air was stifling and stinky. Recycled water, corn hogs, and guinea pigs on a stick were piled in the corner. They descended into the twists and turns following the log run and found little River sitting in a jail. Xavier steamed River out of the prison bars and Ember and Jason rejoiced.

Ember picked him up. "What happened? How did you end up here?"

River sniffled. "When Mr. Dismay found I didn't have a ticket or any money, he threw me in the jail cell and told me I would stay here and rot with the others."

Appalled, Ember and Xavier looked around at the rides and saw that other children were trapped, working in the hot, horrible conditions with no pay or food other than discarded leftovers from park visitors.

Jason spoke to the air, and Ember asked, "Who are you talking to?"

"That was my lawyer, and he will release all of the adolescents now. They are going to get on the elevator and go to Nebularis, where a new, abundant world awaits them."

"Nebularis?" inquired Ember.

Xavier pulled on Ember's hand. "All in due time, honey. Let's go."

A throng of children stampeded through the front gates of Dismayland and boarded the elevator. Xavier led Ember, Jason, and River to an amusement park by the sea called Pacifica Pier. There, they boarded another plane.

Xavier announced, "Next stop: Zuredon."

Many Babies

Aphrodite was heavily pregnant, her belly stretched taut as it quivered wildly. She called out to Cottus.

"Honey, I think it's time. Can you catch them with your hands?"

Babies started popping out of Aphrodite's mouth, and Cottus ran around busily trying to catch them.

"Look!" Aphrodite remarked. "They only have one head!" Two hundred babies arrived and quickly latched onto Aphrodite's two hundred breasts. "Let's show the others!"

Cottus carried Aphrodite to Castle Clarity. When Aphrodite saw the dead bodies of the gods, though, her joyous news was swept aside. She fell to her knees and exclaimed, "Oh no!"

"Look, there's the Kraken," Cottus said. "How did it escape from Tartarus?"

When the Kraken saw Cottus, it glared at him and gulped down Poseidon, Triton, and Jack in one bite. Cottus roared, ready to take on the beast, but the babies leapt off Aphrodite and dove into the moat, where they devoured the Kraken just as quickly as he had eaten the others.

Cornitropus and Positron crawled out of the water, helping Alexander and Ruby out, too. Ruby was crumpled on the grass, badly injured. She breathed her last breath and turned into a narcissus plant. Alexander was bleeding profusely. Persephone handed him a skin of wine, which he downed just before he died.

Cornitropus pulled a shiny piece of metal out of his pocket and handed it to Positron. "Here, I made you another flail out of our old wedding rings. I wove some of Berty's feathers in it to make a strong alloy, for a lost love is even more powerful than love itself. With this, you should be able to destroy the keystone."

"But it's so small."

"Your touch will activate its powers."

Positron took the tiny flail and it grew to the size of a cow. It dazzled them all with gold and crystals. With a grin, Positron swung her flail high into the sky, whipping up the remaining souls into a twister. Persephone opened her bottle and captured the ghosts. When the flail hit the keystone, it exploded with a flash of light that spread all over world of Fractasia.

Zuredon

The plane to Zuredon was more luxurious than the last. Ember, Xavier, Jason, and River were able to sit together in first class. A large blob sitting in front of them grumbled and oozed green goo on Ember's feet. She tried to clean off the slime, but it was stuck.

The repulsive gel winked. "You're welcome."

Ember wondered why she should be thanking the rude passenger. As the ooze soaked into her foot, her skin tingled. Ember felt like she was floating, and she was happy as a lark for the rest of the flight.

Once they deplaned, they boarded a shiny train with purple people who stared at them suspiciously. Xavier produced some cloaks, which partially concealed them, after which they sipped on warm, spicy drinks in the dining car, and dipped biscuits into the mysterious but tasty beverage. As they entered the city of Zuredon, Ember noticed that every building looked like a clock. Ticking could be heard all along the streets, and purple people walked along, staring at their clocks. The train pulled into a station and they took to the streets to search for Chance.

Jason and River marveled at the street performers that decorated the streets. Ember noticed a poor marionette that was dancing for tips. Next to the boy was a spectacled man who pulled levers to make the boy dance. Ember pulled her family over to see the boy. The boy danced faster and faster until he became tangled in the cords. The ropes rubbed purple residue off his skin to reveal tan skin beneath.

River cried, "It's Chance!"

"Mommy!" Chance screamed. "This man is making me dance for money. Save me!"

To Ember's surprise, Xavier clocked the man with the spectacles in the face and knocked him down. She untied Chance and they ran down the streets until they came to a dock, where they boarded a ship to the Columbus Isles of Britannia to find September.

As soon as they hit the high seas, Ember began to vomit. She never got her sea legs, so she stayed holed up in the cabin the rest of the journey while Xavier taught the tykes to fish. She could not wait to step back onto solid land when they finally arrived six days later, having forged through dangerous, stormy waters with twenty-foot waves.

Upon arriving in the Columbus Isles of Britannia, Ember and her companions hiked to a ski resort, where they spent days searching the slopes on skis and snowboards. Ember felt much more at ease riding the mountains than the undulating sea.

On the seventh day they spent searching for September, Xavier called, "Look over there on that mountaintop! There is a little girl, walking with a yeti."

They tracked the yeti for two more days until they came to a cave. Xavier walked into the cave first, and the yeti tried to attack him, but he dispersed into billowy clouds before the magical mammal could catch him. Ember sprinted forward to greet September, who jumped into her arms.

September called to the yeti with a roar, and it reappeared and joined them by a fire.

Ember asked, "Why are you with a yeti?"

"He saved me. I was on the slopes of corn kernels when a ski patrol tried to investigate me because I wasn't with my parents. I screamed, and the yeti rescued me. His name is Bingo, and he's also an outcast here. He says people thinks he smells bad, too, but I love him."

After hearing September's tale, Ember had an idea. "I wonder if he would like to go back to Fractasia?"

Bingo looked pleased and nodded heartily. Jason decided to accompany the shy yeti and the werewolf back to Fractasia.

The next stop for Ember and her crew was Tropticopus, a paradise made of cascades and tropical flowers. The travelers linked hands as they walked along the black sands of a beach. Floral perfume hung thick in the air. They walked into the ocean to cool off.

A group of villagers approached then and invited the entire family to a party. When they arrived at the gathering, April was sliding down a water slide into a never-ending pool.

She swam over to Ember and said, "Hi, Mom and Dad."

Ember couldn't believe her ears. She wondered if it was really possible that Xavier was the father of her darlings. After all, her DNA had danced in the primordial stool with his. He was certainly acting like a father on this little adventure of theirs.

Ember sat in the grass to enjoy the scenery. Her kiddos gathered around her, and April handed her a colorful drink. Before she could try it, though, a group of elders covered in soft, plum-colored fur approached them.

"When your daughter arrived, we thought she was an orphan and took her in. Now that her family has arrived, you all must leave. Your kind, whatever you are, is not welcome here."

The elders stared with their grey eyes and cataracts. Ember imagined each of them as wild animals. She pretended the tall man was a giraffe; the man beside him resembled a platypus. A short lady adorned with jewelry was clearly an angry mink. Ember burst out laughing.

"We can read your minds, you know!" barked the bejeweled woman.

Ember chortled, "Read at your own risk!"

She felt their minds crawl into her brain and search through her thoughts. They were enraged, and accused Ember of hurting their pride, which was punishable by death. While they screamed at each other like the wildlife she had envisioned, Ember and Xavier slipped away with the brood and ran.

They rushed to the bank of the river, but found they were trapped there. Just then, a rectangular box floated up to the bank. It was the elevator!

As they boarded Ember asked, "Xavier, where is Elderberry?"

"She's in Aguptus. Let's go!"

Nebularis

The keystone of Castle Clarity exploded. Shards of the sky broke and hurtled toward the ground. The world vibrated.

Finally, all became still. A pale little girl stood where the keystone had been. She shielded her eyes from the bright light. "Where am I?" she asked, before turning into a small sparrow and flying away.

Persephone put her hands on her hips. "Well, that was odd."

Positron suggested, "I can control matter. What if we take these souls and turn this into a new world like Ember mentioned? That way, Persephone doesn't have to worry about taking them all back to Hades."

Cornitropus rushed into the fields and cut down swathes of grass. He then gathered the hair of the deceased gods and goddesses and began to weave a cloth. He summoned the leptons from the fabric, which formed a composite he called positronium, and then threw it over the entire world.

Minutes later, Fractasia was transformed into a land they named Nebularis. The souls were converted into humanoids who built dwellings and cities. Cornitropus roamed the fields and forests of Nebularis, taking care of the forest and its inhabitants. Cinder and Sergio married and settled with Tobias in a cottage next to a forest.

Positron built a gilded castle on a beautiful high mountain suspended above a lake of aquamarine. As she lounged on a large throne, a flock of tiny dragons the size of ladybugs surrounded her. With one large swat, she squished their guts all over her arm. "Pesky things," she complained, though she was smiling.

Persephone appeared by her side. "Do you want me to take that bug juice to Tartarus?"

"Nah, I got them all! They're dead."

Positron then sang a song.

Atrayu Is Not Trey Anastasio
You sat beside me along a stream that's because
I thought the sun would set low so slowly
And then the bats flew low so-oh low
Physics; and you knew what a positron was
Anti the matter to build chemistry on
And Golgi asparagus
Can't infringe upon Phish!
Atrayu, is not Trey Anastasio
The Never-ending Story had a wolf and a nothing
Not like Trey Anastasio,
Who had a guitar and a crowd.
A dragon in the dark
A white and furry funk
Rocks that whined a lot
But were really not
Fans that jumped and hopped
Tripped and tra-laad around
La da dip doo da dee drum
Tip the bouncer run afoul
Like Atrayu
And not Trey Anastasio
Never-ending not

Setting the Sphinx Free

In the land of Flourdough, Jagger served Rayne a generous slice of golden baklava. "I harvested the sugar from canes, made the flour from grains I grew, and gathered the spices from the bark of the brown trees over there. The oil came from the seeds of those fruits over there."

Rayne tasted the treat. "*Delicioso!* I see you *have* been busy. Good job, brother." She looked up at the sun in the sky and remarked, "My, look at the time!"

Jagger took her plate. "I thought you were a time master or something?"

"Yes, but I forgot to pay attention because your baklava was so good. Now, let's go to Aguptus."

Rayne snapped her fingers, and they were transported to a sandy beach.

"Where are we?" asked Jagger.

"Sharm-el-Shark," Rayne answered.

"Look, that little girl is being chased by an angry mob!" Jagger exclaimed.

"That's Elderberry!"

Elderberry leapt into the sea and started swimming. Rayne and Jagger raced into the ocean after her.

"Ouch! This must be a coral reef!" Jagger yelled. "It's so shallow that we are going to have to float on our bellies so we don't get stung."

Rayne called out, "Elderberry, don't touch the coral!"

Elderberry cried back, "I know!"

The three met up and made their way to the coral shelf, where the ocean was deeper. The current carried them down until they were far down the coastline. Soon, a group of sharks surrounded them, so they stayed as close to the coral as they could.

Elderberry treaded water. "The villagers have trained the sharks to attack anyone they fear is a foe."

"Dear, why would they consider you a foe?" Jagger asked, looking at the little girl in undisguised wonder.

Elderberry gesticulated wildly. "Because the villagers are vicious aliens with snakes coming out of their heads! Two years ago, they invaded the lands and took over the cities. They killed all the adults now there are only minors left. Good thing kids are good at hiding."

"Good enough reason for me!" Jagger cried. "What happens when the tide goes out? We'll be trapped on the coral bed!"

Elderberry nodded. "And the coral is deadly here. I don't know what we'll do!"

A boat started in from the distance and whizzed toward them. A group of girls, all about Elderberry's age, beckoned them to board their boat. They traveled up the coast to a group of caves in the sand, which were decorated with gold, jewels, and bright furs. Elderberry, who could speak the language, translated when they said that they were welcome to stay the night in their underground shelter. They zipped through the ocean until they came to cliff that hung over the sea. The boat continued into a hidden hollow, where they jumped ashore.

That evening, they dined on a variety of grilled fish, roasted vegetables, and flat breads. Elderberry and Rayne joined the girls as they danced and played music with a variety of delicately carved stringed instruments.

After the merriment was over, Elderberry took Jagger and Rayne through a tunnel that led to a smooth, windblown desert.

"Here, I want to show you something."

Triple moons bathed the sands in a surreal, spooky light. They walked along a path until they came to a great sculpture of a lion. Jagger cheered, "It's a sphinx! But is that a goat's head coming out of its rear? And a snake's head on its tail?"

"It's a chimera, silly." Rayne stood in front of the chimera and levitated. She breathed into his mouth and the sand began to fall away from the sand statue's visage. The beast came to life, shaking mud and mortar out of its fur and onto Jagger, who promptly passed out in the sand with a soft thud. The chimera crouched down at Rayne's feet and nodded before grasping Jagger's pantleg between its teeth and dragging him back to the underground dwelling. It then sat in front of the entrance and froze.

In the hours before dawn, Elderberry screamed, waking the others. An angry man with snakes slithering out of his head held her at knifepoint and babbled in the local dialect. As Jagger and Rayne approached, Elderberry translated what he was threatening her with. "He says that if you call the chimera, he will kill me."

An elevator dropped from the sky and smashed the man's head. The door opened, revealing Ember, Xavier, and the rest of their offspring. Elderberry leapt into Xavier's arms. "Daddy!"

The girls from Aguptus and the chimera piled in the elevator with the rest of them just before the door closed and the button labeled "Nebularis" lit up.

The End

When Ember set foot on Nebularis, she instantly felt at peace. She joined her little ones and friends at Positron's citadel, which overlooked the new cities below. Technology was built into the world. No one needed a cell phone because everyone had the ability to read minds, but only if both parties allowed it. Houses grew up from the ground like plants. Transport was made possible by flying on little chimera beasts that the creature had cloned from itself. Each of Ember's children had their own chimeras to watch over them.

Ember twirled around in a long, flowing dress that danced in the warm, soft breeze. Cottus and all the whippersnappers played instruments while Aphrodite led them in harmonious song.

Ember thought about her adventures, her many companions, and the characters who had died along the way; she even missed the meddling gods. She would never forget Berty, who had gone back to Hades with Persephone to replace Hermes.

Jagger approached her tentatively. She felt she had to say something. "I'm sorry I made you feel like these were your children when Xavier was really the father."

Jagger said solemnly, "I know."

Xavier stepped forward and embraced Ember before taking her hand. "Ember, there is something I have to tell you, too."

Elderberry grasped her other hand. "There is something important *we* need to tell you."

Ember's kids gathered around her, looking up at her with somber faces. She wondered what was going on; something felt wrong. She looked into Xavier's eyes, which were welling with tears.

"Darling, we are real, and you made that all possible. But *you* aren't anymore. You are only in a dream—your dream. You have to go home now."

Ember froze. She tried to laugh, to lift her arms—anything—but she could not. She was numb. She couldn't even speak, and yet all she wanted to say was, "No! This is all real! This is *not* a just a fantasy!"

Xavier and her children squeezed her tightly, but she could not hug them back. Their faces started swirling before her.

Xavier cradled her face, but she could no longer feel his hands on her skin. "Nebularis is real because you created us. You have saved so many lives."

Elderberry said confidently, "Don't worry, Mommy, I'll be safe."

The rest of the children chimed in. "We love you, Mommy!"

Ember screamed and screamed until finally no sound came out of her mouth. By then, she realized she was no longer on Nebularis.

A slight hand brushed her shoulder. Ember turned her head to see Tanzanite Chrysalis's face.

"Wake up, Ember! I'm so glad you invited me over. This sleepover was so much fun, but you talk in your sleep, you weirdo! You tried to hug me, too, so I fended you off with this book."

Ember froze. "What?"

"Yeah, this book landed on your head. That's when you started screaming, so I smacked you with it to wake you up."

Ember flipped the book open. *Ashe.* "Tanzanite, this looks like an awesome book! Do you want to read it with me?"

But Tanzanite still looked skeptical. "It looks like it came from the future. 'The evening was dark and damp.' Hey, isn't that how most mysteries start out?"

Ember jumped up and down on the bed. "You betcha! Let's keep reading. I love a good story."

To New Beginnings

Berty soared up into the sky of Nebularis and faded from view. The great blue jay reappeared in a grand, oval-shaped, gilded office where the elderly man with strawberry blonde hair stared at his own reflection in his shining, golden apple. The man's face contorted and he began to shape-shift into a reptile, but that caused him to drop the precious fruit, which rolled to Berty's feet. With a loud caw, the giant bird consumed the orb in one gulp. He soared up into the air just as the man, whose bottom half had transformed into a monitor lizard, tried to whip Berty with his tail. Berty turned into a tall, well-dressed man and strolled to the door.

The bewildered chimera stared at his lizard legs and declared, "I am not wearing any clothes!"

"It's a miracle, the blind man can see!" Berty laughed before closing the door behind him.

About the Author

Sara is a space-time traveler who grew up in a strange world void of modern luxuries like cell phones, hoverboards, or the worldwide web. Even so, Sara's childhood was rich, because she was a latchkey kid who did pretty much whatever she wanted. If she was hot, she jumped in the creek. If she wanted to fly, she swung through the forest on giant grapevines. One day, Sara brought slices of watermelon to her neighbors, and a visitor told her exciting stories about swimming with manta rays. Another day, a missionary at summer camp told Sara about a country shaped like a string bean called Chile. Sara listened intently, and she longed to see the world, too.

Eventually, Sara found herself in a different dimension, where she kayaked over waterfalls in a tropical paradise, sped down Alpen ski slopes, and studied quantum physics. In 1999, while living in a city called Konstanz, Sara started writing a story about a girl she called Ivory. Somewhere along the way, Sara misplaced the original draft, so she started over and created yet another parallel universe. Merging the narratives of Ivory's adventures made Sara's brain hurt, so much so that she wanted to give up entirely.

When life was toughest, Sara completed her quest to bring her characters to life. She encourages her readers to embrace their experiences, both the good and the bad, to create a better future, and to never stop dreaming.

9 781951 490706